Dedication

To my wonderful daughter

Thank you for sharing your amazing
underwater adventures with me.

Love,
Maman

Acknowledgement

BWL Publishing acknowledges the Government of Canada and the Canada Book Fund for its financial support in creating the Canadian Historical Mysteries collection.

Funded by the Government of Canada | Canada

BWL Publishing acknowledges the Province of Alberta for their ongoing support through the Alberta Publisher's Cultural Industry Operating Grant.

Alberta Government

Deep Beneath the Surface

J. S. Marlo

Print ISBNs
Amazon print 9780228637462
Ingram Spark 9780228637479
Barnes & Noble 9780228637486
BWL Print 9780228637493

BWL Publishing Inc.

Books we love to write …
Authors around the world.

http://bwlpublishing.ca

Table of Contents

Chapter 1

"Forget it, Dylan." Upset over the senseless incident that cost him a diver, Hauk Ludwig paced the office of Dylan Carr, a master scuba diving instructor at the Northern Ballard Institute. "I'm not hiring some green kid."

Behind his desk, the instructor leaned back in his chair. "I said young, Hauk, not green."

Semantics, Dylan. Hauk inadvertently kicked a pair of silver fins lying on the floor. They landed with a thud against an open cardboard box filled with technical manuals, nautical charts, and dive logs. "The Model T has been underwater since Ford mass-produced them. It's too brittle to move, but I still need to gather evidence from it. I want an experienced diver, not some amateur who'll breathe bubbles on my wreck."

"Fisher's a pro." The intensity of Dylan's stare contrasted with the casual tone of his statement. "She's been diving around wrecks for longer than any of your current crew members."

"*She?*" Water would turn to blood before Hauk hire a female diver again.

Looking as smug as a pirate on looting day, Dylan clasped his hands behind his neck. "Yes, and *she* is the best I can recommend."

Hauk paused in front of Dylan's desk, placed his hands on the dark cherry wood surface, and glared at the instructor. "Who's your second-best?"

"You know, Hauk, for an intelligent man, you can be unreasonably pigheaded."

In desperate need of a new diver, Hauk ignored the insult. "Women have caused me enough trouble. I just want a good diver."

"Fisher is a topnotch diver, a mechanic, and an investigator." A smile tugged at Dylan's lips. "She's a three-in-one deal."

To Hauk's annoyance, Fisher's description fit his needs. "That's your only recommendation?"

"Yes. So do yourself a favour and go meet her in the basement before she leaves. You can thank me later."

* * *

Holding her pencil tight to stop her hand from shaking, Star logged her last dive entry in her journal. Every muscle in her body ached from her winning fight against the strong current.

Trapped in the training tank, she had escaped the imaginary waterfall looming beyond the wall and resurfaced within the safety parameters. She allowed a satisfied smile to reach her lips. Only two divers in her group of eight accomplished the feat.

Done with her journal, she set aside it and looked around the pool area. At the sight of the obnoxious diver ogling her, she clenched her hands. He had been harassing her since her arrival at the Institute, alternating between sexual innuendos and distasteful remarks about the scar on her cheek.

"Great job, everyone." Their instructor picked up an oxygen tank. "Your recertification papers will be mailed to you. Make sure we have your current address on file."

The obnoxious diver walked by her. "You missed your chance, Fisher. You'll never get a better deal than me."

"Get lost, Donny." Being swarmed by jellyfish was a better deal any day of the week.

* * *

On his way down the familiar corridors of the Institute, Hauk made a few inquiries about Fisher. At twenty-four, she had already built a solid reputation in her field and came highly recommended.

Intrigued despite himself, Hauk headed to the basement where a petite woman with wavy blonde hair shoved the contents of a locker into a red duffel bag.

A large scar closely resembling a star marred her otherwise lovely features. Hauk found it refreshing that she chose not to cover up the imperfection.

She paused and stared at him with dark brown eyes. "In case you're not aware, this is a restricted area."

"Star Fisher?"

Her brows knitted together over the ridge of her nose. "And you are?"

Taken aback by her guarded attitude, Hauk casually leaned one shoulder against a locker. "Hauk Ludwig. I talked to Dylan. He told me you investigate wrecks for a living."

Her gaze narrowed down to two glittering slits. "I mostly investigate vehicles that are dumped in lakes and rivers for insurance fraud. Why the interest?"

"I run a salvage operation." Despite the recommendations, Hauk preferred to rely on his own evaluation of her qualifications. "Do you inspect the vehicles while they are still under water, or after they are extracted?"

"I'm usually called in when the water is too deep, or the vehicle too far from the shore, to justify the cost of retrieval. So, to answer your question, I usually inspect it underwater." She pulled out a dive hood from the top shelf then shoved it in the side pocket of her bag. "Sometimes the damages match the story given by the owner, and others it's staged to look like an accident."

Low-cut jeans hugged her hips, and a black midriff shirt exposed a slender waist. Hauk's imagination ran away from him, and for an instant, he pictured a pirate flag with a skull and crossbones tattooed on her lower back.

Unsettled by the wild image, Hauk gripped the open door of her locker in an effort to rein in his imagination. "Do owners ever dispute your findings?"

She shrugged her muscular shoulders. "They can argue, or bribe, as much as they want, it won't change my report."

Integrity and confidence were qualities that Hauk sought in a diver. "I'm looking to hire a new diver. The job is yours if you're available."

"I'm not." She slung her bag over her left shoulder, contracting a muscle above her scar. "Good day, Ludwig."

The irony that she dismissed him as quickly as he had earlier dismissed the idea of employing a woman left a sour taste in his mouth. "If you change your mind, I'll be in the back parking lot."

* * *

Upon gathering her personal effects, Star stopped by Dylan's office before exiting the building by the back entrance.

In the parking lot adjacent to the loading zone, Ludwig sat on the hood of a grey Jeep, his gaze focused in her direction. The sun accentuated the reddish highlights in his tousled blond hair while the shadow of a beard underlined his roguish appearance.

Foolish butterflies fluttered in the pit of her stomach. She silently chided them. *Stop acting up. If I take the job, it won't be because he looks like Julian.* If anything, the resemblance was a strike against Ludwig.

"Fisher." Ludwig slid down the hood then dug his hands into his jeans pockets. "Have you reconsidered my offer?"

"No, but I talked to Dylan." The master instructor had fed her an interesting underwater tale, unleashing her curiosity. "He told me it was safer to accept a ride from you than to take a cab."

"Is that so?" Amusement shimmered in his steel-blue eyes, softening his prominent Scandinavian features and dispelling some of the resemblance with Julian. Ludwig appeared to be in his late twenties or early thirties, younger than he had looked in the confines of the Institute but older than Julian when tragedy had struck.

Star pushed the memory to the back of her mind and forced a smile. "Dylan seems rather fond of you, Ludwig."

"What can I say? I'm a friendly guy." Ludwig unlocked the cargo hatch of the Jeep and loaded her duffel bag and diving gear. "So where am I supposed to drop you off?"

"Bus station." She climbed onto the passenger seat while he eased behind the wheel. "Feel free to fill me in about that job offer. I'll admit I'm curious."

"Really?" A grin embedded a cute dimple in his left cheek. "I should charge you a fare."

"I promise to leave you a tip, if I get to the bus station alive," she teased, intrigued by the man and his wreck.

He chuckled backing out of the parking lot, and as he turned the steering wheel his elbow grazed her arm. Shivers coursed under her skin, stirring a yearning she thought she buried with Julian.

"I'll bite, Fisher." Amusement spiked his words. He appeared oblivious to the effects he had on her. "What else did Dylan say?"

"He mentioned a Tin Lizzy." Star had never seen a Model T in person, under or above water. No doubt it would surpass the oldest wreckage she had ever investigated. A 1972 Beetle.

"A month ago, a geological team surveying Henstridge Lake discovered a Model T rusting at the bottom, over six hundred metres from the closest shoreline." He smoothly merged into the traffic. "I need to figure out how and why it ended up there."

"Have you considered a winter joyride gone awry?" Throughout her career, she had investigated many similar incidents. "It wouldn't be the first time a car falls through the ice of a frozen lake."

Ludwig cocked his head in her direction. "Sensible explanation but impossible in June."

Baffled by the assumption that the car had sunk during the summer, she stared at his profile. "What makes you think it was dumped in June?"

"In June 1912, the car, and the wife, of a rich banker disappeared near Henstridge Lake, and neither were ever found."

Though skeptical over his theory, Star sought to keep an open mind. "Many cars could have ended up in the lake over the course of a century. Why do you believe the Tin Lizzy belonged to that banker?"

"Back then, only a handful of people owned a Model T, but only one of them, Banker Watson, also owned a property on that shoreline. What can I say? I don't believe in coincidences."

A dubious smile sneaked past her guard. "Have fun solving that mystery."

"My offer still stands, Fisher. I lost one of my divers and Dylan told me you were the best one on the market."

"I'm flattered, but I can't squeeze in a case of that magnitude." The tempting offer conflicted with her current work schedule. "I'm too swamped right now."

Ludwig raised a brow. "Your secretary told me you were between cases."

"My what?" Money was too tight to hire a secretary. "I don't have a secretary, so I'm not sure who you talked to, but you were given the wrong information. June is one of my busiest months of the year." She had loose ends to tie up, lots of paperwork to finish, and since she had left for her three-day recertification course at the Northern Ballard Institute, three new cases had landed on her desk.

"I talked to someone named…" Ludwig lifted one hand from the steering wheel to scratch his head. "Jimmy Fisher. He said you could afford a change of scenery."

"You called my father?" Technically, Jimmy was her uncle, but he had raised her since she was four years old. He was her mentor, her friend, and the only family that Star had ever had. Together, they had been running investigations since she was twelve years old. Everything she had learned, she learned from him, and while Jimmy was right about her benefiting from a change of scenery, it didn't negate the fact that she was still swamped. "You won't mind if I call Jimmy, will you?"

"Of course not." Judging by his confidence, Ludwig had done his homework when inquiring about her.

Ambivalent about accepting Ludwig's offer, she retrieved the phone tucked into the back pocket of her jeans and dialed home.

Her father answered on the second ring. "Hello, squirt. Did you get an offer from Captain Ludwig by any chance?"

No one but Jimmy got away with calling her *squirt*. "I haven't accepted Ludwig's offer yet."

"Why not?" Jimmy's voice rose, a sign that he was either excited or annoyed. In this case, she guessed a mix of both. "Listen to your old man, squirt. You can't let the chance of examining a century old relic slip by. Such an opportunity may never arise again."

"But what about those three new cases we just landed?" Since his accident, her father had been unable to dive. Without her, he wouldn't be able to make the initial assessments, let alone start the investigations.

"I reviewed the claims. We may have to turn two down. The third one can wait until your return."

The money she would make accepting Ludwig's offer would undoubtedly compensate for the cases they would drop. "It may take weeks, Jimmy. Are you sure you'll be fine without me?"

Deep laughter reverberated through her handset. "Yes, I'm sure. You enjoy the experience and try not to give your new captain too much trouble."

Trouble? Me? Her father knew her too well. "I'll try. Love you."

"Love you too, squirt."

She hung up. "Ludwig, you got yourself a new diver."

Chapter 2

Her new captain drove through a forest on a winding dirt road, hitting bumps and collecting dust. The scenery reminded Star of home.

On the side of the road, a yellow sign indicated a sharp curve ahead. Ludwig slowed before negotiating the next bend, and then the forest released the Jeep from its grip.

Star sucked in a breath.

A basin of shimmering blue water nestled between gentle hills opened in front of her. On the opposite shore, colourful cottages and boathouses blended with the landscape. Ludwig parked the Jeep near a launch ramp on a patch of gravel between a green SUV and a battered red car.

A white research vessel was anchored in the middle of the peaceful lake. Star ogled it with envy. "Yours?"

"Yep." There was no mistaking the pride in his voice.

"Nice research vessel, Ludwig." His vessel beat the last watercraft on which she had worked, a corroded aluminum Jon boat that defied the floating laws of physic.

"No argument here." He transferred her belongings into a Zodiac tied to a log at the edge of the lake. "Hop in."

The lightweight, inflatable craft bounced over the water and the wind played in her hair. Star relished both sensations equally. The short ride ended when he docked alongside his vessel near another Zodiac. He carried her diving gear onboard. Her duffel bag slung over her shoulder, she climbed the ladder after him.

"Listen up, everyone. This is Star Fisher. She's replacing Macey." With a tilt of his head, Ludwig indicated a burly man baked by the sun and seated at the helm. "This is Arnie."

The helmsman removed his blue baseball cap embroidered with the old logo of the Montreal Expos and used it to wave.

"Arnie also doubles as the best cook in the Great White North." Ludwig took a step toward the open door of the cabin. "Scott! Scott is our house scientist and research expert. Come out here for a sec!"

A boyish face framed by a mass of unruly black hair peeked around the doorframe. "Yes, boss?" The researcher looked like a teenager fresh out of high school.

"Scott, meet Star Fisher." A courteous nod was all that she received from Scott before Ludwig drew her attention to the stern of the vessel. "And peeling off his wetsuit is Kyle."

Cold, dark eyes scraped over her like sandpaper. "Does she know how to swim?"

Inflamed by the stocky diver's scornful attitude, her temper flared. "Why? You need lessons?"

His broad tanned chest puffed out, Kyle walked toward her. "This isn't diving school, kid. I'm—"

"Kyle." Ludwig's commanding voice stopped the diver in his tracks. "Did you set the underwater lights?"

"Yes, boss." Kyle turned his gaze away from her. "Every metre around the perimeter. She's a beauty."

"Perfect. Fisher and I will have a look." Ludwig dropped her gear at her feet. "Get ready to dive."

* * *

The artificial illumination gave the underwater site an eerie appearance, like a sleeping lighthouse on a misty morning. Happy with the setup, Hauk mentally commended Kyle's groundwork.

Aquatic creatures, attracted by the light, cast shadows over the wreck. The Model T stood on its four wheels, sunk into the soft sand, a ghostly reminder of a past era.

That it landed perfectly after dropping twenty metres was fortunate. It made their inspection easier. The metal was corroded and the wood rotten. Strangely, the glass of one headlight had remained intact. The leather roof was long decomposed, and its rusted frame trailed behind the car like a broken skeleton.

Hauk hovered above Fisher, studying her as much as the car. With slow and deliberate movements, she examined the hull from every direction and snapped pictures.

As she swam closer to the wreck, she prolonged the length and decreased the intensity of her flutter kicks. The cautious maneuvers minimized the water and sand disturbance.

Pleased by the attention she paid to small details, something young or inexperienced divers too often ignored, Hauk silently thanked Dylan for his choice.

From the lakebed, she picked up a handful of sand and let the grains slip between her gloved fingers. The significance of her gesture escaped him, and he wished he could read the expression behind her mask. He would await her contribution to their evening brainstorming session with anticipation.

* * *

Star hadn't realized how closely Ludwig watched her underwater until he asked why she had scooped sand from the bottom.

Seated across from him at the rectangular table occupying part of the main cabin, she rubbed the tips of her fingers with her thumb in recollection. "I needed to feel the texture of the grains to estimate how deep the fragments could seep under the sand."

His left eyebrow rose. "Your estimate?"

A thick layer of fine sand covered the lakebed, making it easy for creatures or water disturbances to conceal small debris. "About five inches."

Ludwig acquiesced before inviting Scott to unveil his latest findings.

"I downloaded the technical specifications of the Model T." The research expert laid on the table detailed pictures of what the antique car would have looked like between 1909 and 1925. "You'll notice that Ford constantly redesigned the skeleton of its Model T. Compared to the pictures taken by Kyle and Star, I'd say we're looking at a 1910 or 1911 Touring."

Each of them took turns examining the evidence.

Like the others, Star agreed with Scott's assessment. "What year was that banker's car again?"

"It's unclear how old, or new, the Model T was when it disappeared, but..." Ludwig rubbed his bristled chin. "The banker bought it before June 1912."

While the men discussed the differences between the Model Ts in circulation in 1912, Star squinted at a photo depicting the front axle. She wished for a better angle, one with her point of interest not obscured by the shadows created by the underwater lamps.

"Something wrong, Fisher?"

Startled by Ludwig's question, she blinked. "Not sure. I think I see a bolt. If you have no objection, I'd like to make another dive."

He arched his other brow. "Tonight?"

No, this morning. Unsure how he would react to her witty remark, she bit it off. "Yes."

"I could dive with her, skip." Unlike Kyle and Scott, who used the term *boss* to address Ludwig, Arnie favoured *skip*. And the skip didn't object.

While she geared up alone on deck with Arnie, she learned that he used to make daily dives in his younger years. In many ways, he reminded her of Jimmy.

She dove in first, quickly followed by Arnie who adopted a stationary position near the lampposts.

Experience, and Jimmy's constant reminders, had taught her not to hurry and to document every step. With a brush she pulled from her belt, she carefully swept the indentation on the front axle, exposing a corroded bolt.

Satisfaction rushed through her. She had guessed right, and to her knowledge, the bolt served only one purpose. Her attention returned to the sandy bottom. Unless the plate had snapped when the car plunged into the lake, it shouldn't be buried too far or too deep.

Hauk left the cabin and stepped onto the twelve-foot deck. According to his watch, Arnie and Fisher had been down less than ten minutes.

The oxygen tanks lined up against the storage bin beckoned to him. He grabbed the closest one and peered at the gauge. Seventeen hundred pounds left. That was enough air for a short dive.

Wanting to witness what had prompted Fisher's request, Hauk geared up and dove in.

The wetsuit didn't completely insulate his skin from the colder water he encountered farther below. With darkness surrounding him, he trusted the guide rope to lead him to the site as he continued his descent. Minutes later, through the shadowy waters, Hauk spotted his two divers. Arnie floated above a lamppost while Fisher knelt on the lakebed in front of the wreck.

An object was in Fisher's hand. Hauk swam toward her to get a better view. The mysterious object disappeared into her bag, and she glided away before he had a chance to satisfy his curiosity.

A few flutter kicks behind her, Hauk stretched out his arm with the intent of tapping her shoulder.

Her hand swiftly swept across her belt. A glint of light reflected off her glove. She spun around. Eyes glazed with fear, she swung her arm. Sharp reflexes allowed Hauk to deflect the blow. It didn't prevent her other hand from sneaking past his defences.

He inhaled sharply.

A silver blade pushed against his hose, ready to sever his air supply with the flick of her wrist.

* * *

Rattled by the close encounter, Hauk climbed onboard behind Fisher. "Were you out of your mind?" Yelling felt good. It felt alive. Hauk couldn't care less if boaters at the other end of the lake heard him.

Fisher briskly turned around. The fury in her eyes scorched him. "Did you have a death wish?"

Angry with her, he brandished the air hose in his hands. The groove made by the blade glared at him. "You drew a knife!"

"You startled me."

"Startled? *I* startled *you? You* panicked, and *you* nearly killed *me.* Dammit, Fisher. You were down there with Arnie. What danger did you think you faced?"

A shadow that Hauk didn't recognize crossed her face.

She chewed on her lower lip. "I'm..." Her voice quavered. "I'm sorry."

"Sorry doesn't cut it." Exasperated by her careless stunt, he tossed his mask onto the deck. "I should fire you."

"I found the licence plate." She extricated a rusted plate from her bag and handed it to him. "And no need to fire me. I quit."

Her duffel bag rested on deck near the bench where she had dropped it when she boarded. She grabbed it and stomped down the ladder onto one of the Zodiacs.

Knowing better than to argue in the heat of the moment, Hauk didn't stop her. Later, he would deal with her. Scott and Kyle, who stood near the cabin door, gathered around him to look at rectangular plate.

"Some indentations are still visible." His researcher took the plate and disappeared inside the cabin.

Hauk followed him to discuss the restoration of the plate, but images of the glistening blade flashed in his mind while listening to Scott's explanations on how he intended to restore the plate.

Hours later, Hauk returned on deck. "Where is she?"

"She wasn't aware of your presence, skip." Seated at the helm, Arnie stirred in his chair. "You didn't give her any warning when you approached."

"I thought she saw me." Hauk recalled the wild fear in her eyes. "I was wrong."

"She's in the small Zodiac. I told her I'd take her to shore in the morning. Are you gonna ask her to stay?"

Good question. Divers fighting imaginary intruders twenty metres below didn't belong on his vessel. "I..." The warm evening breeze brushed Hauk's bare chest but didn't appease the tumultuous frenzy raging inside. "I don't know, yet."

He descended the ladder debating her fate, but halfway down, Hauk stopped and sat on a rung. His bare feet dangled inches from the rubber craft in which she lay with a blanket covering her lower body.

For a chilling instant, he had been at her complete mercy, as vulnerable and powerless as a newborn child. Her survival instinct had triumphed over his sheer strength. Within the blink of an eye, his life, his entire future had rested solely in the hands of a petite and feisty woman—and Hauk didn't like that feeling one iota.

"Do you also want me out of the Zodiac?"

The melodious modulation of her voice enthralled him. "Are you always that impetuous, Fisher?"

"Yeah, it's one of my most endearing qualities." She pushed her back against the side, facing him. "Don't worry. I'll be off your vessel before you discover the other dreadful ones."

As much as he wished otherwise, he had acted recklessly underwater, and to further complicate the situation, he still needed her. "I'd like you to stay."

"I almost killed you, Ludwig." Her voice held no rancor. "I can't stay."

He joined her in the inflatable craft. "I should have known better than to sneak up on you."

"Undoubtedly not your finest moment," she muttered under her breath.

Mere inches separated them. A small gap, but as deep as the abyss. He had to strain his ear to catch her remark. "Why did you draw a knife? Did you panic?"

"I don't panic. I react."

The difference eluded him. "Would you mind explaining your... reaction?" *Disproportionate reaction.*

A heavy silence settled between them, a silent that he was afraid she might not break, until she draped the blanket over her shoulders. "Two years ago, Jimmy and I investigated a river dump. We didn't know about the drugs stashed in the trunk of the car until we were ambushed underwater. I didn't react fast enough. Jimmy was stabbed and never completely recovered. I've been diving alone ever since, and I've learned to be leery of intruders. Very leery."

No wonder his unexpected appearance had set off a defensive response. Hauk was lucky she didn't kill him. "How about you? Were you injured?"

Her arms hugged her knees. "Yes."

Resisting the temptation to move closer, he waited. When she didn't volunteer any more details, he chose not to pry. "For what it's worth, Fisher, you make a formidable opponent." He appreciated her frank answer. "The licence plate is a partial match to the banker's car."

"How partial?"

"Three numbers correspond. The other two are indistinguishable." Glad that he somewhat rekindled her interest, he carefully chose his next words. "If we figure out how or why the banker's car ended up here, we may find out what happened to his wife."

"You realize his wife is long dead by now, don't you?"

He chuckled. "Yes, but I love to solve mysteries. Every wreck has a story, and someone has to tell it."

"You write about them?" The higher pitch in her voice conveyed her surprise.

"I write a lengthy article about each of my salvage operations." Three magazines competed to publish his articles, enabling him to reach a vast readership on four continents.

She dropped her chin onto her knees. "In a way, it's like investigating an insurance scam and writing a report, but way more fun."

"Not sure about the fun part." Some of his deadlines were atrocious. "But we both search for the truth."

A short nod loosened a blonde curl from behind her ear. "While I looked for the plate, I noticed a suspicious gash in the front tire."

Her readiness to share her observations pleased him. "Does that mean you're staying?"

Her bashful smile stirred a longing he thought he had learned to control years ago.

"I suppose I could stick around awhile longer, but beware, I'm an early riser. I like to go for a swim and make a dive before breakfast." Wrapped in the blanket, she reverted to her previous position at the bottom of the Zodiac.

An early riser himself, Hauk could live with that condition. "Any other special considerations?"

Her gaze washed over him. "Could you turn off the lights around the vessel so I can sleep?"

Amused, he suppressed a grin. They both knew that even if he wanted, he couldn't turn off all the lights without creating a collision hazard. "Wouldn't you be more comfortable on a cot in the cabin?"

"No, not unless it's raining. Good night, Ludwig."

"Good night... Star."

Chapter 3

Hauk cracked an eye open. The rising sun shone through the only porthole in the cabin. Based on its position on the horizon, it was between 6:30 and 7:00 a.m. He sat on his cot and looked around the room. Only one of the other four cots pushed against the inside walls contained an occupant.

Curled in a ball with a blanket at his feet, Scott showed no signs of waking up anytime soon. Ruffled sheets lay crumbled on Kyle's empty cot while crisp white linen tightly hugged Arnie's and Star's.

For as long as Hauk had known Arnie, the older man had preferred sleeping in his chair at the helm, but Star's choice to spend the night in the Zodiac baffled him, unless she felt uncomfortable sharing a cabin with members of the opposite sex. Whatever her reasons, Hauk couldn't offer her different accommodations. Aside from a tiny bathroom and a small galley that couldn't accommodate more than two people at a time, his vessel only provided this crowded cabin where the sleeping and research areas were separated by an invisible line drawn on the floor.

"One day I'll get a larger boat," he whispered to himself.

The tantalizing aroma of fresh coffee reached his nostrils. Careful not to wake Scott, Hauk stepped out on deck.

"Morning, skip." Arnie presented him with a steamy cup of his famous brew.

"Thanks." Hauk savoured his first sip. After all these years, he still hadn't guessed Arnie's secret ingredient. "Where's Kyle?"

"I sent him into town for supplies. He made a point of using the Zodiac in which the girl was sleeping." A smile wrinkled the corner of Arnie's eyes. "She wasn't too impressed."

"No doubt." Hauk's quick glance around the deck didn't reveal her presence. "Did she go with him?"

With a crooked finger, broken too many times, Arnie pointed east. "She's a darn good swimmer."

Star was a dot in the golden reflection of the rising sun over the lake. Mesmerized, Hauk watched her while drinking his coffee. The seamless strokes and graceful glide bared her communion with the water. That wasn't something anyone could fake, though some women tried, and he had been young and foolish enough to believe them.

"I guess I should go cook breakfast. She'll be hungry when she returns."

"No rush. Star and I will make a dive first." Hauk's stomach growled in disagreement, but he ignored it.

"Star?" His helmsman drummed his fingers on the railing. "What happened to calling her Fisher?"

"She's part of the crew, Arnie." Aside from *boss* and *skip*, the crew operated on a first-name basis. Hauk didn't need to justify the use of her first name.

"Good job convincing her to stay." Arnie patted Hauk's shoulder. "I like her. She'll keep you on your toes."

Hauk glanced at his helmsman. "I hired her because she was the best diver I could find on short notice." Being a woman was a strike against Star, an unfair strike, and while Hauk stood by his decision to hire her, it didn't change how he felt about women. "Weren't you on your way to the galley?"

"Yeah... I was... I am..." Arnie rested his elbows on the railing, his stance contradicting his words. "You do realize some women are worth their weight in gold, right?"

After striking out twice, Hauk had written them off. He suffered enough aggravation and humiliation at the hands of his last mistake to last him a lifetime. "Star's assignment is temporary *and* strictly professional. Don't get too attached."

"If you say so, skip." Arnie walked away, but the sarcasm lingered in the air.

* * *

"Dubbing my experiment a futile demonstration won't stop me from carrying it out, Ludwig." Using spare parts that she found at the bottom of a red toolbox, Star had designed a suitable adaptor to blow air into the tires of the Model T. "We're not dealing with an accidental wreck. The undercurrent of the lake didn't drag the car all the way to the middle, and it sure wasn't dropped by a helicopter."

Busy donning his wetsuit, Ludwig rolled his eyes. "Establishing the tires were slashed won't explain how the car plunged into the lake."

"Maybe not, but the reason behind the deed may provide clues." She strapped on two scuba tanks, connecting her own personal tank to her regulator and fitting the other one with her manmade adaptor. "Flat tires are commonly used to immobilize vehicles. It could mean the car sat on an unstable floating device."

Scott ate his breakfast on the outdoor bench next to the open toolbox. "Or a simple, flat raft without railings or bindings to secure the cargo—" His fork hung in midair between his mouth and his plate of bacon and eggs. "I need to research something."

33

Her gaze locked on Ludwig, Star brushed off Scott's sudden departure. "Are you ready to dive or not?"

Ludwig slapped on a weight belt in response.

Her descent into the cold, dark water heightened her senses. The silence of the depths enveloped her and brought an inner peace that eluded her above the surface. Her breathing slowed. Her reality shifted. She became attuned to the aquatic life swarming around her.

She approached the wreck from the driver's side and knelt by the front wheel. The adaptor fit perfectly into the valve of the left tire. She pumped air from her spare tank into the tire. Air bubbles instantly escaped from a three-inch gap. Its smooth edges weren't the product of wear and tear but of a sharp blade. She repeated the experiment on another tire. It appeared intact, but then bubbles seeped from the sand.

Aware of Ludwig's scrutiny, she dug around the second wheel.

* * *

Kyle took advantage of his visit into town to stop by the bar and pay his tab. While the place never closed, he had always assumed that the patrons eventually went home. The morning crowd seemed to indicate otherwise.

As his gaze skimmed over the customers, Kyle did a double take and frowned. He wasn't aware his friend and former dive partner had been released from the hospital, but there was Macey, nursing a drink in the corner. Alone.

Kyle walked to his table. "You should go home, Mace."

Heedless of the suggestion, Macey ordered another beer. "If you're here to babysit me in case I run into more shady characters, don't bother."

The double-edged remark scraped over Kyle's back, leaving a scratch. He pulled the opposite chair and sat. "How are you?"

A waiter removed Macey's empty mug and replaced it with a full one, leaving no indication of how many drinks had previously been served.

"I'll survive." Macey's bitter tone betrayed his misery. "I may even dive again."

It was unlikely with a perforated lung, but for his friend's sake, Kyle faked some enthusiasm. "That'd be great, Mace."

"Did the boss replace me?"

"A careless rookie kid named Fisher. Don't worry, it's only temporary." Sooner rather than later, Hauk would come to his senses and get rid of her before she assaulted someone else. "She dug out a licence plate. It's a close match to the Model T that disappeared in 1912."

Macey's glassy eyes lit up. "The rich banker?"

"Yeah." Patrons glanced their way, but Kyle dismissed their interest in their private conversation. "The car is a beauty, Mace. You should have seen her." The shadow drifting across Macey's face deadened Kyle's enthusiasm. He didn't mean to rub salt into his friend's wound. "Sorry, Mace."

"Stop feeling responsible." Macey growled. "I was the fool and I paid the price."

Kyle's deep resentment toward the blonde woman who almost ended his friend's life simmered just below the surface, obscuring his guilt-ridden conscience.

* * *

Back from their morning dive, Star enjoyed a quiet breakfast on deck with Ludwig and Arnie.

A door banged against a wall, prompting her to look up from her plate.

A grinning Scott exited the cabin. "You're back already?"

"We resurfaced fifteen minutes ago." Ludwig placed his empty coffee mug on the bench he shared with her. "Did you find something or are you just having fun disrupting our breakfast?"

The researcher waved papers in the air. "I knew it sounded familiar, but it took me a while to remember where I saw it. I've browsed so many newspapers, I swear I can recite all the headlines from 1912."

Amused by Scott's exuberance, Star leaned toward Ludwig. "Is he always this cryptic?"

"He spends too much time alone with Wowsy," Ludwig whispered in her ear. "His special laptop."

His breath tickled her skin, generating tiny pulses along her nerve endings. It was a physical response, one upon which she had no control. Nothing more and nothing less. She tilted her head in his direction to see if he had noticed her meaningless reaction.

Ludwig's attention was fixed on the researcher. "Cut to the chase, Scott."

Standing in front of them, Scott handed Ludwig some papers. Star peeked over his shoulder at a printed copy of a newspaper article recounting the disappearance of Mary Watson, the rich banker's wife. The article ended with a black-and-white picture of Mary, her husband, and their infant son, taken in front of their cottage.

Star skimmed over the article only to be sickened by the mother's behaviour. "Mary abandoned her newborn son to run away with her lover?"

"You're not seeing it, are you?" Scott pointed a finger at something behind the banker.

Perplexed, Star took a closer look at the image. On the lakefront, a floating dock was attached to the end of a wooden jetty with loose ropes. "You mean the large dock?"

The researcher's head bobbled up and down. "Now look at the width of the jetty."

The jetty extending into the lake wasn't as wide as the floating dock, but based on the objects and people near the structure, Star felt comfortable venturing a guess. "It's about six feet wide, which is a respectable size for a cottage jetty." A dubious idea crossed her mind. "Are you suggesting someone drove the car down the jetty and borrowed the floating dock to dump it in the middle of the lake?"

"Why not?" Scott held her gaze. "The dock appears level with the jetty. It looks large and sturdy enough to transport a car. It'd be feasible to untie the dock from the jetty and use it to ferry the Model T."

"You can't be serious," Kyle thundered.

Absorbed by the discussion, Star hadn't noticed the diver who climbed onboard with the supplies until he butted in. How much of the discussion Kyle overheard, she had no clue. Still, even if he heard most of it, he hadn't seen the picture, and thus, he didn't have sufficient grounds to dismiss the theory offhand. So, she felt compelled to defend Scott. "I doubt the four tires were slashed for no reason. It could have been done to prevent the car from moving, or rolling overboard, while it was transported."

The muscles in Kyle's arms rippled as he balanced the bags on his hips. "And how would they have pushed the car into the water without tipping the dock and sending everyone overboard?"

"I—" It pained Star that she couldn't further argue with Kyle. "That I can't explain, but dumping a vehicle in the middle of a lake in the summer takes some efforts. I don't dispute the assumption that the car disappeared around the same time that Mary Watson ran away with her lover, but it makes no sense that she stole it to drive away only to waste her time ditching it in the water nearby."

Ludwig rubbed his chin, something he seemed to do when he mulled over something. "It seemed too much of a coincidence that Mary Watson and the Model T disappeared around the same time, but if this is indeed the Watson's car, and I believe it is, then it is unlikely that she used it to get away. I wonder if the authorities back in 1912 considered the possibility they were dealing with two separate incidents."

"Think you could get your hands on an old police report, skip?" The helmsman had remained silent until now, but he obviously followed the discussion.

Ludwig checked his watch. "I may be able to catch Murphy at the Country Club."

The name *Murphy* held no meaning for Star. "Who's Murphy?"

"A retired police officer and a valuable source of information." From the description Ludwig gave, it sounded like he had dealt with Murphy on multiple occasions. "Scott, dig up everything you can on Mary Watson, her husband, the son she abandoned, the cottage—"

"Got it, boss." The researcher dashed inside the cabin.

"Star. Kyle." Ludwig stood, his gaze equally encompassing them both. "Start documenting every inch of that car. Arnie, you're in charge."

Kyle walked by her with the supplies. "I'm not sure how you stopped Hauk from firing you," the diver snapped under his breath. "But your tactic won't work on me. Stay out of my way."

The words stung Star like a whip.

* * *

Seated on the outdoor bench, Hauk read Kyle's latest report. On paper, Kyle supported Star's observations, but in person, they couldn't agree on anything.

For two weeks, his two divers had independently processed the car. Tired of their behaviour, Hauk tossed the sheaf of papers on the storage bin by the cabin door.

Arnie's head popped up from underneath the navigation panel. "Something wrong, skip?"

"No, but they try my patience." Hauk didn't understand the root of Kyle's hostility and had no idea how to curb Star's mounting reciprocity.

His helmsman raised a greyish brow. "I hope you're not thinking of firing one of them."

A headache burgeoned in Hauk's skull. "Not yet…" Those two were the best divers he had ever hired, and he couldn't lose them. Hoping to alleviate the throbbing, Hauk lay on the bench and closed his eyes.

The news of his discovery had reached the media, and journalists taking pictures from watercrafts loomed in the distance. While Hauk had no patience for them, experience had taught him that the fascination would wane as his operation progressed. In the meantime, to ensure the safety of his crew, he had obtained a court injunction forbidding any watercrafts of approaching within sixty metres of his salvage site.

In contrast, the authorities showed no interest in the Model T and had turned a blind eye to his expedition. Still, Hauk was grateful to Murphy who had provided him with a copy of the original police report.

After his wife's disappearance, Banker Watson disclosed her affair with a former employee and accused the lovers of stealing his car and running away together.

"So much for that theory," muttered Hauk.

Since no indication of foul play or contrary evidence were ever found, the lead investigator at the time had accepted the banker's explanation and shelved the case.

"Are you ready for this, boss?" The resourceful young man towering over him had spent all his waking hours either on his computer or on the phone gathering invaluable information on the Watson clan.

With his right hand, Hauk shielded his eyes from the glaring sun. "I'm listening, Scott."

"By accident, I stumbled onto the society column. It's amazing the juicy gossips—"

"Only the relevant parts, please." As entertaining as Scott's famous scenic detours could be, Hauk preferred the expressway.

"Watson, our grieving banker, remarried four months after Mary's disappearance."

A slow whistle escaped Hauk's lips. "It didn't take him long to seek comfort in another woman's arms."

"Not just another woman. His new wife was also the mother of an infant son named Erwin. It says in the article that the banker immediately adopted the *fatherless* boy."

The emphasis on fatherless caught Hauk's attention. He sat up on the bench. "The banker married his mistress and adopted the son *he'd fathered* with her?"

"I can't say for sure, but lots of rumors were circulating about Erwin." Scott pointed west. "If you look in that direction, you'll see a red roof crowning a white house."

Hauk squinted to get a better view. "You mean the white mansion with a matching boathouse and a large gazebo?"

"Yes, that big white house." His researcher chuckled. "You'll be interested to learn that the Watson's cottage used to stand in place of that large gazebo."

Interesting indeed. "Was the property sold after Watson died?" Earlier in the week, Hauk had learned that the banker jumped out of a window from the eleventh floor of his office building in October 1929.

"No, but it burned to the ground in 1931. Watson's *adopted* son, Erwin, rebuilt it a year later."

"Erwin? His second son?" The line of succession surprised Hauk. "Shouldn't his first son, the one he had with Mary, have inherited the property?"

"I'm still searching for Mary's son." Scott's voice carried a hint of frustration at his lack of success.

"Keep searching." Hauk didn't doubt that Scott would eventually find the baby. "Meanwhile, what happened after Erwin rebuilt the cottage?"

"Nothing until his death. Then his daughter Eleanor Watson tore the structure down and erected that big white... that mansion with the red roof. She lives there year-around with her son, Paul Robert."

"Paul Robert?" Hauk had met with a Paul Robert earlier in the morning. "Not the lawyer?"

His researcher nodded. "The same, boss."

The high-profile lawyer had offered Hauk a considerable sum of money to abandon his salvage operation and spare the surviving members of the Watson family from reliving the terrible events surrounding the disappearance of their matriarch, Mary.

Paul Robert obviously forgot to mention his affiliation to Eleanor Watson or that his branch of the family wasn't biologically related to the late Mary Watson. The voluntary omissions—or outright lies—rubbed Hauk the wrong way.

Chapter 4

Star preferred eating on deck rather than in the cabin. Outdoors, she could always count on Mother Nature to provide riveting scenes.

Tonight, a white canoe glided over the lake along the eastern shore. The orange lifejackets of the paddlers contrasted against the blue water and verdant forest in the background.

"Star, do you have something decent to wear in your duffel bag?"

Wary of Ludwig's sudden interest in her wardrobe, she eyed him over her plate. "Why? Something wrong with my shorts?"

"No, but you and I are going on a boat ride to pay a visit to Watson's descendants from his second wife. I'd like you to wear something a bit more dressy... dressier... You know what I mean."

"Why me?" She enjoyed dressing up as much as she enjoyed sunburns.

"Why her?" To hear Kyle question Ludwig's plan didn't bring her any satisfaction.

Ludwig's gaze travelled back and forth between her and Kyle. "Eleanor Watson and her son may be more forthcoming if I show up with a woman."

"You mean *me*?" Not much appealed less to Star than wasting her evening making small talk with strangers.

"You mean *her*?" Kyle's objection was unwarranted.

This time, Star resented his condescending attitude.

"Do I hear an echo?" A shadow darkened Ludwig's expression. He stood with his supper in hand. "We're leaving in one hour, Fisher."

Fisher? Ludwig hadn't called her Fisher in weeks. And from the smirk on Kyle's face, the insolent diver had noticed.

* * *

Hauk moored the Zodiac to the jetty facing Eleanor's mansion.

The current waterfront showed similarities to the historical newspaper photograph of the happy Watson family. Hauk could almost picture the floating dock tied at the end of the jetty or the cottage standing where vestiges of its the foundation were still visible around the gazebo.

Clad in a short, lime skirt and a white tank top that offered a stunning contrast to her suntanned skin, Star walked a few steps ahead of him. With each step she took, her hips swayed back and forth with the rhythm of the waves crashing against the jetty. His gaze travelled up from her slender waist to—

She stopped abruptly and spun around. "I still don't understand what you hope to gain by meeting them."

Caught staring at her remarkable attributes, Hauk grinned sheepishly.

"Fine," she groaned. "Don't tell me."

"I want to know why they tried to stop me from investigating." His hand sought the delicate curve at the small of her back. "Let's go."

"No pushing, Ludwig." Her back arched inward. "It won't get me there any faster."

He dropped his hand. "You know you can call me Hauk, right?" Calling him Ludwig sounded too impersonal, and he wanted to project a friendly impression during their visit.

"Sure, *Hauk*."

They approached the front veranda.

An elderly woman stood behind a screen door. "Mr. Ludwig. What a lovely surprise."

"Good evening." Though they had never met, the woman knew his name. "Would Mrs. Watson be available by any chance?"

"Call me Eleanor." A smile added wrinkles to Eleanor's ageless face. "Please come in."

Invited into a large living room, Hauk joined Star on a dark blue leather loveseat.

The local newspaper lay on the coffee table. The first page featured an article about his salvage operation along with a photo of his crew.

Across the table, Eleanor sat in a blue, flowery armchair near a wood fireplace. "Your diving operation, Mr. Ludwig, is provoking quite an uproar around our quiet lake." She had skipped the pleasantries and offered them no drink.

"Quite unintentional, though I admit I didn't realize the extent of the disturbance until I met your son this morning." Hauk discreetly glanced around the sunny, luxurious interior. A curved stairwell led to a second floor. "Is he here?"

"Paul works late. Lawyers." Eleanor sighed. "You know how they are."

"Yes. I do." *Unscrupulous and contemptuous.* Hauk couldn't care less if they worked all day or night.

"Paul phoned me today." Eleanor crossed her left leg over her right knee and rested both hands on her lap. "I learned you declined his proposition. Are you, by any chance, reconsidering?"

No, not a chance. "Truth be told, Mrs. Watson, his proposition sounded a lot like a bribe."

"A bribe? I'm sorry to hear you misinterpreted Paul's intentions," Eleanor apologized, but her clouded blue eyes remained impassive.

He glanced at Star to gauge her reaction to Eleanor's expression.

Star leaned forward, her gaze locked on the older lady. "Mrs. Watson, doesn't it strike you as odd that the car your grandmother allegedly stole ended up at the bottom of the lake?"

"You're reopening an awful chapter in the family history, dear." The older woman's fingers tightened slightly, creating crinkles in her white linen skirt.

Star reached out and placed her hand over Eleanor's forearm. "Please, would you share with us what happened a century ago?"

* * *

On good days, the bar drew rowdy patrons in. On bad days, the bartender kicked sorry carcasses out. Drink in hand, Bruce pushed his way through the raucous crowd and blue smoke. His friend Dusty waited for him in a dark corner, away from prying ears and eyes.

Bruce grabbed a stool and sat beside Dusty. "What's up?"

His long-time friend slapped a newspaper on the round table. "Look at the star on the girl's face. Right cheek, just like the ugly bitchling."

A colour picture of Ludwig's crew was posted on the first page. Bruce looked at the girl's scar then shrugged off the resemblance. "Last I remember, she drowned."

Dusty took a swig of his beer. "Her body was never found."

"Dead people don't resurface twenty years later." Tempted to smack Dusty over the head with the newspaper, Bruce grabbed it and folded it in half. "She's dead."

"What if the nanny stashed—"

"Chill out." Debating the child's fate with Dusty only fed his paranoid tendencies. "We have another problem. I heard one of the divers describe the car they found at the bottom of the lake. It's Watson's Model T."

Dusty's face lit up. "Your cunning grandpa?"

The crazy, old crook wasn't my grandpa. "Step-great-grandfather, and this isn't funny." The implications should have stared his friend right in the face. Bruce shouldn't need to spell them out. "If the police decide to reopen the Watson investigation, it'll lead to the murders, and we don't want that, do we?"

His friend grumbled through gritted teeth. "You want me to stop the divers' expedition?"

Short of a better option, Bruce nodded.

* * *

A storm brewed on the horizon. Pushed by strong winds, dark clouds swirled over the lake. The Zodiac sliced through the rising waves, spraying a fine mist over Star's clothes and skin.

"Eleanor didn't correct me when I used the term grandmother." Star had to shout to cut through the noise of the engine and Mother Nature's angry sounds.

"I noticed." Seated at the back, Hauk steered the Zodiac toward his vessel. "What did you make of her story?"

Sobs had stifled Eleanor's voice while she recounted her grandfather Watson's scheme, but Star didn't buy the story. "Too much of a theatrical performance."

A muscle twitched under Hauk's taut, blue shirt. Two more buttons had come undone since their departure from Eleanor's mansion. A third tugged against its hole, almost begging for assistance.

A mischievous grin played on his lips. "I agree."

Heat rushed to Star's face. In his presence, her imagination had a tendency to run wild. Calling him Ludwig had helped to rein it in, but now that they were on first-name basis, she had to find a way to stop it. Permanently. She forced her gaze to meet his before glancing toward the vessel they were fast approaching.

Once Hauk turned the engine off, she hurried to secure the Zodiac with the rope hanging near the ladder. They climbed onboard.

On deck, Arnie awaited their return. "Glean any useful information?"

The vessel swayed under Star's feet, and she relished the feeling. "Growing up, Eleanor Watson heard rumours of her grandfather, Banker Watson, taking advantage of his first wife's disappearance to report his car stolen and collect the insurance money."

"Insurance money?" The doors of the storage bin rattled when Kyle slammed them shut. "It doesn't make sense."

"Why not?" Chin held high, Star stared at her dive partner.

He slouched on the bench. "Why would the banker dump his car in the lake? And why would the lawyer offer the boss thousands of dollars to hush the discovery? The shifty banker is dead. The insurance company won't sue four generations later— why are you smiling?"

Despite playing devil's advocate, Star agreed with Kyle. "Hauk and I also think she lied. We just can't figure out why."

"Her grandfather committed suicide after he declared bankruptcy." Hauk paced the deck. "Eleanor claims she wants to preserve what's left of his reputation, so she begged me not to add fraud to his deeds."

"It still doesn't make sense." Kyle bolted off the bench. "We can't prove fraud. We can't even determine for sure how the car ended up at the bottom. For all we know, the missing wife sank it to spite the banker before taking off with her lover."

Scott cleared his throat. How long he had stood inside the cabin doorway listening, Star couldn't tell. "It's possible Eleanor Watson is truly trying to avoid another stain on the family tree."

Hauk's jaw tightened. "Based on what?"

The researcher rocked back and forth on the balls of his feet in rhythm with the boat. "Based on the information I collected on her ex."

"Ex?" Star didn't recall Eleanor mentioning any ex-husband or lover, and from Hauk's mystified expression, he didn't either. "Which ex?"

"Six years ago, Eleanor's husband, a lawyer named Frederick Robert, embezzled over two million dollars before his firm partners became suspicious. To—"

"She married a crooked lawyer?" Kyle snorted. "Corruption runs deep in that family."

A grin spread across Scott's boyish face. "My nana would say *birds of a feather flock together*. Anyway, to avoid prosecution, Frederick Robert fled the country with his secretary. Eleanor filed for divorce and changed her name back to Watson. The scandal nearly cost their son, Paul Robert, who was a junior partner in the firm, his law career. Fun fact, Eleanor was Frederick's second wife. They got married a month after he divorced his first wife."

"Fred left his first wife for Eleanor, and then he left Eleanor for his secretary? That's what I call karma, but—" Arnie lifted his baseball cap and wiped his bald head with a red handkerchief. "Isn't an old insurance scam trivial compared to her ex-husband's embezzlement and betrayal?"

"I suppose it's possible that Eleanor is afraid to face another public humiliation." On a primal level, Star empathized with the older woman. She understood the constant battle against crude stares and inconsiderate remarks. They both had to live with the consequences of someone—or something—else's malicious actions. "Still, I doubt an insurance claim alone accounts for the efforts spent to dispose of the car."

* * *

Dusty parked his commercial van in the bushes, not too far from the patch of gravel where boaters kept their vehicles. From his hiding place, he enjoyed an unobstructed view of the intrusive vessel and its nosy crew.

As the evening progressed, the sky darkened.

A sudden downpour forced Ludwig and his crew to take refuge inside the cabin. An hour later, someone turned off the lights,

54

leaving only the white anchor light glowing in the night.

Elbows on the steering wheel, Dusty lowered his binoculars. By the time he reached the boat, the crew should all be asleep. He exited the front seat and walked to the back of his van. The wind whipped at his clothes and the rain drenched everything he wore. Heedless of the discomfort, or the danger, he threw his wet shirt and pants into the cargo area, donned his black wetsuit, and fins in hand, ventured into the stormy night.

Wary of prying eyes, Dusty glanced around. Seeing no one, he stepped into the water and slipped on his fins. The storm raged over his head. He swam below the disturbance created by the waves. On the lake, the white anchor light shining at the top of Ludwig's vessel acted as a beacon every time Dusty resurfaced to get his bearings.

Two Zodiacs blocked the access to the ladder. He circled them with ease and dropped his fins into the last one. The rocking of the vessel masked his ascent onto the deck.

During his evening surveillance, he had watched the male diver ready the gears then stow them in the storage bin. Dusty opened the lid and cringed at the creaking. The hinges needed grease, but the crashing of the waves had drowned the noise.

He pulled pliers from his belt and sabotaged every regulator neatly aligned on the lower shelf.

On their next underwater exploration, the divers will gasp for air and wiggle like fish on hooks. Proud of his handiwork, Dusty put away the pliers. *It's too bad I won't be there to witness their demise.*

* * *

Tiptoeing down a hallway toward the bathroom, a little blonde girl played with a rabbit-shaped button of her nightgown. She stopped in the doorway and peeked inside. Her gaze wandered to the cupboard above the toilet.

The left door slid open. Red blood dripped from the shelf onto the floor. The heads of a woman and two young children stared back with empty brown eyes.

Horrified, the child screamed.

High above the little girl's head, a blade shone under the lone light bulb hanging from the ceiling. The long knife swept through the air—

Star bolted upright on her cot, gasping and shaking. The light cotton blanket she had wrapped herself in didn't prevent the cold from invading her body or the tears from pooling in her eyes. She forced herself to take deep calming breaths.

The disturbing images slowly faded away. It was only a nightmare, a horrible nightmare that had plagued her for as long as she remembered.

As the tremors and the pounding of her heart subsided, she became aware of her surroundings. The rain thumped on the roof drowning the regular breathing sounds of the sleeping crew. At least she didn't scream out loud and wake everyone. In need of personal space, she sneaked out of the cabin.

She sat on the bench. In the shadows created by the anchor light, she pulled her knees up against her chest and gazed into the stormy night. The rain plastered her clothes and hair to her body, but she didn't care.

"Taking a shower?"

Startled by Hauk's sudden appearance, she recoiled against the back cushion.

He raised his hands in surrender, a mock gesture captured by the anchor light. "No knife, please."

The light banter eased the tension warping her body. "You're safe."

He sat beside her, his leg brushing her foot. "Would you like to talk?"

"About what?" With great efforts, she relegated the nightmare to the back of her mind, where it belonged.

"About whatever got you out of bed to brave this wonderful weather?" His gravelly voice rumbled across her skin. "In case you haven't noticed, it's pouring ducks."

"Ducks?" Grateful for the colourful mental picture, she relaxed. "Just a bad dream. Nothing really."

His wet undershirt hugged his chest, accentuating his chiseled muscles...

Caught fantasizing again, she shook her head, chiding herself. It had been too long since a man held her in his arms and saw past her scar, but this was a temporary assignment. Getting attached to any crew member would only lead to a broken heart. It had taken all the strength she could muster to survive Julian's death. She couldn't fathom experiencing that pain again let alone mending another wounded heart.

"You're drenched." His gaze wandered over the deck.

Rain poured down her face, and Star smiled at the irony. "I spend my life in the water, remember?"

He pushed a dripping curl from her cheek, his fingers gently skimming over the creases of her scar, and leaving behind the illusion of a feathery caress.

"A dog," she volunteered before he asked. "As a child, I was mauled by a dog."

His eyes widened. "A dog?" The tip of one finger traced her scar. "I'm amazed by the dog."

"Amazed?" The only amazing thing about the dog was that it bit her entire cheek but missed her eye, her nose, and her mouth by the skin of its teeth.

"The star design suits your personality." He dropped his hand. "It adds a hint of mystery and mischief to your expression."

To her dismay, foolish butterflies fluttered in the pit of her stomach. "You seriously need glasses, Hauk."

"Perfect vision, even in the dark. Tell me, is Star a nickname?"

Growing up, she often wondered about the coincidence. "No. I was named after my mother, Stella. She died when I was four."

He bowed his head. "Sorry."

The loss happened so long ago that Star couldn't remember the feeling of losing her mother. Of her younger years, she only recalled the big black dog that attacked her near the water. She dreamed of dead strangers, saw their faces, their eyes, but for the life of her, she couldn't picture her own mother.

A four-year-old child shouldn't have forgotten her mother. Maybe the lack of memories—and not the scar—caused that void inside her chest. "I'm sorry too. Good night, Hauk."

Afraid to reveal too much, she left him in the rain.

Chapter 5

Annoyed at Star, Kyle marched up and down the deck. Ready to dive, he was forced to wait for her. Her morning swim impeded on their work schedule, and if it were up to him, he would ban the ritual—or fire her.

The sound of footsteps on the ladder alerted him to her ascent. He didn't wait for her feet to touch the deck. "Hurry up."

She glared at him. "What's your problem this morning?"

You. During the night, her moaning and twitching had roused him. He had caught a draft of cool air when she left the cabin, then another one when the boss followed her. Intrigued, Kyle had ventured outside only to sneer at her sweet act toward Hauk.

Impervious to Arnie's presence, Kyle threw her a towel. "We're paid to work not swim."

To add to his frustration, it took her forever to don her wetsuit and she refused the tank he offered her.

Instead, she retrieved her own smaller tank. "Just dive without me, Kyle. I'll be down in a minute."

"Your sorry butt better follow me, kid."

* * *

Fast approaching her lethal dose of confrontation with the insufferable diver, Star growled. "Does he hate women in general or is it a special treatment he reserves just for me?"

Arnie helped her with her jacket. "You took Macey's place."

"And?" From the random tidbits that Star had picked up, she understood Kyle and Macey had been good buddies, but the reason behind his departure remained unclear. "What happened to Macey? Did Hauk fire him?"

"A woman robbed him after stabbing him with a pocketknife."

No wonder Kyle was hostile toward her. Hauk had replaced his friend by a woman. *Me.* "I guess it explains Kyle's attitude."

"But it doesn't excuse it. You're working hard and you're detail-oriented. You deserve to be here."

"Thank you, Arnie." The kind words lifted her spirits. "Would you get me a second regulator, please?"

"Why?" The man retrieved one from the storage bin for her. "Something wrong with yours?"

"No." She snapped the last strap of her jacket into its buckle. "I'm conducting another experiment."

After connecting the regulator to the tank that Kyle had originally presented her with, she tested it.

Arnie knelt by her side. "You don't trust anyone, do you?"

"It's a matter of caution, not trust. I always double-check my equipment."

She turned the valve off, then on again. According to the gauge, the tank was full, except something was disrupting the airflow into the regulator.

Arnie tapped on the gauge. "Something's wrong with the pressure."

"Probably faulty. That happens." Undaunted, she nabbed a different one and tested it. "This one isn't functioning properly either."

She tried a third one and felt a rising panic in her chest. "I need to get Kyle out now. Call an ambulance."

* * *

Star's heart pounded against her ribcage, adrenaline flowed through her veins, and hairs prickled all over her body. Her senses in high alert, she scanned the dark water surrounding her, listening for sounds she couldn't possibly hear.

If Kyle's regulator failed, he would meet a fate worse than death—a fate she didn't wish on anyone.

Haunted by the gruesome memory, she continued her cautious descent, one hand on the guide rope and the other on her belt. Something brushed her leg. She drew her knife, and stopped short of slicing a walleye below its gill. The fish swam away. Still, the encounter left her rattled.

Above the wreck, she spotted Kyle, twisting and jerking.

Ruling out a direct physical confrontation that would undoubtedly result in both their deaths, she approached the strong, desperate man and slapped him with the tip of her fin.

He spun, and his arms missed striking her by mere inches. Agony and terror contorted his features. He suddenly lurched at her with incredible agility and speed.

Too late to retreat, she bent her knee and raised her leg. He grabbed her wrist and twisted it. Pain coursed through her arm. She pressed her foot against his chest, ready to thrust him away if he threatened her life.

A flicker of recognition appeared in his dark eyes. She took a deep breath, removed her mouthpiece, and in a fluid motion, offered it to him.

As he breathed air into his lungs, the fear in his eyes subsided and the grip on her wrist loosened.

Star stopped believing in a coincidence after discovering the third faulty regulator.

Now that Kyle was on his way to the hospital, she lined up all the regulators on the deck, including the ones that Kyle and she used.

Even though her regulator worked, she still examined it and tested it like all the others.

"It wasn't a fluke." The blood in her veins boiled with rage. "Arnie? Come here."

The man instantly abandoned his post at the helm to squat beside her. "Find something?"

"Tool marks. See?" Her hands shook showing him the suspicious tool marks on each regulator. "They all bear similar signs of sabotage, except mine."

The helmsman gaped like a fish in an empty bucket. "This... this looks intentional, but no one onboard could have done this."

"I agree, Arnie." The notion that a crew member was a saboteur went in one ear and out the other without brushing her brain. "Someone systematically disabled all the regulators, I'm guessing to stop or hinder the salvage operation by causing an accident, but unlike every member of the crew, whoever is responsible didn't know I keep my gear behind the bench. This can only be an outside job."

"Okay, but who?" Arnie toyed with the brim of his baseball cap. "Kyle prepped the equipment last night. He would have noticed if something was amiss."

"Kyle and I may have our differences, but he isn't careless." Despite how she felt toward her dive partner, Star couldn't deny that Kyle was meticulous. "I'm convinced the equipment was in perfect working order last night. You'll think I'm insane, Arnie, but..." The likelihood that an intruder sneaked onboard during the night seemed too farfetched to entertain, but she couldn't think of any other explanation. "You and I don't usually sleep in the cabin unless Mother Nature brews up a storm, which is exactly what happened last night. I would wager that someone took advantage of the storm to board the boat while we were all sleeping inside."

"You're not insane, girl, but only insane or desperate people would venture in the water during a storm." Arnie grabbed one of the regulators. "And this can only be the handiwork of an insane person."

It frightened Star to hear Arnie agree with her, but it also spurred her to dig deeper into the intruder's motivation. She marched to the back of the deck, grabbed a full tank, then strapped it to her jacket.

Arnie got hold of her last buckle before she could fasten it. "What do you think you're doing?"

"Someone took an awful risk tampering with the regulators." To her annoyance, she couldn't conceal the tremors in her voice. "I want to know why that someone didn't want us to dive this morning."

"You're not going down there alone." He raised his voice, something he had never resorted to since she joined the crew. "It isn't safe."

* * *

"You let her dive alone?" Hauk roared upon his return from his morning visits to the insurance companies in town. "Were you out of your mind?"

During his absence, Kyle and Star had been instructed to examine the car, not get killed. To learn that Arnie had hooked her up to a safety line, or that she had waited forty-five minutes before making her second dive, didn't lessen Hauk's apprehension.

"She's vigilant, Hauk." Arnie only called him Hauk when he made a strong point. "You need to trust her judgment."

Hauk had tested her instincts, but the knowledge that she could defend herself didn't stop fear from constricting his chest. "It's not her judgment I'm questioning,

Arnie, it's the lack of judgment of whoever sabotaged the equipment."

"I've kept the safety line taut, and Star hasn't made any abrupt moves." Arnie leaned against the railing, the line sliding back and forth between his fingers. "I'd feel it if she was struggling with someone or something."

Hauk was tempted to yank the line from his helmsman's hands and reel her in against her will, but without knowing the exact nature of her underwater activities, he couldn't risk startling and injuring her. His stomach tied into a reef knot, Hauk stared helplessly at the diver's flag attached to a floating buoy.

Red with a broad diagonal white stripe, the flag fluttered in the breeze, signalling the presence of a diver below.

* * *

Frustrated, Star circled the wreck a second time for something that she or Kyle might have missed. The corrosion had eaten away the identification number engraved on the engine, and the other mechanical components held no particular interest. They had searched the trunk, the—

She briefly stopped kicking as she recalled the Tin Lizzy specs. *The seats consisted of two padded, rectangular, wooden boxes with a dorsal panel attached to them. Replacing the nails on the horizontal plank with hinges would transform the wasted space underneath into a storage area.*

It was the only place they had overlooked.

Without touching the rotted wood, she examined the seats. No hinges, only nails embedded at irregular intervals. Using her knife, she extracted half a dozen. Some were longer than others by half an inch. *Ford wouldn't have used two different sizes of nails to hammer that seat. Someone else made modifications after purchasing it.* Unable to remove more nails, she pulled on the plank. It crumbled under the pressure. *Oh, oh... Hauk won't be happy.*

She swept her hand back and forth to clear the debris floating above what used to be the back seat. The bottom had caved in, but to her great disappointment, the search of the bottom yielded no result.

In the name of thoroughness, she should subject the front seat to the same fate, but she hesitated. Destroying seats wasn't included in her job description, nor was listening to her gut feelings. However, over the years, she had relied on them to perform her job, and her gut feelings had never failed her.

She extracted as many nails as possible from the front plank then lifted it as gently as she could. To her dismay, the wood disintegrated in her hands, clouding the water with swirling particles. *I'm very sorry, Hauk.*

Once the dust settled, she peered inside the front compartment. Not only had it not sunk in, but it revealed several small objects.

Well, that wasn't for nothing. She picked up the biggest object, a two-inch long fragment. Unable to visually identify it, she placed it in the bag strapped to her belt. The next piece, roughly an-inch long, was shaped like a cross. Then she retrieved a round item that reminded her of an earring and four more misshapen fragments. After they were all placed inside her bag, she carefully swept the bottom. In a corner, she made another discovery. A ring.

Pleased with the results of her search, she rose to the surface—and met Hauk's angry gaze.

* * *

Parked in front of the police station, Hauk vented his frustration by kicking the front tire of his Jeep.

The police officer had first dismissed Kyle's tragedy as an unfortunate accident. Granted, his diver should have tested his equipment before diving and not relied on his evening preparation, but it didn't explain why all the regulators became dysfunctional overnight. The suggestion that someone on his crew fiddled with them hadn't impressed Hauk. He trusted each of them implicitly. In the end, the officer had opened a case file and recorded his complaint.

"Did the cop want a dead body to go with it?" Hauk was too infuriated to care that bystanders could overhear him. "The tool marks prove sabotage."

Standing by the passenger side, her arms crossed on the edge of the roof, Star stared at him. "Yes, but the police officer also made a valid point"

Hauk glared, groaning. "When?"

"When he said an intruder would need inside knowledge of Kyle's routine. I know you think I'm reckless because I dive alone, but you're wrong. I am an overcautious diver who only takes calculated chances and always checks her gear before every dive. That's how Jimmy trained me and that's how I operate." And thanks to that training, she had been able to save Kyle in the nick of time. "The point is, if I were the intruder, I wouldn't risk boarding a boat during a storm unless I was certain my evil deeds wouldn't be compromised by a diver like me."

"For the record, I don't think you're reckless." *Just headstrong, and fierce, and trustworthy, and—* As Hauk mentally listed all the qualities he admired, another thought crossed his mind. "What if the intruder didn't mean to harm anyone? It could have been a scare tactic to stop or delay the operation.”

“He gambled with a storm that could easily have produced lightning, Hauk.” Blonde curls bounced over her shoulders, sensuously brushing her bronze skin. “That’s high risk for a low stake like a scare tactic, but then I do value my life. Maybe the intruder doesn’t.”

“Maybe... Get in.” Both doors, his and hers, opened and closed at the same time. “I’m dropping you off at the hospital so you can question Kyle.”

Her hand froze on her seatbelt buckle. “Me?”

“You see someone else here?” He didn’t mean to snap, but he was frustrated, and a part of him was still angry with her for diving alone. *Not for diving alone. For diving. Period.*

An intruder could have been lurking around the site, waiting to dispose of her. The few relics that she discovered hidden under the seat were not worth risking her life.

Her beautiful brown eyes narrowed into two dark slits. “What exactly am I supposed to ask Kyle?” The seatbelt clicked in place, and she clasped her hands together on her lap. “And where are *you* going?”

“Looking for Macey.” While Hauk didn’t pin his former diver as a saboteur, Macey might have unknowingly shared his inside knowledge of Kyle’s routine with someone else. "If he spends his days at the bar like Kyle hints, Macey may have heard, or told someone, something important."

"And if he drinks, he may not remember anything he heard or said," she countered with a mischievous smirk.

"Not funny, Fisher." Hauk chided himself for admiring her features. *Dammit, she's ten years my junior.* Furthermore, no woman was worth a third strike. "You're going to visit Kyle. End of discussion."

Chapter 6

Clueless as why Hauk delegated the task to her, Star grumbled all the way to the fifth floor. Scott and Arnie would have made better candidates to visit Kyle. The diver would have appreciated their visit. *Unlike mine.*

To her disappointment, no medical personnel stopped her from roaming the hallway of the hospital after visiting hours.

Her impromptu arrival inside Kyle's room interrupted his flirtatious exchange with a pretty nurse, dissipating his broad smile, and chased away the brunette. Had a patient occupied the other bed, Star would probably have managed to scare him away as well.

Propped against his pillows, Kyle glared coldly at her. "Were you crazy pulling a stunt like that without an octopus?"

Unlike her own, the regulators onboard came equipped with an octopus, which consisted of a second mouthpiece and an auxiliary air source designed to make a rescue effort safer for the rescuer. During her underwater struggle with Kyle, she had secretly wished she hadn't relinquished the somewhat cumbersome appendage.

"I'm so glad your brush with death didn't alter your charming personality." She sat on the ledge of the large window overlooking the parking lot, waiting for another harsh comeback.

"I was choking. It took every ounce of strength I had not to snatch that mouthpiece from you and keep it." His milder tone, more than his confession, stunned her. "You risked your life to rescue me. Why?"

"Because..."

Years ago, she had registered for a deep diving course in a submerged quarry. A dozen divers, mostly middle-aged men, attended the seven-day course. Among them was Julian, a young university law student who needed a change of scenery after writing a series of gruesome exams. They met at lunch on the first day, fell in love by nightfall, and spent every minute of every day together, above and under water. On the last day, they ended up with different underwater partners. No one noticed Julian was in trouble until he reached the second ledge and began thrashing in the water. His partner tried to help, but Julian lurched at him. Too far to intervene, Star watched them fight, and drown. Her heart shattered in thousand pieces, all sinking to the bottom while she carried Julian to the surface. She had sat in silence at the edge of the quarry under a scorching sun, and to this day, she could still feel the shivering cold that invaded her body.

"Because..." *Because I couldn't bear the burden of another tragedy.* She briefly closed her eyes to prevent tears from spilling over. "Because I value life, Kyle, including yours. But make no mistake, had you threatened mine, you would be dead."

A smile softened his chiseled features. "Fair enough, kid. So what went wrong?"

"Well..." She never had to tell anyone that he had been the victim of a murder attempt, so she wasn't sure how to proceed. "Your regulator failed. Someone tinkered with it."

Kyle's mouth dropped open and closed, and opened again. "You mean it wasn't an accident?"

She shook her head. "Someone sabotaged all the regulators onboard, except mine."

"All of them?" Kyle sank into his pillow. "You didn't dive *knowing* I was in trouble, did you?"

Of course I did. The man was her dive partner, and while it might not mean anything to him, it mattered to her. "My sorry butt felt obligated to rescue yours. Call it a lack of judgment."

His gaze momentarily lost its focus, and during the brief introspection, Star sensed a subtle change in his demeanor.

"If you don't mind staying for a while, kid, I would appreciate all the details."

* * *

The bar swarmed with customers. The smoke didn't offend Hauk's sense of smell as much as the odours of onion rings and rotten fish did. He scanned the dimly lit room for Macey.

Yells and laughter drowned out the country music playing from a jukebox. A crowd had gathered near the restrooms where a cheerful storyteller entertained his rowdy audience. Recognizing Macey's voice and the sailboat tale, Hauk dodged scantily clad waitresses and inebriated patrons to get to him.

"Hey, boss!" Macey waved at him from the stool he occupied at the head of a rectangular table. "Long time, no see. What brings you to this dump?"

"Ain't no dump," the portly owner yelled. "Skip? Want lunch or a beer? It's on the house."

His stomach still reeling from his last culinary experience in the joint, Hauk gestured for a beer.

"Rumour says an ambulance was dispatched to the lake." Macey raised his mug, spilling some of its content on his shirt before it touched his lips.

Hauk scrutinized his injured diver. Dirty brown hair, unkempt beard, hollowed eyes, and rumpled clothes that left no doubt as to where Macey spent his days and nights. Someone had transformed the responsible diver that Hauk hired two years earlier into the shell of a man.

"Waw 'appen?" slurred an elderly man with a grubby white T-shirt. "Nyone got 'urt?"

"They say they pulled one of your guys out of the water," shouted a beefy guy with a psychedelic tattoo on his bicep.

Hauk raked his gaze over the crowd. How and where these people obtained their information mystified him.

"Was Kyle injured?" Macey's voice had sobered up. "Or that rookie who replaced me?"

A waitress approached Hauk carrying a tray filled with drinks. Foam dripped down the side of the mug she handed him. He nodded in thanks toward the owner before addressing the patrons. "Nobody's injured."

Faces dropped and patrons jeered at the lack of tragedy.

Disgusted, Hauk grabbed Macey by the front of his filthy shirt. "We need to talk in private."

* * *

Seated at the end of the bar top, Bruce nursed a drink while listening to the lively discussion, his keen interest hidden behind dark aviator sunglasses.

Ludwig dragged his young diver by his shirt to a quiet table. The crowd dispersed and the noise died down.

Under the pretense of lighting a cigarette, Bruce shifted on his stool so the pair remained in his line of vision.

Dusty had called earlier to say he took care of the divers and their quest. Busy with clients in his office, Bruce didn't ask for details. Unlike his disturbed friend, Bruce derived no personal satisfaction from hurting or killing, but what needed to be done had to be done, at any and all costs. Ending the salvage operation had been necessary to protect the past.

Too far from the pair to eavesdrop, Bruce had to be content with watching the one-sided discussion during which Ludwig's lips moved and the diver's head either shook or nodded. Still, Ludwig's solemn demeanor seemed to attest to Dusty's success.

A few minutes later, Ludwig pushed his mug to the middle of the table and rose, mimicked by the young diver.

Bruce downed his beer, crushed his cigarette butt in an ashtray, and followed them outside. The pair left together in a grey Jeep.

Leery of the reasons that prompted Ludwig to seek his injured diver, Bruce jumped into his truck and tailed the Jeep through town, always keeping a few cars between their respective vehicles.

Ludwig stopped at a rundown motel then hauled luggage from a room into the back of the Jeep.

Unhappy with the development, Bruce seethed out loud. "If Ludwig is planning on reinstating the injured diver, then the operation has been merely delayed, not terminated."

As soon as Ludwig drove away from the motel, Bruce resumed his tail, which ended at the bus station.

Seeing the young diver grab his belongings and enter the station lifted a weight from Bruce's shoulders. "The diver is leaving town. So far, so good." He kept following the Jeep across town, and it got even better when Ludwig pulled into the hospital parking lot. "Someone must have been admitted, or else Ludwig wouldn't be here."

Desperate for irrefutable bad news, Bruce parked in the back alley and entered the lobby of the hospital where he spotted Ludwig near the gift shop. Afraid to be noticed, Bruce picked up a newspaper conveniently discarded on top of a garbage can and held it open in front of his face. A few seconds later, he peered over the edge in time to see Ludwig step into an empty elevator.

The numbers over the left door lit up, then paused on the fifth floor.

Bruce approached the second elevator. Its door opened, and a distracted young woman bumped into him.

She lifted her head. "Sorry, I wasn't paying attention."

Shocked, Bruce stumbled back and stared in disbelief at the scar on her right cheek. Her gaze narrowed, and she strode away. For a stunned moment, he considered following her but changed his mind. There was no point arousing her suspicion when he knew exactly where to find her.

On the fifth floor, the nurses' station was deserted. Bruce leaned over the counter and peeked at the computer screen. *Diving accident. Room 513.*

At least one of them was injured, but it didn't say how badly. Needing answers, Bruce approached Room 513, only stopping when he could overhear the voices loud and clear.

His newspaper open to the sports section, Bruce leaned against the wall near a linen cart and listened.

"Boss, I'm fine."

"Sure you are. Doctor?"

Bruce recognized Ludwig's voice from the bar. Apparently a doctor was in the room with Ludwig and the male diver.

"To be cautious, I'd like to keep him overnight."

"Overnight? I've been poked enough." The diver sounded desperate. "There's nothing wrong. Star saved me in time."

The name *Star* didn't ring a bell in Bruce's mind, but the *nothing wrong* didn't bode well for him and Dusty.

"You do as the doctor requests. I'll pick you up in the morning." Ludwig's voice left no room for argument.

"Come on, boss."

Bruce smiled as the diver's plea fell on deaf ears.

"Don't overstay your visit, Mr. Ludwig." The nasal voice of the doctor could be heard over the ruffling of a curtain. "My patient needs to rest."

Bruce let out a derisive snort. *Needs to rest?* That had to be every doctor's favourite expression.

The doctor walked out of the room without glancing in Bruce's direction.

"Did Star pay you a visit?" Ludwig asked.

There's that name again. Remembering the newspaper article that Dusty had shown him yesterday, Bruce peered at the date written at the top of the sports page. *Yesterday's edition. Lucky me.*

"She left five minutes ago. She told me you went to see Macey. What did he say?"

Five minutes ago? That was around the time that Bruce bumped into the disfigured woman. He quickly flipped back to the first page where he found the colour picture of Ludwig's crew. Under the girl's photo was her name. Star Fisher.

"He said nothing. I sent him home, Kyle. I even called his old man. He'll make sure Macey receives adequate care."

Bruce was glad to hear they knew nothing and that at least one diver was permanently out of the picture. However, it didn't solve his problem, and it didn't explain why the girl changed her name. Or how she survived.

"Listen, boss, I didn't screw up down there."

The diver might not have screwed up, but Dusty obviously did. *All the divers should be permanently disabled. Or dead.*

A loud chime announced the end of visiting hours.

Bruce dropped the newspaper onto the linen tray and left the floor before Ludwig came out and stumbled onto him.

Once inside his truck, Bruce wiped sweat off his forehead and called Dusty. *Come on. Pick up.*

On the seventh ring, his friend answered. "What?"

Bruce pulled the phone away, his ears ringing. His first reaction was to hang up and call back when his friend was in a better mood, but the urgency of the situation stopped him. "We have a big problem."

"What problem?" Dusty panted. "And make it fast."

A stronger wave of anger washed over Bruce. He wedged his phone in the crook of his neck then lit up a cigarette to calm his nerve. "The female diver is alive, and she rescued the other diver."

"I sabotaged their gear. The divers should all be dead." A thud resounded in the background. "Back on my lap, you—"

"Lose the hooker," Bruce shouted back, his frustration growing exponentially.

"Can't do, Bruce." A female moaned on the line. "She ain't done."

"Get rid of her. Now." *How, but how, did I end up friend with a guy whose brain falls off his pants every time they get unzipped?* "The—child—never—drowned." Bruce slowly articulated each word to get Dusty's attention. "I bumped into her."

"You did what?" Dusty's exclamation was followed by the slamming of a door. "Did she recognize you?"

"I doubt it, but we can't risk that she remembers anyone or—" Bruce's gaze wandered out his side window. "I think I see her."

A young woman resembling Fisher walked through a vacant lot near the hospital. Alone. In a minute or so, she would either turn onto the sidewalk or cross the intersection.

Bruce glanced around and couldn't believe his luck. No bystanders and no traffic. "I'll call you back."

* * *

Medical facilities made Star jittery, so after visiting Kyle, she sought a sunny haven.

A few blocks from the hospital, she stumbled on a waterpark where kids splashed and played under giant sprinklers. She watched them for a while before strolling back to meet Hauk.

Within view of the hospital, she cut through a vacant lot, walked through rubbles and tall grass, then proceeded to cross a quiet intersection.

An engine roared to life and tires squealed on the asphalt. The sudden racket startled her. Stopped in the middle of the intersection, she looked up and down the street for the source of the noise. Her breath caught in her throat at the sight of a white pickup speeding in her direction.

She hurried toward the sidewalk. To her horror, the driver changed course. The ram on the radiator grille lunged toward her, cutting off her escape. In a desperate attempt to save her life, she leapt onto the hood. The bumper grazed her legs, and she smacked her shoulder on the windshield. Shrieking in agony, she sought something to hold on to. Her fingers closed around the wiper blade. A sudden swerve of the vehicle made her lose her feeble grip. Tossed like a rag doll by another abrupt change of direction, she landed on the hot pavement with an agonizing thud.

Sprawled face down in the middle of the road, Star gasped for air. "Help..."

Pain rippled through every muscle in her body. She forced her head up. The simple gesture cost so much effort, it didn't seem worth the trouble of moving. Tears built in her eyes. She looked through a mat of tangled hair and glimpsed a truck negotiating a sharp, right turn only to disappear seconds later.

Afraid another car might hit her, she pushed onto her hands and knees, and crawled to the sidewalk. An eternity later, she reached a fire hydrant. Her palms were scraped and her teeth clenched. Breathing heavily, she gripped the fire hydrant and wobbled trying to pull herself up. Assailed by a wave of dizziness, she sank to her knees.

Tears streamed down her cheeks. "Help... please help."

* * *

Slumped against the side of the Jeep, Star slipped in and out of consciousness, waiting.

"Hey, you! Get off my Jeep!" Hauk's voice pierced the heavy cloud choking her brain. "Star?" He wrapped her in his arms. "Star, what happened?"

Relieved to hear him, she collapsed against his chest. "Water..."

"Hold on." He opened a door then gently eased her onto the passenger seat. "Don't move. I'll get you water." He reached behind her then pressed a bottle against her lips, slowly tilting it back and forth. "Easy." His voice was husky and low. "That's it. Keep going."

The lukewarm water appeased her parched mouth and the darkness threatening to engulf her dissipated. "Thank you."

He brushed a strand of damp hair off her forehead. "I've been looking all over the hospital for you." His gaze travelled from her torn clothes to the bloody cuts and scratches on her arms and legs, and his expression hardened. "Did someone attack you?"

Fresh tears pooled in her eyes.

His thumb caressed her cheek. "Talk to me, havfrue."

The tender gesture soothed her sore body and her aching heart. "A truck."

He cupped her face, compelling her to meet his gaze. "What truck?"

Seeking solace in his steel-blue eyes, she leaned against his palm. "A truck hit me. The driver never stopped. He ran me down and left me in the street, like..." A sob racked her body. "Like roadkill." *Like I wasn't worth a second thought.*

A kiss grazed her forehead. "It's over, havfrue. You're safe. We'll get a doctor to—"

"No." Reality struck amid the emotional storm battering her, shifting her brain into high gear. As she grappled with the situation, reason overrode feelings, but a thin layer of embarrassment lingered in the air. "I'm fine."

"Really?" His stare conveyed his disagreement.

"I don't need to see a doctor." The last time she paid an impromptu visit to a physician for a minor accident, he forbad her to dive and ordered her to rest for a week. The *rest* almost drove her insane. "I didn't hit my head or break anything. I just got scared. I'm fine now."

Hoping it would prompt Hauk to drop the subject, Star sank in her seat and crossed her arms over her chest, creating a physical barrier between them.

"You may have suffered internal injuries." Hauk stood outside the Jeep, keeping the passenger door open. "Like it or not, you are seeing a doctor. Now."

Chapter 7

Onboard his research vessel, Hauk leaned against the railing to monitor Star's late-afternoon swim in the lake.

Instead of resting, like the doctor at the hospital recommended, Star chose to swim, hoping the exercise would loosen her stiff muscles.

Hauk didn't disagree with her, but he was reluctant to let her out of his sight. Even for a moment.

"According to Star, the driver went out of his way to hit her head-on." The near tragedy had rattled Hauk more than he cared to admit out loud. "This wasn't an accident, Arnie."

"That's two attempts on the crew in two days." His helmsman stood by his side, his left elbow inches away from Hauk's fingers. "What did the police say?"

"Let's just say the officer wasn't overly optimistic about finding the culprit." The trip to the police station had been as useful as the one to the hospital. "Did you know they average a dozen hit-and-run cases a month? Most remain unsolved for lack of resources. Star's only a statistic."

Arnie shook his head. "She gave a good description of the truck. You'd think that would help narrow down their list."

"Too many white Dodge pickups in circulation." While driving back to the lake with Star, Hauk had counted twenty-two white trucks. Granted, not all of them were Dodge, but it validated the officer's statement.

A dragonfly flew by Arnie who swatted at the insect with his baseball cap. "Too bad she didn't see the driver."

Hauk couldn't agree more.

A few minutes later, the subject of their conversation climbed the ladder. Blood dripped from her shoulder.

Hauk was amazed the x-ray hadn't shown any broken bones. "Arnie, get me the first aid kit, please."

"No need." Star walked right past him. "It'll stop bleeding on its own."

Compelled by some mysterious forces to take care of the feisty spitfire, Hauk grasped her hand and drew her back. "Didn't the doctor put a bandage on it?"

She sat next to him. "No." A defiant smile lit up her face. "He said I didn't need one."

Undeterred, Hauk opened the first aid kit. "The doctor was an idiot."

Silent chuckles shook her shoulders. "I told you we wasted our time at the hospital."

Swollen and purple, the skin around the narrow gash matched the colour of her tight swimsuit.

"Stop squirming." He held her arm still while pouring antiseptic over the wound.

Her muscles tensed. "It stings."

"Good." Hauk inwardly grinned. "How did you get that cut?"

"The wiper blade, I think. Maybe the antenna." She shrugged. "I don't remember. Are you done?"

Contrary to the doctor, Hauk applied a large bandage and let his fingers trail along her arm. "You make a lousy patient."

"Lousy?" Her voice quavered. "You're not the greatest doc—"

"Boss!" Scott shouted from inside the cabin. "We have a problem."

* * *

Inside the cabin, the crew stood around the table. Two fluorescent lamps lit the artifacts that Star had retrieved from underneath the front seat.

Hauk and Arnie whistled in admiration, and Star shared their reaction. The researcher had outdone himself transforming the grimy objects into sparkling jewelry.

She skimmed her fingers over a striking gold cross embedded with seven tiny round diamonds, a lone gold stud earring missing its gemstone, and a superbly crafted filigree ring featuring a delicate rose design. The other missing earring had probably slipped between the cracks and fallen in the sand. Star was tempted to dive back and search for it. "They're beautiful, Scott."

"Yes." A bittersweet expression adorned Scott's face. "Beautiful, expensive, and very distinctive."

Hauk raised an eyebrow. "What do you mean by distinctive?"

"See for yourself." The research expert handed Hauk a copy of an old newspaper article.

From across the table, Star could see a close-up picture of the banker, his wife, and their newborn son, but she couldn't read the fine print.

"Christening of the newest member of the Watson clan," Hauk read aloud. "You found his first son?"

"Yes and no. The baby's name was Samuel, but I still haven't tracked him down." Scott fidgeted. "Now look at Mary's jewelry."

Intrigued, Star approached Hauk for a closer look. The new mother cradled her newborn son against her chest with her left hand cupping his head. The same delicate ring displayed on the table adorned Mary's left ring finger.

"Mary's wedding ring?" Astounded by the discovery, Star looked at Scott for confirmation.

The researcher nodded before pointing a skinny finger at the cross nestled in the valley of Mary's swollen breasts and the earring peeking through her dark curls. "A visual match for every item."

"This is good." Hauk's smile reached his eyes. "The jewelry indicates a correlation between Mary's disappearance and the car."

Scott winced. "That would be an understatement."

"So what's the problem?" Frustration laced Hauk's voice. "Scott?"

"Well... I ran some tests on the porous fragments that Star also brought back."

Star's pulse increased with excitement. "And?"

The researcher rubbed his hands together. "They're bones. Human bones. Star may have found the missing Mary Watson."

* * *

Amid the pink and purple streaks colouring the western sky, the sun dipped into the lake.

Star leaned against the railing. The soft breeze whispered through her hair, taming the tumult inside her chest.

Footsteps alerted her to someone's presence. From the corner of her eye, she caught Hauk's approach. He stopped behind her.

"What's wrong?" His breath caressed her ear, sending chills down her spine.

"They were bones, Hauk." Her voice quavered with guilt. "I picked them up and shoved them into my bag like... junk." The last word barely passed her lips.

After the plank disintegrated in her hand, particles had risen around her. Star had believed them to be debris from the rotted wood. The idea that she might have unceremoniously dispersed Mary Watson's remains unsettled her.

Hauk placed his hands gently over her shoulders and slowly turned her around. His tender gaze enveloped her. "You didn't know."

Ignorance wasn't an excuse. "I... I'm no longer sure what to think of the insurance scam story that Eleanor Watson fed us."

He cupped her elbow and guided her to the bench where he invited her to sit beside him. "Me neither."

"What did your morning search yield?" During Kyle's ill-fated dive, Hauk had been in town investigating Eleanor's insurance story, but he hadn't shared the details of his trip with them yet. Then again, it wasn't like the occasion presented itself with everything else that happened.

"Nothing." His steel-blue eyes wandered heavenward. "Banker Watson's insurance company doesn't exist anymore. I couldn't find any records of his policies or claims."

An unladylike snort escaped her mouth. "So much for disproving Eleanor's story."

Hauk intertwined his hands behind his head and leaned back. "Well, if the story is true and the banker intentionally submerged his car the same night his wife disappeared, he had to have known she was dead under the seat."

If Mary wasn't already dead, she would have drowned at the bottom of the lake, trapped in her makeshift coffin, which was a horrible death to contemplate.

"I suppose it doesn't prove the banker killed her or that Eleanor knew about Mary's death. On the other hand, it's also possible that Eleanor knew her grandfather was responsible for his first wife's death, and she used the insurance story as a smoke screen to prevent us from adding murder to her family name." Either way, Star suspected the banker had escaped justice. "Do you think Eleanor Watson could be behind the sabotage of the equipment?"

"I honestly don't know." His arm moved behind her back, and his fingers grazed her neck. "How are you feeling?"

Shivers coursed through her body. "I'm fine, Hauk." *Except for when I'm around you.*

A low growl rumbled from his chest. "You and Kyle are saying that a lot today, and I'm having a hard time believing either of you."

Me and Kyle. Diplomatic way to remind her that he cared about her but as a crew member, not as a woman.

As a child, Star learned the hard way how to stand up to bullies in the schoolyard. At the time, it seemed unfair that she was the one who ended up in detention for hitting them when they were the ones who harassed her. Nonetheless, it achieved the desire effect. They stopped pulling her hair and calling her names, and for a while, she almost forgot she looked different, but then she became a teenager. In high school, the pretty girls dated the popular boys. If there were any strings attached to the dates, Star didn't see them. On the other hand, the boys who invited girls like Star on a date expected some sort of compensation at the end of the evening. When Star made it painfully clear for them that she didn't play that game, the invitations stopped. Julian was the one who made her believe that beauty was in the eye of the beholder.

Star stopped reacting to people's open stares and side glances years ago. Curiosity was a natural phenomenon. It drove people to ask questions, to investigate, to seek answer. Star valued curiosity but she hated the pity, distaste, or disdain reflected on their unblemished faces.

No one looked at her strangely when she first came onboard Hauk's vessel or any time afterwards, except for Kyle, but his animosity was directed toward her gender, not her appearance. Her crewmates were comfortable around her and she felt at ease among them. It became easy, too easy, to forget that a world of difference existed between being unfazed by her scar and being attracted to her.

"Star?" Hauk's voice caressed her heart. "Talk to me."

Maybe one day I'll risk the pain of falling in love again, but not here and not now. Hauk was her captain. He hired her to work on the Model T. This salvage operation would eventually come to an end, and then he would move on with his regular crew. She didn't belong in his future. "I was just reminiscing. Would you like me to make another dive to see if I missed anything?"

"I called the police to tell them about our discovery." His jaw hardened. "As of five minutes ago, the site has become off-limits. I lost my salvage rights."

"That sucks." Sorrow sat like a heavy weight on her chest.

"It does, and I should have known better than to sell the story of the wreck before I finish uncovering all the facts." Mary's story deserved to be written one day, and Hauk would have undoubtedly done justice to her life and her untimely death.

"If that's your way of telling me that you can't pay me, don't worry. I enjoyed the opportunity." The operation had come to a sudden and unfortunate end. Her work here was over. "You can drop me off at the bus station in the morning on your way to the hospital."

"Star, I..." A peculiar expression flitted across his face. "I wish things had turned out differently."

Me too. She nodded in silence before walking away.

* * *

As Hauk paced the cabin, visions of Star danced in front of his eyes.

The moment he first spoke to her, he realized how different she was from the other women seeking his name and nonexistent fortune. Star never begged him for the job, asked for special treatment, or made any attempt at seduction. Quite the opposite. He doubted she would have disembarked upon learning that his expeditions were funded by an eccentric great-aunt with too much money and no children, that the artifacts he salvaged were donated and not auctioned to museums, or that his modest earnings came solely from the articles he published.

He valued the good working relationship he enjoyed with her, a relationship that bordered friendship, but it wasn't like she harboured any feelings toward him.

A life awaits her on shore. A life she needs to go back to. A life in which I play no role. Hauk envied the men who lined up at her door for a chance to spend an evening with her. *Younger men who can offer her more than this rocky vessel.*

"Skip?" Arnie entered the cabin. "Do you think it's safe for Star to sleep in the Zodiac?"

* * *

"Let's get this straight, Ludwig. I'm not sleeping in the same room as a dead body."

"A few bones, Star, not a dead body." Hauk muffled his frustration with a silent sigh. The woman was more stubborn than a clamshell. "Sleeping in the Zodiac isn't safe."

"Why not? You already reported what's left of the dead body to the police. It's too late to cover it up." Despite his objections, Star gathered a pillow and blanket from under the bench on deck. "I'll be fine."

He clenched his fists to keep from strangling her.

After he told the police about the human remains, they assigned a detective Pratt to the case. Detective Pratt reviewed the previous accident reports involving his crew and didn't take the sabotage of the regulators or the hit-and-run lightly. After three decades on the job, the detective had never heard of a century-old murder worth killing for, unless ramifications of Mary Watson's alleged death extended into the present time.

Officers were supposed to arrive in the morning to secure the underwater wreck and collect the bones and artifacts. In the meantime, Hauk had been asked to preserve the integrity of the site in whatever capacity he saw fit.

"Star, someone tried to kill you and Kyle."

Her dark brown eyes shot daggers at his chest with great accuracy. "I—"

"I found him!" Scott stepped on deck. "I found—" His hands dropped to his sides. "Is this a bad time?"

"Perfect timing," Arnie quipped from his chair, clearly eavesdropping on their argument.

Not amused, Hauk grabbed Star's pillow and blanket, tossed them back into the bench, closed the lid, and sat on it to make a point. "What did you find, Scott?"

"Mary's son." A gust of wind tussled Scott's hair. "After Mary's disappearance, her parents were awarded custody of their grandson. Mary's boy was raised as Samuel Rutherford, not Samuel Watson."

Hauk was impressed by Scott's successful search. "Did the banker disown

Samuel, or did Samuel die before inheriting the cottage?"

"I found his obituary. Samuel died in 1985. Donations to the cancer society were requested. He was survived by a daughter, Amy. No wife mentioned." Scott's words came out in ragged breaths. "Samuel would have been around seventy-five years old, so he did die long after the estate was passed down to his adopted-step-half-brother Erwin. Since the two *brothers* were about the same age, I'm guessing that their daughters should be somewhat within the same age bracket. Since Eleanor is still alive, the odds are that Amy is too, but I haven't found her yet."

"Good job, Scott." Samuel's descendants might have a different version of Mary's disappearance than Erwin's descendants, and Hauk was eager to hear Amy's version. "Keep searching for Amy."

* * *

Wide-awake, Hauk lay on his cot with his hands behind his head.

The only light in the cabin emanated from Scott's computer screen, and the only sound stemmed from his fingers flying over the keyboard. Once in a while, his researcher paused to grab a drink or write in his notebook.

Hauk diverted his attention to the porthole. The battle to convince Star to sleep inside had ended in defeat. Her preference for the Zodiac didn't make any more sense than the unshed tears glistening in her eyes when he bade her good night.

At least she wasn't alone. Arnie slept at the helm. If something happened in the Zodiac, his helmsman would hear it, not that it gave Hauk much peace of mind. "Anything, Scott?"

The young man jolted in his chair. "Maybe. I'm cross-referencing."

* * *

Tiptoeing down a hallway toward the bathroom, a little blonde girl played with a rabbit-shaped button of her nightgown. She stopped in the doorway and peeked inside. Her gaze wandered to the cupboard above the toilet.

"No, little girl." Star's heart thumped inside her chest. "Go back."

The left door slid open. Red blood dripped from the shelf onto the floor.

"Don't look, little girl."

The heads of a woman and two young children stared back with empty brown eyes. Horrified, the child screamed.

"Run, little girl. Run!"

High above the little girl's head, a blade shone under the lone light bulb hanging from the ceiling. The long knife swept through the air—

Terror swelled inside Star's mind.

She screamed.

* * *

A feral scream echoed in the night.

Hauk bolted out of the cabin and down the ladder without giving any more than a passing glance at Arnie's silhouette.

Kicking and thrashing at the bottom of the Zodiac, Star fought an invisible assailant. Hauk jumped onboard, rocking the craft and shifting her struggle toward him. Fists and feet pounded him incessantly.

He grabbed her wrists in an effort to immobilize her. "Star, it's me."

For a petite woman, she packed a wallop. Her knee connected with his groin. Searing pain ripped through his entire body. Gasping for air, Hauk lost his balance and tumbled on top of her. Her eyes popped open. She screamed again.

"It's over," he croaked, the pain in his lower parts slowly ebbing away.

She blinked at him. "Hauk?"

Propped up on his elbows, his body covering hers, he gave her what he hoped was a comforting smile, not a distorted grimace. "Your bad dream is over." Very much aware of her soft curves brushing his bare chest with every strenuous breath she took, he kept a low voice. "You're safe."

Under the shining stars, her parted lips and her flushed cheeks proved almost impossible to resist, but she was leaving in the morning. It was too late to ask her to stay.

She wiggled underneath him. "You're crushing me."

Polite way of telling me to get off. "Sorry. Let's get you sitting."

"Skip?" Arnie called down from the deck.

"She's fine, Arnie. We'll be up in a minute."

In the cool night, her teeth chattered. Hauk picked up her blanket and draped it around her shoulders. His hand lingered behind her back. To his surprise and pleasure, she leaned into his embrace.

"Wanna talk about it?" Hauk whispered once she stopped trembling.

She shook her head back and forth. Her mouth grazed his bare chest and his skin sizzled at the contact.

With the back of his hand, he lifted her chin. Her lips, mere inches away, tantalized him. "Star, whatever is haunting you—"

"I found her, boss! Boss?"

Hauk silently cursed Scott's radar for untimely interruptions. "Coming, Scott."

Chapter 8

Star didn't resist Hauk's nudge up the ladder. Reliving the nightmare had put a damper on staying in the Zodiac alone. She was more than happy to enter the cabin and listen to Scott.

"Samuel Rutherford, Mary's son, was in his early fifties when his daughter Amy Rutherford was born in the Yukon. Samuel appeared to have been in a common-law relationship with Amy's mother who died in childbirth. I found records of Amy attending Lakewood Elementary School, so at one point Samuel moved back to Ontario with Amy. A few years after her father's death, Amy married Adrian Humphrey, and she became known as Amy Humphrey. Together, they had a son, Jonathan, then twin daughters, Christine and Vanessa. Tragically, the entire family died when the twins were four years old." Scott's solemn tone chilled the air. "They are buried at Lakewood Cemetery."

"Mary's descendants are all dead?" Stunned by such a twist of fate, Star slumped on her bed. "How did they die?"

"The tragedy that struck the Humphreys happened twenty years ago, almost to this day. On July 27th, Adrian Humphrey, an insurance representative, came home late to discover his wife, his son, and one of his twin daughters, slaught..." Scott's voice quavered. "Slaughtered on the bathroom floor. The next day, Adrian died in a suspicious car accident. A week later, the Lakewood Police fished the other twin's nightgown from a nearby creek where she presumably drowned. The body of four-year-old Vanessa was never found."

Star sat on her cot, her stomach reeling. The monster who committed such heinous crimes deserved a fate worse than death. "Why were they killed? What sentence did the murderous monster get?"

"No motives were established. No suspects were identified. And no arrests were made. The crime was never solved." Scott turned his laptop toward the crew as a picture appeared on the screen. "This is the Humphrey family."

Star stretched her neck to get a better view and froze. Bile rose inside her throat. *It can't be them.* Surely her eyes were betraying her. "I need air."

* * *

Star hugged her knees against her chest

and gazed at the sky for answers. The stars twinkling in the night simmered over the lake without shedding any light on her dark, unconscious mind.

"You look like you've seen a ghost." Hauk spoke softly as though he were trying to calm a wild animal.

Her whole body shivered. "Ghosts. Dead people. Same difference."

"You're not making much sense." He joined her on the bench. "What happened in the cabin?"

"I know it's impossible but..." Sane people didn't dream of severed heads, not when they belonged on real people's necks.

"But what?"

Star diverted her gaze onto the man next to her. "I have nightmares about them, Hauk. About Amy and her children."

"The Humphreys?" Confusion clouded his expression. "Why don't you tell me about the nightmares? It may make you feel better."

Somehow, Star wasn't convinced about the latter part of that statement.

As a child, every night she screamed, Jimmy rocked her back to sleep. When she grew too big for the rocking chair, he switched to cookies and milk to appease her fear. Not once did Jimmy inquire about the nightmares, and not once did she volunteer details.

"That nightmare's been haunting me forever. It always starts with a little blonde girl walking down a hallway in a blue nightgown with pink, rabbit-shaped buttons." Jimmy used to buy her pajamas, not pretty nightgowns like the one worn by the child. "Her chubby fingers always toy with the second button."

Hauk slipped his hand around her shoulders and caressed her arm. "How old is she?"

"The little girl? I... I'm not sure." Unlike the other children, the features of the blonde child remained blurry throughout the nightmare. "Three, maybe four years old. She enters a small bathroom at the end of a hallway. I tell her to run, not look up... She never listens."

He hiccupped a chuckle. "Sorry, I didn't mean to laugh, but I have a soft spot for rebellious children. So, what happens next in that bathroom?"

"She looks up at the cupboard. The doors are yellow. Bright yellow." To this day, Star refused to wear or paint anything yellow because of that cupboard. "A door slides open. It's always the left one. Blood spills from a shelf down onto the floor. The little girl tips her chin up to look... and she screams." The gut-wrenching scream echoed in Star's ears. Giving in to the emotions bottled up inside, she let the tears stream down her cheeks.

Hauk tightened his embrace. "What does the girl see, Star? What do you see?"

"The severed heads of a blonde woman and two children, a brown-haired boy and a red-headed girl, like—" She lifted her chin to meet his eyes. "Like in the picture that Scott downloaded."

"I'm so sorry." His gaze enveloped her, draping an almost tangible security blanket around her. *Sorry* was good, much better than the other terms he might have been tempted to use to describe her, like *weird*, *disturbed*, or *crazy* for having such nightmares. "I'm sorry the Humphreys resembled the—"

"No." Dismayed by the misunderstanding, she recoiled on the bench. "I see *them*, Hauk. In my nightmare, I see Amy and her children."

"That's not possible." His arm dropped from around her, his reaction finally mirroring the one that Star had anticipated. "There has to be a logical explanation."

"Like what?" Anger rose inside her chest, anger directed at herself for having those nightmares. "I dream someone chopped their heads off. There's no logic in that. I even see the light shine on the blade before the knife sweeps..." New images played in front of her eyes. Her struggle with Hauk had allowed the nightmare to continue.

"Star?" A hint of panic spiked his voice. "Talk to me."

"The monster missed. The blow didn't kill her." A wave of relief washed over Star.

The blade missed and the child with the pretty nightgown escaped. "The little blonde girl fled."

* * *

Seated next to Arnie at the helm, Scott eavesdropped on the uncanny conversation taking place on deck. "Blue? Pink? Yellow?" he whispered. "No one dreams in colour."

Arnie shrugged. "I doubt it matters much to her."

"I wonder which dead twin she sees." His comment met Arnie's reproachful scowl. "I have a theory, you know." Eager to share his theory with Hauk and Star, Scott pulled himself up.

The helmsman grabbed his arm. "It better be good, boy, or you're gonna end up as fish food if you interrupt for nothing."

Scott cleared his throat approaching the bench. "Star, would it be too much to ask which twin you're seeing dead?"

* * *

Hauk watched the scene unfolding inside the cabin with disquieting interest.

Bent in front of Scott's computer, Star studied the colour picture haunting her nights.

"I see Amy." The tip of her index finger brushed over the image of the woman who gazed tenderly at her children. "And Jonathan." The brown-haired, dark-eyed boy stood erect by his father's side. A miniature version of the man who rested his large hand on his son's narrow shoulder. "And this little girl." She pointed at the girl with long red hair sitting in the grass beside her fraternal twin who wore her blonde hair shorter.

"The red-headed twin is..." Scott checked his notes. "Christine. She was found dead on the bathroom floor. Do you see Vanessa in your dream?"

"I'm not sure..." Star's nose twitched. "In my nightmares, the face of the blonde girl tiptoeing toward the bathroom is always blurry, but I suppose she could be Vanessa."

"Star, is it possible you somehow heard or read about the tragedy, and confronted with such evil, you buried the memory in your nightmares?" The researcher's possible explanation raised the questions of how, where, or when Star would have had access to that story.

She gave Scott a dubious look. "You're kidding, right?"

Seemingly unfazed, his researcher folded his skinny arms across his chest.

"Dreams act as a coping mechanism. It's a proven fact."

Her mouth opened and closed without making a sound. The objections she didn't utter resonated loud and clear in Hauk's mind. In the end, she surprised him by quietly retiring to her cot despite the presence of Mary's remains inside the cabin.

That she preferred to sleep with the bones rather than alone in the Zodiac spoke of the intensity of her dream.

Her reaction unsettled Hauk.

* * *

Ignoring the throbbing ache in her muscles and the dull pain in her heart, Star loaded her gear into the Jeep. Her plan to share a conversation with Hauk during their ride to the bus station vanished when his phone rang.

He handed her the keys. "Would you mind driving?"

From behind the wheel, she listened to his side of the conversation with Murphy. Losing his salvage rights hadn't deterred Hauk from inquiring about the Humphreys. Maybe one day he would write about Mary and her descendants, and Star would read his article.

Hauk hung up as she pulled into the bus station parking lot. Considerate to the end, he helped her carry her luggage into the lobby.

A long line welcomed them.

The three inches she gained on tiptoe didn't allow Star to see past a tall guy with a dark blue backpack. "Hauk, can you see to the front of the line? Is there a problem?"

With his height, Hauk towered over the crowd. "Only one teller on duty." The ghost of a smile floated across his lips. "An old lady is balancing a cage in front of the teller. I think she disagrees over Fluffy's travel arrangements."

"Very funny, Ludwig. I—" Two destinations blinked in red on the departure screen located high on the wall. "My bus is delayed."

"Wait in line. I'll try to find out what is going on."

"No need. Kyle will soon be discharged from the hospital and he'll be waiting for you to pick him up. You should go." She was able to manage on her own. "Besides, I can be patient."

"Patient?" Visibly amused, he tapped her nose gently with his index finger. "I knew I'd eventually discover one of your endearing qualities."

The playfulness he too rarely displayed smoothed the worry lines that had crinkled his face over the past few days. "Star, what do I need to say or do to convince you to—"

"Luv!" A tall, exotic beauty hurried in their direction and grabbed Hauk's arm. "Where have you been?"

"Excuse me, but you're mistaken." The efforts that Hauk made to distance himself from the possessive woman seemed to fall on deaf ears. His expression hardened. "Listen, lady. I—"

"Lady?" The bombshell batted luminous green eyes. "Don't you remember me, luv?"

A twinge a jealousy pinched Star's heart. Whatever proposition Hauk almost made before the interruption had become irrelevant. On a professional level, her job here had ended. The police took over the investigation of the wreck and sent Hauk and his crew packing. And on a personal level, she shouldn't have entertained the silly idea that Hauk might be interested in her. Men like him dated women like that green-eyed beauty.

Flawless women. "I have to go, Hauk." The time had come to rein in her wayward fantasies and face reality. "Thanks for the ride."

"Star. Wait."

* * *

Hauk's frustration toward the arrogant woman grew exponentially with each step that Star took away from him. He shook his arm. "Let go, woman."

Oblivious to his command, the woman tightened her grasp. "But I've missed you, luv," she purred in his ear.

Losing all patience, Hauk gripped her wrists, forcing her to let go. She yelped in pain, a highly exaggerated reaction considering he barely squeezed and his fingers didn't leave any imprint on her skin.

She pouted. "What was that for?"

Fed up, he was tempted to walk away, but he didn't want her to follow him and make another scene in front of Star. "I'm not sure what kind of game you're playing but I'm not remotely interested—"

"Name is Nicky. Don't you remember?" Her sulky voice did nothing to abate his fury. "We met at the bar a couple months ago."

The bad memory resurfaced in his mind.

"We shared a drink, luv." She had hunted him all evening and offered him a drink. "You said you'd call."

The phone didn't ring for a reason. "In case you didn't notice, I was with someone."

"Her?" Nicky's eyelashes fluttered. "She's disfigured, luv. You deserve better."

The urge to strike the woman surged inside him. In the end, his fierce, angry glare proved to be just as effective. She recoiled under the invisible blow.

"Get away from me." His icy tone expedited the woman's departure.

Freed at last, he scanned the lobby, searching for Star. A teller had opened a second booth, and Star had lined up behind it.

The steps he took toward her were halted with the ringing of his cell phone. "Ludwig."

"Boss? I got discharged early, but I can take a cab if the timing sucks." His diver had picked up on the curt greeting.

Hauk looked in Star's direction. A middle-aged man had struck up a conversation with her. Her head nodded graciously and her hair caressed her shoulders. Hauk didn't need to see her expression to know she had already moved on with her life.

"Wait at the hospital. I'll be there shortly." Resigned to a future that didn't include her, Hauk exited the bus station.

* * *

Parked across the street, Bruce waited in his truck, his gaze glued to the revolving doors of the bus station.

On his way to work, he had spotted Ludwig's grey Jeep at an intersection, and on a hunch, decided to follow it, only to end up at the bus station again.

That the girl managed to walk away from the accident dumbfounded him. She should be lying at the morgue, not hauling luggage inside the station with Ludwig on her heels.

One of them was obviously going on a trip. Bruce wanted to know which one and more importantly why.

Sometime later, Ludwig exited the station. Alone.

Once the Jeep disappeared down the street, Bruce stepped out onto the sidewalk. He took one last puff, dropped his cigarette butt onto the concrete, and crushed it with his shoe. Maybe he exaggerated the threat she posed. Thinking back, he had no memory of his early childhood days. It was possible she forgot. And if she were adopted, like her new last name suggested, her parents wouldn't have dwelled on her past.

So far she hadn't exposed them. Bruce wanted to keep it that way, preferably without any more bloodshed, but before he let her leave town, he wanted to know where she headed.

Upon entering the station, he spotted Fisher in line at the ticket counter. Afraid his presence might accidently jog her memory, he picked up a schedule and pretended to look at it while slowly walking along the wall. The teller called her next.

A wide, square column near the counter offered a convenient hiding place. His gaze on the pamphlet, Bruce eavesdropped on their conversation. The name of her destination raised the hair on the nape of his neck.

Hauk entered the lobby of the hospital and spotted Kyle near a vending machine.

In as good a shape as possible, his diver walked toward him. "Why the long face, boss?"

Everything had gone wrong, and to top it all, Hauk lost his chance. Star would have been worth a third strike, but he didn't even go to bat for her. "I'll explain in the Jeep. Let's go."

Once Hauk eased behind the wheel, Kyle broke the silence. "What's going on?"

While driving toward the lake, Hauk recounted the events of the last twenty-four hours. The human remains. Star's weird nightmares. The murders of the Humphreys in Lakewood. Star's being hit by a truck behind the hospital.

"The hit-and-run victim was the kid?"

Star wasn't a kid, but the question still prompted Hauk to pull over to the side of the road, near a shallow ditch. "What do you know about Star's accident?"

"Take it easy." Kyle raised his hands in surrender. "A nurse saw it happen."

Eager for more details, Hauk scowled. "Speak."

"It was quiet on the floor, and one of the nurses, she's new and young—"

"Skip the conquest details, Kyle." Hauk's patience had flown away back at the bus station.

"One of her colleagues witnessed an accident from the nurses' lounge. A white truck ran over someone in the street. By the time the nurse rushed outside, the victim and the truck had disappeared."

A witness no one had been aware of saw Star's accident. That was excellent news.

"Okay, here's what we're going to do. Murphy called me this morning." After Star's nightmare, Hauk had contacted the retired police officer and requested the file on the Humphrey murders. While Murphy hadn't appreciated being awakened in the middle of the night, he still promised to look into it. "Murphy can't give me access to the Humphreys case since it's technically still an open investigation, but he's arranged for me to meet with the inspector who investigated the murders twenty years ago."

Kyle's eyebrow arched in apparent surprise. "And this inspector is willing to talk?"

"Yes. He retired a few years back, and he's also Murphy's golf buddy. While I'm at the Country Club talking to them, you'll take the Jeep and go back to the hospital. Talk to that nurse. Note all the details. And make sure you convince her to report the accident to the police."

"Got it. Want me to pick you up afterwards?"

"No." Someone at the club was bound to give him a ride. If not, Hauk would hail a cab. "I'll meet you at the lake."

Kyle nodded. "The boat's still in the water?"

"Arnie is keeping it in an inlet at the south tip of the lake. I'm not ready to leave yet."

A grin appeared on his diver's face. "Just tell me the kid isn't in the water spying on the wreck and the cops?"

An invisible hand squeezed Hauk's heart. Star's departure had left a giant void inside his chest.

"Is something wrong?" His diver's sixth sense unsettled Hauk. "Did something else happen to the kid?"

"No, she went home this morning." Hauk glanced at the clock on the dashboard. Assuming she didn't experience any more delays, she should be boarding shortly. "Listen, after your trip to the hospital, do me a favour and stop by the bus station to make sure Star departed without a hitch. Her bus was late, and I would hate for her to be stranded downtown."

Chapter 9

Lady Luck struck twice.

Not only did Kyle secure a date with the pretty young nurse, but he also met with her colleague who had been more than eager to discuss the accident. He patted his shirt pocket. The scrap of paper tucked inside would make his boss extremely happy.

Kyle stopped at the bus station.

In the parking lot, an employee loaded Star's diving gear in the underneath luggage compartment of a green bus. Glad to be given the chance to thank her and bid her farewell, Kyle waited by the gate where people lined up.

A bell chimed, announcing the boarding of her bus.

Surprised not to see her in the crowd, Kyle went to talk to the teller on duty, a middle-aged woman with a mole on her chin. When she refused to answer his polite inquiry, he barged into the manager's office.

A short, round man sat in an armchair. "May I help you?"

Hopefully, yes. "Care to explain why luggage is leaving without its owner?"

The frown of surprise on the manager's flaccid face didn't bode well. "You must be mistaken, sir. We're not allowed to accept luggage unless the passenger travels with us."

"Someone loaded my girlfriend's diving gear into the luggage compartment of one of your buses." Kyle concocted the lie in hope to obtain the manager's assistance. "And she ain't there. Trust me, I checked."

"Diving gear?" The manager tapped his forehead. "I do remember the young woman." The tap had apparently turned on a light bulb inside the man's skull. "She boarded a different bus. Here it is. She paid to ship her equipment home as cargo. This is perfectly legal."

Not inclined to debate legal practices, Kyle approached the manager's desk. "Where did she go?"

"I'm not authorized to—"

His patience running thin, Kyle slammed his palms on the cluttered desk and scattered paper onto the floor. "Which bus?"

"The Lakewood bus."

Lakewood? The name sounded familiar. Then Kyle remembered his conversation with Hauk. The Humphreys had been murdered in Lakewood. "I need the itinerary."

The jittery manager handed him a schedule. "It's a fifty-eight-minute trip. Four stops. It left ten minutes ago."

At the Country Club, Murphy introduced Hauk to his good friend, retired inspector Jay Kenneth.

With their military haircuts, golf shirts, white shorts, and beers half empty, the two older men looked like brothers in arms.

An old photo of the Humphrey family lay haphazardly across the patio table. "The children were crumpled over their mother, suggesting she was killed first." Kenneth tapped the corner of the picture as if he were afraid to touch the mother's face. "Three sets of bloody footprints led from the bathroom through the kitchen and out the patio door."

Hauk arched a brow. "Three sets?"

"Barefoot prints matching the missing four-year-old girl, a man's size eleven running shoe, and a narrow size six."

None of the articles that Scott had found mentioned two suspects. "Was the husband, Adrian, a suspect?"

"No motive and..." Kenneth paused while the waitress refilled their drinks. "And a solid alibi for the night in question. He was with a client. The next day, his car ended up in a ditch."

Under suspicious circumstances, if Hauk recalled correctly. "Accident, suicide, or murder?"

"We don't know for sure. It's possible he drove too fast and missed the curb. The man would have been distraught enough." The inspector took a swig of his beer. "We found no obvious mechanical failure, no indication he struggled with his seatbelt before he died, but then he may have been unconscious from the massive blow he'd received to the back of the head."

"He hit the *back* of his head?" Accident victims usually hit the front of their head, either on the steering wheel or the windshield, and to Hauk's knowledge, a padded headrest couldn't account for a massive blow. "How?"

With his right index finger, Kenneth absently traced the handle of his mug. "No idea, but now you understand why we called it suspicious."

Hauk sank back in his chair. "Before his death, did Adrian shed any light on what might have happened in that bathroom?"

"No." A vein pulsed in Kenneth's neck. "And he couldn't think of anyone who would want to harm his family."

No enemies? Hauk had yet to meet a man who hadn't made a few enemies along the way. "Any leads on the bloody prints?"

"The child's footprints stopped outside the patio door. We assumed the nanny picked her up and carried her to the creek where they drowned."

Scott had never mentioned a nanny, or else Hauk would have remembered. "They had a nanny?"

"Yes, a young woman named..." The inspector glanced at Murphy who had remained silent throughout the conversation. "Ella. Mr. Humphrey couldn't remember her last name. His wife had hired her a few days prior to the tragedy."

The timing didn't sit well with Hauk. "Was she a suspect?"

"The correct term would be a person of interest, Mr. Ludwig." Kenneth's politically correct term didn't mean she wasn't a suspect. "The victims' throats were slit with such force, their heads were almost severed."

"Severed?" Star's nightmare resurfaced in Hauk's mind.

"That's the deed of a strong person, not a small woman. As far as being an accomplice?" The retired inspector shrugged. "Anything is possible, but I doubt it. To gain access to the house, the killer slashed the screen door leading inside the garage. One would think the nanny would have unlocked the door for him if she'd been an accomplice. And why would any of them take the child outside at the risk of being seen by the neighbours?"

Hauk nodded at the assessment. It made more sense that the nanny fled the house in panic with the surviving twin and ended up by the creek where the killer cornered them.

"And neither the nanny's nor the child's bodies were ever recovered?"

"Correct." Kenneth's gaze lingered once more on the picture. "The creek flooded that spring, and the water remained high and treacherous throughout the summer. We dragged the bottom and found the girl's nightgown near the mouth of the creek where the water flows into the Woodland River. Once in the river, the bodies would have been at the mercy of strong undercurrents. Mother Nature never released them."

That part confirms Scott's account. "Were you absolutely certain the nightgown belonged to the missing twin?"

"Yes. We collected two strands of hair coiled around a button and compared the DNA extracted from the follicles to her parents' and siblings' DNA. They matched. And in the family photo album, we found a picture of the child wearing the same blue nightgown."

"Blue?" *The child in Star's nightmares wore a blue gown.*

A sad smile tugged Kenneth's mustache down. "A blue nightgown with pretty, pink buttons."

"Pink buttons," Hauk repeated, his casual tone concealing his unrest.

"We kept the description of the nightgown confidential with the hope of eventually confronting the murderer. My... my granddaughter had a similar nightgown with the same rabbit-shaped buttons. I asked my daughter to throw it in the garbage. I just couldn't look at my little Felicia without seeing Vanessa."

Cold sweat dripped between Hauk's shoulder blades. He would have accepted a blue nightgown as a coincidence, but not the shape of the pink buttons. "Are you sure the description of the gown was never leaked to the press?"

"I am certain, Mr. Ludwig."

At one point, Star had become privy to the description. And while Hauk didn't believe she possessed psychic abilities, the only other explanation sounded even more ludicrous.

* * *

Less than a kilometre separated the Jeep from the green bus.

"Damn it, kid." Annoyed by her irresponsible behaviour, Kyle chased after the bus, determined to catch up with it. "What possessed you to board that bus?"

Someone had run over her, almost killing her, for no apparent reason. Travelling to Lakewood where the murders occurred sounded like a bad idea.

"Are you tempting fate?"

The bus rode onto the bridge over Dead Man's Ravine. Beyond the bus, farther up the road on the other side of the ravine, a cloud of dust drew Kyle's attention. A white pickup emerged from a dirt trail onto the main road. It raced toward the bus, gathering speed on the entry ramp of the bridge.

Kyle gripped the steering wheel with both hands, foreshadowing an impending catastrophe.

The truck rammed into the side of the bus. The impact sent the truck spinning out of control and the bus skidding against the railing. The truck came to an abrupt halt in the middle of the bridge, turned around, and sped off in the direction it had come from.

Horrified by the scene, Kyle stopped on the side of the road and watched the reckless driver flee the scene.

The screech of metal scraping against metal echoed with the frantic beating of his heart. Sections of the top railing began to collapse. One after the other, they plunged into the murky rapids looming below.

Kyle's stomach twisted into a knot. If the bottom railing fell into the ravine, the bus would follow.

Teetering on the edge of disaster, the heavy bus slowly moved forward, each spin of its tires bringing it closer to the end of the bridge.

Kyle held his breath. Only a few more metres before it reached the exit ramp built above the grassy slope of the ravine.

The entire railing collapsed in shrieking agony. The bus tipped on its side and tumbled down the slope, flattening shrubs and bushes on its way. It stopped with a final, sickening lurch near the water's edge.

* * *

Wearing her seatbelt on the bus saved Star's life, but it didn't prevent the suitcase stowed in the compartment above her from smacking her on the head.

"Stop staring at me and concentrate on the road." The slightest noise exacerbated the pounding inside her skull. "I can't take another accident."

From the driver's seat of the Jeep, Kyle kept glancing at her every few seconds. "Hauk will be furious when he learns I didn't take you to the hospital."

"I don't have a concussion." The paramedic had cleared her. She didn't need or want a second opinion. "Besides, my contract is over. Hauk won't care."

Kyle gave her an exasperated look. "Listen, kid—"

"What?" she groaned, eager to go home and forget.

A long sigh whooshed out of his mouth. "Do me a favour, stop talking and rest."

She closed her eyes, and as exhaustion claimed her, she vaguely registered Kyle's phone call.

Upon Kyle's return to the lake, Hauk replaced his diver behind the wheel and drove away with the woman asleep in the passenger seat.

Under different circumstances, he might have enjoyed the ride in the countryside, but he was too worried about Star to give more than a passing thought to the landscape.

She stirred, and her elbow brushed the middle console where rested a travel cup filled with cold coffee. Her arm was scratched, her hand was smeared with dry blood, and some of her nails were broken. She appeared small and fragile, and yet, he knew it to be only an illusion. What she lacked in size, she more than possessed in spirit and determination.

Her eyes slowly opened. "Where am I?"

"You're still in the Jeep. How are you feeling?"

"I feel like..." She ran her fingers through her hair. "It feels like someone is playing ping pong with the bump on my head. Where's Kyle? Where are we?"

"Kyle is aboard the vessel." His crew were also instructed to remain vigilant. "And you and I are heading toward Lakewood."

She straightened up in her seat. "Why?"

"Didn't you want to go there?" Maybe he had been wrong to assume she intended to go home when he dropped her off at the bus station. Still, Hauk was disappointed that she didn't trust him with her plan to travel to Lakewood. "Why didn't you tell me at the bus station?"

Her eyebrows met over the bridge of her nose. "I... I didn't know."

"You didn't know if I'd want to go with you?" The Jeep hit a pothole, and he quickly gripped his travel cup to stop it from spilling. "You could have asked."

"I didn't know I'd be going to Lakewood." She sank in her seat, wincing. "When you left the bus station with that woman, I—"

"Wait a sec." Anger at the woman in question rose inside his chest. "That woman wasn't—"

"It doesn't matter, Hauk." Star brushed him off without giving him a chance to explain. "While I waited in line, I struck up a conversation with a real estate agent from Lakewood, and he talked about Amy Humphrey's house. Former house."

Understanding dawned on Hauk. "Is that why you took that bus? The realtor roused your curiosity, and you couldn't resist satisfying it?"

"Yes and no... I didn't feel like waiting three hours for my bus, so I boarded the bus to Lakewood." She shrugged. "I figured I would spend the day there, then catch a bus home in the evening. I obviously made the wrong choice."

"Not wrong, just untimely, but I'm grateful you got off relatively unscathed." From what Hauk had gathered on the news, some passengers weren't so fortunate.

"Me too," she whispered. "Were there any fatalities?"

"Two passengers are in critical condition and the driver was declared dead at the scene." According to a reporter, many passengers praised the driver for saving their lives. "Kyle talked to a witness this morning. A nurse. She saw the truck hit you."

Star's expression hardened. "Why didn't she help me?"

"She tried, Star. She ran outside and searched the street, but you'd already picked yourself up and made your way to my Jeep." Knowing someone had rushed to her rescue might never erase her lone struggle, but Hauk hoped that in time, it would bring Star some comfort. "The nurse didn't see the driver, but she scribbled a partial licence plate."

"She did?" Her dirt-streaked face lit up. "Did you give it to the police?"

"The nurse had already reported the accident, but the police didn't know you were the victim. Now they do." Hauk also asked Scott if he could somehow look up the licence number. "Star, the nurse saw you dash out of his way, but she also saw him change direction so he wouldn't miss you." The nurse's story confirmed Star's version, that the driver had every intention of hitting her.

"This wasn't a random accident, not unless the guy enjoys running people over."

A blank mask obscured her expression, but Star couldn't hide the small tremors shaking her body. Afraid she had gone into shock, Hauk pulled over and parked alongside the road before draping the plaid blanket he kept on the backseat across her shoulders.

She hugged the fuzzy fabric to her chest with tight fists. "I'm fine."

Skeptical, he arched a brow.

"Honest. I'm just... I'm angry, Hauk. Angry for not looking at the driver, angry at not knowing why, angry... angry at him for scaring me." Acknowledging her fear and the attempt on her life out loud spoke of her strength and resilience.

Rattled by the same emotions, Hauk brushed back a lock of hair stuck to her forehead. "It's okay to be angry and scared."

"If you say so." Shadows crossed her eyes. "Why did you send Kyle to the bus station?"

"I didn't want you to be stranded at the station all day in case your bus was further delayed or cancelled." A voice inside his head had insisted that he checked on her, but saying it aloud would have sounded lame, even ridiculous "Did you see the truck that hit your bus?"

She shook her head. "I was sitting on the other side, reading. Why?"

Hauk had wondered if Kyle mentioned the white truck to her. Based on her casual response, it sounded like his diver didn't. "A white pickup truck caused the accident, and the driver sped away."

Her dark brown eyes widened instantly. "White? Like the truck that... that..."

"Kyle didn't see the make or model of the truck, but..." Hauk wished he could protect her from the guilt she might feel learning people were hurt and died because she rode on that bus. "We can't rule out the possibility that whoever ran you over tried to finish the job."

"This is insane, Hauk." Laced with anger and indignation, her voice rose in the confines of the Jeep. "Dozens of innocent people were on that bus. Children with runny noses, toothless grannies—"

"Just hear me out, please." Hoping to get her attention and curb the flow of objections before her temper flared up and aggravated her headache, he laid a hand on her forearm.

She crossed her arms over her chest, and glared at him. "I'm not worth the death of anyone." Her words carried the finality of the conversation. "This was an accident. Period."

A sigh built inside his chest. No woman had ever managed to exasperate and fascinate him at the same time. "You're right. Lots of white trucks and irresponsible drivers roam the roads. It was a coincidence."

Except he didn't believe in coincidences, and he doubted she did either.

* * *

Bruce paced the kitchen of the ramshackle house that Dusty had inherited from his deceased mother.

Everyone on the bus should be dead, but his plan had derailed as badly as the bridge. The fate of the other passengers had been of no consequence, a means to an end, a simple yet effective way to deflect attention from the targeted girl.

His initial scheme had been to enter the bridge seemingly out of control and sway into the wrong lane, forcing the bus onto the railing and down the ravine. The bus driver had accelerated to avoid him, leaving Bruce with no choice but to ram him. "The girl was on her way to Lakewood. I had to stop her."

Dusty hit the table with his fist, leaving a dent. "If a single dumb ass on that bus recognized you or wrote down your plate number, you're screwed. We're screwed."

"Muddy plate and baseball cap," Bruce bragged with feigned confidence. "I would never stand out in a police lineup." Even if the police succeeded in apprehending him, they wouldn't be able to prove premeditation. At worse, charges for speeding, reckless driving, and fleeing the

134

scene would be laid. With the help of a good lawyer and his prior record sealed, Bruce would probably get away with a hefty fine but no jail time.

"If you say so." Dusty sounded anything but convinced. "You know the cops will be looking for your banged up truck, right?"

"Why do you think I'm here?" Dusty's remote acreage made the perfect hiding place. No one risked venturing into this part of the woods, not with the threatening *No Trespassing* signs nailed to the trees bordering its perimeter. "You'll keep my truck in your garage until I fix it."

His friend slumped onto a kitchen chair. "What are you going to drive? And don't say my van."

Bruce sat opposite Dusty at the table. "One of the courtesy cars from the shop." Being the boss had its advantages. None of his employees would dare question his motives or his unscheduled absence this morning. "It won't attract any attention, but we have a more pressing problem. The girl is still alive but she disappeared. No idea where."

Chapter 10

Hauk wanted to rent a nicer room for Star to freshen up, but Lakewood lacked adequate accommodations. His tired body sprawled across the bed, he stared at the cracked ceiling yellowed by decades of cigarette smoke.

"A fresh coat of paint would go a long way to improve the state of the room," he muttered under his breath.

All the motels in the small town looked like they were built in the fifties, with some owners placing more emphasis on restoration than others. The friendly, young man working the registration desk had assured them that the room was clean, the beds comfortable, and the bathroom recently renovated.

The water in the bathroom stopped running. Hauk approached the door and knocked. "Star?"

"Yes? Do you want something?"

He leaned his forehead against the doorframe, wanting the last thing he should covet. "I'm heading out for a few minutes. Need anything from the Jeep?"

"Don't think so."

"No opening the door to strangers," he cautioned. "I'll be back before you miss me."

He left the motel, crossed the street, and walked into the real estate office he had noticed before checking into the motel.

His long discussion with the realtor provided interesting information regarding the Humphrey family. An hour had passed by the time Hauk thanked the relator and returned to the motel.

An eerie silence welcomed him into the room, disturbed only by the humming of the air conditioning unit. Hauk scanned the room and caught sight of a body slumped across the bed.

"Star?" A jackhammer pounded inside his chest. He rushed to her side and ran his fingers through her blonde curls. His fears eased with her regular breathing, he inhaled the delicate scent of lilac lingering over her skin.

"Hauk..." She trailed off in a sultry voice.

"Am I in your dreams?" he whispered, his gaze travelling down her slender body.

Her beige tank top and khaki cargo shorts did little to conceal the scratches marring her legs and arms.

* * *

Star peeked through hazy eyes, her mind

searching for the path from dreams to reality. "Hauk?"

He sat at the edge of the bed. "Did you have a nice nap?"

"A nap?" She only laid down waiting for him, never intending to fall asleep. "How long?"

"An hour or so." He trailed his fingers along her cheek, pushing a lock of hair near her ear. "How's your head?"

The innocent brush against her skin awakened idle feelings. "Bump is still tender, but the headache is better."

"Good." He pulled away, to her disappointment. "Would you like to visit the Humphreys' house?"

The startling offer chased the last vestiges of sleep from her brain. "Really?"

He pulled a set of keys from his pocket and dangled them in front of her eyes. "I'm a resourceful man. Want something to eat first?"

Her empty stomach rumbled in response.

* * *

The leaves of the towering trees lining the residential street rustled in the breeze, and the late afternoon sun shone through the branches, casting shadows on the road.

Hauk slowed down approaching a playground filled with children.

In the passenger seat, Star propped her elbow on the ledge of the open window. "When you talked to Inspector Kenneth, did he say he looked for a connection between the murders and Adrian Humphrey's caseload?"

During their lunch, Hauk had recounted his meeting with the inspector, but at the time, Star had mostly listened, so he was pleased to hear her asking questions. "He did, and nothing stood out. You think they might have missed something?"

"I..." She nibbled on her lower lip. "I'm not sure, but I find it strange that Eleanor fed us an insurance story and that Adrian reviewed insurance claims."

An intersection lay ahead. "That one could be coincidence."

"Maybe..." She leaned back in her seat. "I dream of dead people, Hauk. Do you think I'm crazy?"

Startled by the unexpected query about her mental state, he slammed on the brakes, abruptly stopping a metre away from the stop sign.

She glared at him. "Are you trying to bash my head against the windshield to beat some sense into me?"

"Sorry." He resumed his drive through the neighbourhood. "No, you're not crazy. Snooping around here, on the other hand, might not be the smartest idea." Visiting the crime scene might affect her brain in ways he couldn't begin to image.

Her eyes narrowed in suspicion. "You didn't break any laws getting those keys, did you?"

"Of course not. I got the keys from a realtor who also gave me the entire history of the house." Astonished by the sharp turns and quick wit of her mind, he kept shifting his attention back and forth between Star and the road. "After the murders, the bank auctioned the property to cover the mortgage. A local builder bought it and renovated it with the intention of selling it and pocketing a hefty profit. With its macabre history, the Humphreys' house remained unsold. Some years later, the builder filed for bankruptcy, and the town repossessed the house. It was transformed into a subsidized daycare until a child escaped supervision and wandered down to the creek."

Star gasped. "Did she drown?"

Uneasy by Star's assumption that the child was a girl, Hauk continued. "No. Lucky for the boy, Lakewood experienced a drought that summer. He was found sitting in the mud with water trickling around him. After the incident, the kiddy school became a homeless shelter, but it also closed after a drug addict fatally stabbed an employee during a psychotic episode."

Star shook her head. "That house is cursed."

Minutes later, Hauk parked in front of what used to be a white two-storey bungalow. The paint, subjected to years of inclement weather, had yellowed and peeled from the siding. On the roof, asphalt shingles curled up at the edges—a warning to potential buyers that expensive repairs awaited the future owner. Weeds sprouted amid cracks in the driveway, and a *For Sale* sign hung from a crooked post stuck in the middle of the dead lawn.

* * *

Thinking it might be best to explore the exterior of the property before the sun dipped below the horizon, Star circled the Humphreys' house.

On the south border grew a well-trimmed cedar hedge. To the north, a faded royal blue and white picket fence provided a demarcation from the neighbour's yard. The missing boards drew a smile from Star's lips. She pictured rambunctious kids sneaking into the neighbour's garden to steal carrots or tomatoes.

An ancient oak stood proudly in the middle of the backyard. Wooden rungs nailed on its trunk led up to a tree house perched on the sturdy thick branches above. In between the makeshift steps, lovestruck kids had carved hearts with their initials on them.

Star ran a hand over a smooth rung curving downward. The steps of countless little feet climbing up and down reverberated through the tips of her fingers, and silent laughter resonated from the tree house.

The image of a child falling from a branch fleeted across her eyes. "She fell." Still, the vision didn't alter the serenity of the backyard.

Hauk placed his hands over her shoulders. "A girl fell?" His chest pressed against her back and his warm breath tickled her ear. "What's the initials of the lucky guy she fell for, havfrue?"

Unruly butterflies fluttered in her stomach. The strange nickname added another layer of mystery to Hauk's behaviour, but then she remembered the encounter at the bus terminal. She didn't measure up to the exotic beauty, to the flawless women that men like him were attracted to.

Mad at herself for harbouring feelings toward him, Star spun around and took a step back. "The little girl—" Her back pushed against the trunk. "She fell from the tree house."

The sparkles dancing in his eyes waned away. "You saw a child fall down?"

"A little blonde girl." *The child from my nightmares.*

"Star, you need to curb those morbid—"

"Sorry to interrupt." On the neighbouring property, an elderly lady peeked over the cedar hedge. "This is private property."

Hauk dangled the house keys in the air. "We're visiting the house."

"Are you thinking of buying?" The neighbour scurried through the backyard. Seconds later, a diminutive figure stood facing them. If she tiptoed, the grey bun at the top of her head still wouldn't reach Hauk's shoulder.

The elderly lady reminded Star of her second-grade teacher. With one glare, Miss Caruthers had possessed the gift of silencing her entire class into submission.

"Buying? Maybe." A white lie on Hauk's part. "We were told the house has a tragic history."

The neighbour tut-tutted him. "It all happened a long time ago, young man. This is a lovely and peaceful neighbourhood. You and your wife would be very happy here."

Something in the sentence brought a smile to Hauk's face while the word *wife* flushed Star's cheeks.

"I'm Hauk, and this is Star."

"Dora. I live next door." The elderly lady pointed at a modest bungalow, similar to the Humphreys'. "I miss not having neighbours since my poor Charley passed away. Laughing children should be playing in this yard, and colourful flowers should be growing in the gardens.”

“How long have you lived here, Dora?” Hauk hadn’t bothered correcting Dora’s erroneous assumption.

“Thirty wonderful years.” With a warm smile, Dora invited them to follow her toward the end of the Humphreys’ backyard.

The ground gently sloped under Star’s feet. No barrier separated the backyard from the creek farther down. “Dora, how come no one ever built a fence?”

“This section of the backyard is too rocky.” Dora’s sneaker-clad foot tapped the ground. “Can’t dig deep enough.”

They stopped near the embankment. The creek extended five metres across and appeared to run half as deep. Rocks and boulders edged the clear, blue water, mercilessly dragging twigs and branches along its sinuous path.

The current grabbed hold of the blonde girl. Tossed against the rocks, the child gasped for air. Shivers of fear coursed through Star’s body. “She drowned here.”

“I see you heard about Vanessa,” Dora noted in a sad voice.

Mentally shaking the disturbing vision away, Star focused her attention on the neighbour. “Did you know them well?”

Dora nodded with a bittersweet smile. “It was such a lovely family and such a terrible tragedy.”

"Could you please tell us all you know about the Humphreys?" Star couldn't explain the feeling gnawing inside her, but something more than curiosity pushed her to inquire.

"Well... Adrian, the dad, worked in insurance. Amy stayed at home with her children, a boy and twin girls. Adorable and quiet little kids except for the rambunctious blonde twin." Dora rolled her eyes in feigned exasperation. "Always in trouble that one. Her name was Vanessa, but everyone called her Nessa. She was my favourite, you know." Dora walked farther up the creek, and Star followed her. "Nessa loved to climb, a real monkey. One day she ventured onto the roof of the tree house and fell without breaking a single bone. If you ask me, her guardian angel was watching, not that it impressed Amy much."

"So much for your uncanny vision," Hauk murmured within Star's earshot.

Unsettled by her vision, Star struggled to keep her voice steady. "Was... was Vanessa's mother upset?"

"Upset *and* terrified. Poor Nessa got grounded, but she still managed to sneak out of the house and go play by the creek. I was pruning my roses when I heard her scream." Dora raised her finger indicating a huge boulder near a series of rapids. "I found Nessa covered in blood near that rock."

"A dog..." The breeze carried the dog's foul breath to Star's nose. The water breaking against the rocks echoed the sharp burning pain as teeth lacerated her skin. Her knees buckled underneath her. Two powerful arms lowered her to the ground. Star unconsciously made a fist, trapping blades of grass between her fingers, just as chubby little fingers grabbed the matted fur to stop the vicious attack. "A big black dog."

Dora knelt by her side and patted her forearm. "Are you all right, dear? How did you know a black dog attacked Nessa?"

"I..." Star touched her own face, tracing the ridges of her scar. "I didn't." A scent had triggered memories of her own attack, not Vanessa's. "I'm fine."

"Star, you're not—" Hauk swallowed hard, but his clenched jaw was a clear indication he disagreed. Nonetheless, he pulled her up but kept an arm around her waist. "Dora, how long after the dog attack did Vanessa drown?"

"A week..." Dora wobbled standing up. "Maybe two."

"Here, Dora." Hauk offered the elderly lady his free hand and helped her up. "Were you home that night?"

"If I had been, I might have seen or heard something." Dora's voice dropped to a whisper. "Every day during that summer I came to check the creek. No sign of Vanessa. The police never found her body, you know, only her nightgown."

Images of the nanny and her young charge trapped between the water and the killer flowed through Star's mind, triggering unanswerable questions. *Did the nanny fight or beg for her life before it tragically ended? Did she jump into the creek in a desperate attempt to escape a brutal death? Did she—*

Hauk's hand gently rubbed her lower back, stopping her pointless musings. "Dora, did you know the nanny?"

"I didn't. Amy had recently hired her to take care of the children in preparation for her upcoming surgery."

"What kind of surgery?" he asked.

Hands on her hips, Dora looked Hauk up and down disapprovingly. "Woman's surgery, young man. None of your business."

The sharp reply brought a smile to Star's face. "Thank you, Dora."

"You look rather pale, dear. You should go home, and let your..." The elderly lady threw another frown Hauk's way. "Let your husband take *good* care of you."

"I promise I will." Hauk pulled Star against him, no doubt to impress the neighbour. "Thank you for showing us around."

After one last look in their direction, Dora left them alone.

* * *

"See something you like?" Hauk teased, hoping to diffuse the mounting tension between them.

Star looked him up and down, just like Dora had done moments earlier, but with a more guarded expression. Afraid he might have overstepped his boundaries, Hauk dropped his hand and took a step sideways before Star had a chance to push him away.

Star folded her arms in front of her, inadvertently grazing his chest with her elbow. "Why did you pretend you were my husband?"

Telling Star that her touch fired up sensations difficult to ignore or that he drew immense personal satisfaction at being called her husband didn't sound like a good idea at the moment. "Dora seemed like a nice, old lady. I didn't want to ruin her opinion of us by telling her that we were just snooping around. Now you want to tell me why you almost fainted?"

"I didn't faint." Her tone lacked its usual verve.

Amused, he waggled his brows. "Oh, I see... you just love falling within arm's reach of me?"

A darker shade of red crept into her face. "Don't flatter yourself, Ludwig. I got dizzy."

"Dizzy?" He modulated his voice to resemble the soft caress that he bestowed over her scar with the tips of his fingers. "You relived your own attack, didn't you?" When she didn't contradict him, he knew he had guessed right. "You and that turbulent child seem to have a lot in common."

"Somehow, coming from you, that doesn't sound like a compliment."

Inwardly smiling, he offered her his arm. "Let's go inside before we meet an unfriendly dog."

* * *

The wooden steps leading to the porch creaked under their weight, and the front door squeaked when Star opened it.

Dust bunnies had invaded the floor streaked with smudged footprints, cobwebs decorated the ceilings, and the stench of stale, hot air churned her stomach.

Hauk flicked the light switch up and down. "No electricity."

It was obvious that no one had bothered to pay the bills or clean in months, possibly years. "No wonder the house hadn't sold," she muttered under her breath. Still, the interior looked strangely familiar.

Across the foyer was the living room and farther down was the infamous hallway.

As Star approached the bathroom, her confident stride faltered and cold sweat trickled between her shoulder blades.

Tiny bare feet had walked on the same hardwood floor and left a trail of blood. *Why am I dreaming about them?*

On a hunch that the ugly bitchling might visit the old Humphreys' house, Dusty drove to Lakewood only to spot Ludwig's grey Jeep parked in front of the neglected lawn flagged with a *For Sale* sign.

To avoid attracting attention, Dusty parked a few blocks up. He slipped on a pair of gloves before approaching the Humphreys' house on foot.

The curtains inside the neighbouring house on the left were drawn and no cars were parked in the driveway. Hoping the neighbours weren't home, Dusty walked around their garage.

A broken fence was all that separated their backyard from the Humphreys'.

Dusty slipped through the fence then rushed toward the Humphreys' garage side door, the same access point he used in his previous attack.

Twenty years ago, the screen door had been locked but not the solid side door. With his hunting knife, he had sliced through the mesh screen, opened the door, slipped inside the garage, and then inside the house.

This time around, the screen door was gone but the solid door was locked. Still, it didn't deter Dusty. Over the decades, he had perfected his breaking and entering skills to include lock picking. With the right picks and a few twists of the wrist, he unlocked the side door. It opened and closed without a squeak.

Now that he had gained access to the garage, he slid a dark hood over his face then tested the door leading inside the house. Not only was it unlocked, but it also opened without a sound.

Farther down the hallway, voices echoed from inside the bathroom.

The thrill of the hunt had his blood pumping through his veins. History repeated itself.

Chapter 11

Hauk entered a small bathroom halfway down the hallway and almost gagged.

The rays of sunshine piercing through the window above the cracked sink, cast shadows on the filthy toilet bowl missing its lid.

Seemingly oblivious to the stench, Star stared, her pupils dilated, at the unlit dome mounted to the ceiling. "A lone light bulb."

"Star?" When she didn't respond, Hauk gently shook her.

"I..." She blinked repeatedly. "I'm fine."

A low growl of exasperation rumbled inside his throat as he lowered his hands from her shoulders. *Stubborn woman.*

Her gaze wandered around the room then appeared to focus on the grey storage cabinet above the toilet tank. "In my nightmares, that cupboard is yellow." She pulled a pocketknife from the back of her shorts, flicked the blade open, and scratched the grey cupboard door.

"Star, you can't damage—" The streak of yellow paint she exposed silenced his objections.

"Hauk? This is..." Her voice quavered. "This is beyond creepy."

No kidding. A part of him wanted to yank the doors open and look at the shelves, but he was afraid his actions might trigger more painful memories for her. "Star, why don't you give me that knife and go into the kitchen? I'll meet you in a few minutes."

* * *

Going to the kitchen, away from that foul bathroom, sounds like an excellent idea. Star walked down the hallway gazing at the floor when suddenly she crashed into something solid.

A hunting knife clattered on the hardwood floor near her feet. Stunned, she lifted her head only to stare at two narrow slits cut through a black hood. "W—"

The masked intruder wrapped his hands around her throat, silencing her surprise, and squeezed. Gasping for air, for sound, she grabbed his wrists and dug her nails into his skin. He winced, and his grip lessened. Emboldened, she dug deeper and yanked on his arms. Her hand slipped, and she ripped his sleeve, exposing a tattoo. Her oxygen deprived brain registered wings and a beak.

He banged her head against the wall. Stars danced in front of her eyes.

153

"Star, no more breaking things. I'll be out soon."

Hauk...Help... A strong, musky scent assaulted her nostrils, jolting her senses. She clawed at the hood, at the slits, aiming for her attacker's eyes. He took a step back, opening a gap between their bodies. With all the strength she could muster, she thrust her knee into his groin.

Her attacker yelped in pain.

"What did I say about breaking—"

The attacker shoved her into Hauk, scooped the knife off the floor, and fled.

* * *

Wary of the wildlife lurking in the nightly shadows of the forest, ready to leap in front of the Jeep, Hauk focused his attention onto the road.

As far as he could tell, no one had been following them since they left the hospital. Still, that didn't ease the crushing sensation inside his chest. Due to his own carelessness, he almost lost her inside the cursed house.

In the passenger seat, Star stirred in her sleep. Hauk reached for her hand. Under the blanket covering her, his thumb found the inside of her wrist.

The small circles he drew over the soft spot seemed to calm her. "Sweet dreams, havfrue." His cell phone vibrated inside his pocket. He answered in a low voice, careful not to wake her. "Ludwig."

"How's Star, boss?"

From the hospital, Hauk had called his helmsman to update him on the situation. To hear Kyle, not Arnie, inquire about Star spoke of the incredible shift in the divers' rocky relationship.

"The doctor said she would make a full recovery, but she was urged not to talk until the swelling goes down."

"Like there's a snowball's chance in hell that's going to happen." Amid the outburst, a sigh of relief resounded on the line. "Are they keeping her at the hospital under police protection?"

"The police are taking Star's attack seriously, and they're not ruling out a connection with her previous hit and run, but the evidence so far points toward a random attack. From what I learned, the neighbourhood watch reports shady characters and suspicious activities around the old Humphreys' house on a weekly basis." The many smudged footprints and the boarded windows in the basement attested to how often the house had been broken into in recent years, and while Hauk didn't see any signs of recent activity or anything worth stealing, he had to admit it made a nice hideout for petty criminals. "I find it suspicious that the assailant wore a face mask, but then a few weeks ago, the police arrested a suspected burglar wearing a similar disguise farther down the street, so who knows."

Kyle muttered some unsavoury adjectives under his breath. "Are you on your way back to the lake?"

"No, not yet." Hauk had a theory about the attacks that he wanted to investigate before sharing it with anyone. "Any luck identifying the white pickup?"

"Fifty-three possible matches. Scott is busy narrowing them down, but it'll take time."

Time wasn't a luxury that Hauk could afford, not if he was right about Star. "Do me a favour. Tell Scott to keep working on it, tell Arnie to move the boat near the limit line imposed by the police." The proximity of law enforcement should reduce the risk of attack on his crew. "And I need someone to track down the insurance claims that Adrian Humphrey was working on before his death."

"I'm on it, boss. Anything else?"

"No, but be careful snooping around town." Too many incidents already plagued his crew, Hauk didn't want to make another trip to the hospital. "Keep me posted."

Hauk hung up, and a heavy silence filled the Jeep.

"You think he's also in danger?" Star whispered in a scratchy voice.

Not as much as Hauk believed she was, but he kept the disturbing thought to himself. "You're not supposed to talk," he chided, softening his remark with a playful tone.

Her gaze, which was directed at him, travelled to the window. "Where are we?"

"Middle of nowhere." The Jeep's high beams only showed ditches and trees alongside the road. "I'm taking you home, Star."

"This isn't the way to—" She coughed out the rest of her remark.

"I'm taking a detour. Just close your eyes and go back to sleep. I'll keep you safe. I promise."

* * *

Star guided Hauk toward a log cabin nestled between a quiet lake and a luxuriant forest.

Home. The air smelled fresher and the sun shone brighter around her remote cabin. Behind the boathouse, the slightly overweight body of her father lay in the hammock tied between two large birch trees.

Her smile broadened. Growing up, she enjoyed disturbing his midmorning nap, more often than not, with water. "Jimmy?"

At the sound of her voice, he opened dark brown eyes, and then he fell off the hammock and onto the grass.

"Squirt?" He stood, and his big, loving arms gathered her battered body against him. "What happened?"

Her head pressed against his chest, she could hear the strong beat of his heart, its familiar thumping easing her aches and pains. "It's a long story."

He kissed the top of her head. "Why don't you begin by introducing me to that tall guy over there?"

Upon her invitation, Hauk approached to meet Jimmy, and the two men exchanged a solid handshake.

At fifty-two, despite a constant struggle with his waistline, her father was in relatively good shape. Small talk sustained his inquiries until they entered the kitchen. Once they were all seated around the table with mugs of coffee, Hauk recounted the mishaps that plagued his crew.

"And you think all those accidents are related to that Model T you found?" Jimmy fidgeted with the spoon he used to add sugar to his brew.

Hauk nodded. "And to Star's nightmares."

At the words, Star winced in imaginary pain.

"Nightmares?" Deep concern wrinkled the corners of her father's eyes. "Are you still having those nightmares, squirt?"

"I'm fine, Jimmy. Honest." *It could be worse. I could be dead.*

Her father frowned. "From where I sit, you don't look too swell."

Amusement twinkled in Hauk's eyes. "Jimmy, may I ask a few questions about Star's parents?"

"My parents?" The empty stainless-steel bowl on the table reflected Star's dubious look.

"Call it a hunch, Star, but it may explain the attempts on your life."

It didn't feel like a hunch, more like a fishing expedition that she didn't want to board. "I don't have a father, and my mother died when I was young." That was it. Short and to the point.

Star then looked up through her lashes at her father. The reasons behind his reluctance to talk about Stella had always eluded her. Over the years, Star learned to squelch her curiosity and live with the sketchy details he had provided of her mother.

"Your mother... Stella... she didn't die."

"What?" Shocked by the revelation, Star went to stand by the window. Resentment built inside her chest and throat, and she coughed out her irritation. "If my mother didn't die, where has she been hiding all these years?"

"Come back to the table, squirt."

Impervious to her father's plea, Star leaned her back against the window frame and crossed her arms over her chest. "I'm not a child, Jimmy. You don't need to shield me anymore. I want the truth and all the sordid details that go with it."

Across the table, Jimmy clasped his hands together. "This isn't easy." To give him credit, he looked at her while he spoke. "You have to understand that my father, your grandfather, was a very strict man. After he lost his wife, his temper worsened. I'd left home long before my mother's death, but Ella was twelve years younger than me and—"

"Ella?" *The Humphreys' nanny was named Ella.* Star glanced at Hauk who shifted on his chair.

"The nickname I gave your mom when we were kids. It stuck. Anyway, your mom, she rebelled against your grandfather's authority, not that I blamed her, but her wild choices led to disaster. She became pregnant, and your grandfather kicked her out. She was fifteen."

"He threw her out at fifteen?" Her grandfather's cruelty outraged Star. "But she was a child."

"I know... At the time, I worked hundreds of kilometres away. When I came home for a visit that summer, Ella had already been gone for two months. I searched for her, but no one knew where she went." Sorrow laced Jimmy's voice. "Five years passed. Your grandfather died. I inherited the house and moved back into town. Then one night, twenty years ago, Ella called. She was hysterical. Years earlier, I'd failed to protect her, but I was determined to make up for my past mistake. I jumped in my truck and drove like a madman, making the twelve-hour ride to Lakewood in less than eight."

"My mom lived in Lakewood twenty years ago?" The murders had occurred twenty years ago. Of all the coincidences that rocked Star's world, that one was the biggest.

"Yes, a shabby apartment building in Lakewood. She was waiting for me in a basement room. I never forgot that place." His expression saddened, and Star braced herself for more painful details. "You lay on a lumpy bed, wearing only an oversized T-shirt. The morning sun shining through the barred window highlighted the bruises and cuts on your body. You were pretty banged up. I approached you with caution, afraid you would bolt. Your haunted expression nearly broke my heart. I picked you up and cradled you in my arms. It seemed to ease some of the fear and sadness in your eyes. You... you were the most beautiful thing I'd ever seen." His words draped a blanket of love over Star's heart. "Come to think of it, you look just as beat up now as you did back then."

Star smiled through her tears. "Not funny. What happened to my mother? Did she do that to me?"

"No. Your mother wasn't in a much better shape than you were. She babbled about a man trying to kill you."

Hauk leaned forward. "What man?"

"I didn't pay attention, son. I figured it didn't matter if he was a boyfriend, a stranger… or a john," Jimmy added in a hushed tone, avoiding her gaze. "That monster attacked them, and Ella was afraid he'd come back to finish the job. She begged me to take Star and keep her safe. I wanted to take them both, but Ella refused." He sighed. "I know I should have insisted, squirt, but I was so angry with your mother for not protecting you in the first place that I left her there. I never heard from Ella again. I suppose she had her reasons. I owed it to her to do the best for you."

"Jimmy, do you remember the date you rescued Star?" Hauk inquired in a sombre tone.

"Of course I do. A man never forgets the day he becomes a father. It was on July 28th."

"The morning after the murders…" Shaken by the timeline, Star grasped the ledge of the window as her mind grappled with the implications.

A chair screeched on the floor. Her father glanced back and forth between her and Hauk. "What murders?"

* * *

The sun dipping behind the trees cast ominous shadows on Star's home—and on her life.

Reeling from the questions spinning in her head, she sat on the floating dock with her feet dangling inches from the surface of the lake, and stared at the darkening water.

Though he couldn't prove it, Hauk was convinced that her mother was the nanny hired by the Humphreys days before the murders.

Star had to admit the coincidences were too striking to be dismissed. Both were named Ella, and her mother had called her estranged brother for help the night of the murders. It would also explain why the police never found Ella's body.

What about Vanessa? Only her nightgown was found. The fate of the little girl haunted Star's nightmares. *Why didn't my mother go to the police? Did she feel guilty because she couldn't save Vanessa? Did—*

A slight tap on her shoulder startled her. She recoiled, almost falling into the lake.

"Sorry." Hauk sat beside her. "I didn't mean to scare you."

If only his touch was the only thing she had to fear, her future might not be so dire. "Why do I have the feeling you knew my mother was connected to the Humphreys even before we talked to Jimmy?"

"You and Vanessa were both mauled by a dog, and you dream about her. A connection had to exist." His gaze wandered over the lake. "Do you recall your mother ever telling you about the twins? Or the murders?"

"Maybe my mother took me with her when she interviewed for the job. Maybe I played with the twins. Maybe I used that bathroom." Star's frustration grew. The memories were buried deep inside her mind, so deep they only resurfaced at night. "I must have seen things or overheard my mother talking—or babbling, like Jimmy said—about the Humphreys, or else I wouldn't remember those details in my nightmares, would I?"

"No, you wouldn't. Like I said in the kitchen, we can't rule out the possibility that the monster who killed the Humphreys, the monster who's roamed free for the last twenty years, somehow resurfaced." Hauk brushed a lock of hair behind her ear, leaving behind the illusion of a soft caress. "You and your mother were beaten the night of the murders. I'm guessing the monster tried to silence you both, but Ella somehow managed to escape him long enough to call Jimmy. I know you don't remember the monster, and a part of me is glad you don't, but Jimmy never forgot what you looked like when he rescued you, and I suspect the monster didn't either. If I'm right, you are a threat to his freedom—a threat he needs to neutralize."

Seeking comfort and reassurance, she leaned her head against Hauk's shoulder and closed her eyes. "Why didn't my mother go to the police after Jimmy took me home? Was she afraid she would be blamed for Vanessa's death?" Her mother's silence didn't make Star safer, it only bought her time. And time had run out.

Hauk slipped an arm around her shoulders and hugged her tight. "Ella trusted her brother to keep you safe, and Jimmy did, but something changed. I intend to figure out what. In the meantime, I want you to rest your voice and stay here, away from—"

"Oh, no." She recoiled, pushing him at arm's length. "Tomorrow, I'm going back to Lakewood to search for my mother." *I deserve the truth, and the children in my nightmares deserve justice.*

Chapter 12

Hauk knew better than to wage a losing battle, but if Star thought he would let her go to Lakewood by herself in the morning, she would learn that he could outmatch her tenacity. Besides, the bus incident brought her back into his life, or brought him back into her life, for a reason. So this time, he intended to step up to the plate and swing. If he got a third strike, he would at least have tried instead of wondering for the rest of his life if she could have been that special one.

Back inside the cabin, Star showed him to a bedroom on the main floor after which she headed up a narrow set of stairs at the end of the hallway.

Hauk lit the pink lamp clipped to the headboard of a double bed then surveyed the room.

A faded blue and purple quilt lay folded at the end of the bed. A recent picture of Star and an alarm clock off by one hour rested on top of a dresser. Two pretty dolls stared with glassy eyes from on a shelf by the window. And posters of aquatic species that Hauk had never encountered in his dives decorated the walls.

This didn't look like an ordinary guest bedroom. It looked like Star's bedroom.

Wearing nothing but his boxers, he lay on top of the bed, turned off the light, and slowly drifted off.

A scream pierced the night, rousing him. He bolted up into a sitting position and listened for more sounds. The floor above cracked under muffled footsteps.

Hauk slipped a pair of shorts on and hurried out of the room. Across the hallway, Jimmy snored behind a closed door, oblivious to the disturbance.

Ominous scenarios played out inside Hauk's mind as he rushed up the narrow staircase that Star had climbed earlier.

Armed with nothing but his fists and a robust determination to keep her safe, he pushed her door. It opened without a sound, revealing a lone silhouette standing by the window.

He expelled the breath he didn't realize he was holding, and relaxed a notch.

The moonshine enveloped Star in an eerie haze.

Afraid to startle her, he kept his voice low. "Star?"

"Hauk?" She didn't move, but her whisper carried through the silent night.

This room was smaller than the one in which he slept. Flanked by a dresser and a rocking chair, a single bed was pushed against a wall underneath a slanted ceiling. A blanket was folded on the back of the chair. He picked it up before approaching her.

The blanket was soft and light. He draped it over her shoulders and gently held it in place. "Would you like to talk?"

She leaned back into his chest. "If I say no, will you leave me alone?"

"No." Emboldened by her physical response, he trailed his hands up and down her arms.

"You're an obstinate man, Hauk Ludwig." The sweet scent of lilac lingered around her.

"Guilty as charge." He grazed her hair inhaling the floral fragrance. "You can talk to me, you know."

In the glass of the partially open window, a timid smile flittered across her shadowy reflection. "Did I wake you when I screamed?"

"I was dozing off, not sleeping." The woman haunted his nights as much as the nightmares haunted hers. "You didn't disturb your father."

"He's a sound sleeper." Low and silky, her voice enthralled him. "After I switched bedrooms and moved into the attic, he couldn't hear me scream anymore, so he stopped worrying about my nightmares. I just never corrected his assumption that they no longer plagued my nights."

It pained Hauk that her desire to protect her father had inadvertently pushed away the only person with whom she could have talked about them. "Will you move down to your old room now that Jimmy knows the truth?"

"No." She gazed out the window. "I love this room and the view of the lake."

A cool breeze whispered through the window screen and the moon's reflection glistened on the surface of the water.

Content to hold her, Hauk wished for time to slow down. "It's beautiful."

"And peaceful, more peaceful than my life," she murmured, almost to herself.

He cursed the words burning is tongue, knowing they would break the spell. "Was your nightmare identical to the other ones?"

"Dream and reality are colliding, Hauk. I saw the hand holding the knife over the child's head, but this time there was a strange bird tattooed near his wrist." Back at the hospital, Star had described the tattoo as a bird in flight to the police officer interviewing her. "My subconscious is adding details of my recent attack to the nightmare, like it's not already disturbing enough. I feel like I'm losing my mind."

"You're not losing it. Your mind is simply trying to make sense of the tragic events that plagued your life, and your subconscious is filtering the details through your nightmares." Clues were hidden in her mind, and until they rose to the surface, Hauk doubted the nightmares would stop. "You're the strongest, most resilient, and most beautiful woman I've ever met, havfrue. We'll get through this."

She turned around, prompting him to drop his hands, and stared at him. "What did you just say?"

"I said we'll get through this, together." With the tips of his fingers, Hauk traced the fine lines of her scar. "No children should go through what you—"

The shadows darkened her face, and she pulled away. "I don't want your pity. Save it for the monster who attacked me because he'll need it when I'm done with him."

Something he did or said had triggered her outburst, but for the life of him, Hauk had no idea where he went wrong.

She hugged the blanket close to her chest. "And stop looking at me like... like that."

"Like what, Star? Like I care? Like I want to protect you? Like... like I'm in love with you?" That was it. He said the words he swore never to say or feel again. "What's going on in that amazing mind of yours, havfrue? I know I may be clueless at times, but I was under the impression... I was hoping you might somehow return my feelings."

Her eyes widened, like a doe caught in the headlights of an eighteen-wheeler. "I... I'm not like her."

"*Her?*" Hauk vigorously rubbed his cheeks, hoping to sway his sleep-deprived brain into making sense of Star's puzzling behavior. "There are no other women in my life, Star. There hasn't been in a long time. Who are you talking about?"

"The—" She chewed on her bottom lip. "The exotic beauty from the bus station."

"Her? She wasn't a beauty, she was a vulgar piece of coal." Had Star not looked so angry, so vulnerable, Hauk would have laughed at the misunderstanding. "One night at the bar, she offered me a drink and slipped her number along with it. I gave the drink to Kyle, left the bar alone, and threw the piece of paper in the thrash on my way out. The scene she made at the bus station was a disgrace. I was never interested in her. Besides, I don't do one-night stand. Never did, never will. After I got rid of her, I wanted to explain but a certain diamond in the rough never gave me the chance."

"A diamond in the rough?" she murmured, her eyes glistening in the moonlight.

"A beautiful and priceless diamond." Heartened by the smirk lighting up her face, he wrapped her in his arms. "I wouldn't change a single thing about you, havfrue, not even that fiery temper of yours. I may not deserve you, but I love you. Would you give me a chance to make you happy?"

She rested her head against his chest. "What does *havfrue* mean?"

"Havfrue is a Norwegian mythical creature. A mermaid." He cupped her cheek, tilting her head up. "A beautiful enchantress who enthralls unsuspecting sailors."

Her lips parted, and he couldn't resist brushing a tender kiss on them. The tip of her tongue grazed his, teasing him. Intoxicated by her taste, he delved deeper into her mouth, savouring the moment he had dreamed of for weeks.

Through his passion-induced haze, he suddenly recalled the beating she had sustained and eased their embrace. "I'm not sure the doctor would approve if I were to kiss you all night."

"Why not?" Her hair tickled his chin. "I wasn't talking."

Afraid she might extend an invitation he shouldn't accept but would be powerless to refuse, Hauk released her. "I need to go back downstairs before we wake Jimmy up. I'll see you in the morning." And he left her room before his willpower burst like bubbles on the surface of a lake.

* * *

After a short stopover in slumberland, Hauk entered the kitchen where Star's father was reading his newspaper while drinking his coffee.

"Good morning, Hauk. Slept well?"

"I..." Hauk silently cursed his hesitation. "Yes."

Jimmy lowered his paper and arched a brow. "Did my snoring keep you awake?"

Relieved that his nightly visit to the attic had remained secret, Hauk relaxed. "No, but it took a while for my brain to shut down." *To relinquish the memory of Star's touch and taste.* "Do you mind if I take a cup?"

"Of course not." Her father pointed at the counter. "Serve yourself."

"Where's Star?" Hauk had checked the attic. The bed was made, and its resident was nowhere in the vicinity.

"In the den, searching the photo albums for pictures of her mother."

Hearing rapid steps, Hauk turned toward the hallway.

Star flagged something in the air. "Found two." Their gaze met, and she greeted him with a shy nod.

Sensing her awkwardness, Hauk pulled out the chair next to him. "Why don't you come here and show me what she looks like?"

She sat near him and placed the photos on the red-and-white checkered tablecloth. Hauk discreetly slipped his hand over Star's bare thigh. A small tremor coursed under his open palm, the only discernible sign that he startled her. From out of the corner of her eye, she glanced at him. A coy smile appeared on her lips as she twined her fingers with his.

Her father lowered his newspaper. "That's your mother all right." In the first photo, a teenage girl with long black hair and a mischievous smile swung on a tire suspended between two huge trees. The second photo was a close-up of her mother's face. "This was taken the summer before she got pregnant with you."

Hauk studied the photographs. Her mother was pretty, but she shared little resemblance with her daughter.

Under the table, Star squeezed his hand. "I don't look anything like her."

"Maybe you take after your father or a distant relative." Hauk shared little resemblance with either of his deceased parents, but he was the spitting image of his great-uncle Isaac. "What do you know about your birth father?"

"Nothing. He's not listed on my birth certificate." She eyed at her adoptive father. "Did my biological father take off? Did my mother even know who he was?"

"I have no idea, squirt." Jimmy's fingers drummed against the rim of his coffee mug. "I never saw your real birth certificate... or knew your real name."

Star's nails dug into the palm of Hauk's hand and a bucketload of apprehension stirred in the pit of his stomach. "What do you mean by *you don't know Star's real name*?"

"Ella, she..." Jimmy seemed to ponder his words at length. "In the apartment, Ella called you her little star. As I drove home with you, I tried to get you to tell me your name, but you barely said a word.”

Hauk could only imagine how frightened young Star must have been to be taken away by a stranger.

“I knew you were traumatized, so I didn’t insist. Short of a better name, I called you Star. I figured you’d eventually remember your real name, but you never corrected me.” Jimmy shrugged. “I assumed your mother named you after herself.”

“Stella and Star.” Both names rolled melodiously off Star’s tongue. “I can’t remember any other name.”

“Maybe it was your real name after all.” Her father tapped his own cheek. “With that fresh wound, it sure suited your personality.”

“You mean Star’s scar?” If Hauk recalled their conversation with Dora correctly, the dog had mauled the missing twin shortly before the murders. The coincidence that Star’s and Vanessa’s mauling occurred around the same time didn’t sit well with him

“Yes. Upon arriving home, I took Star to good old Doc. I needed to ascertain she was all right.” Jimmy’s gaze travelled back and forth between him and Star before settling on his daughter. “Despite the cuts and bruises marring your body, and the wound on your cheek, you showed no sign of prolonged abuse. Doc thought you might have been bitten by an animal a week or so earlier. It seemed your mother took much better care of you than I gave her credit for.”

Tears glistened in Star’s eyes.

Unsure how Star would react to a public display of affection in front of her father, Hauk resisted the temptation to slip his arm around her shoulders. Instead, he caressed her hand with his thumb. “That still doesn’t explain Star’s birth certificate.”

“Well, when it became apparent that Ella abandoned you, I went to see Doc for help. He made inquiries to hospitals but came up empty-handed and...” Again, Jimmy hesitated. “You needed an identity, squirt, so Doc filled a new birth certificate with your name, a date of birth, and—”

“You mean my birthday may not even be November 27th?” Star grew paler by the second.

“I know I should have told you long ago, but I never knew how.” Jimmy cupped his coffee mug with trembling hands. “November 27th was Ella’s due date. I had to pay a huge fine because I was late registering you, but with the paper that Doc signed, we were able to get you a new birth certificate.”

“Your doctor forged a new identity for Star?” Huge fine or not, Hauk questioned the legality of the practice. “Neither of you alerted the authorities?”

“Doc was an old friend of the family and ready to retire. He suggested the idea. I couldn’t let the authorities take my little girl, could I?” With sad eyes, her father pleaded for understanding, and maybe forgiveness. "I was a single guy in his early thirties with an odd job, no steady income, who lived in a rundown cottage by a lake in the wood. Not what a social worker would have deemed as a suitable guardian or environment to raise a child."

"For what it's worth, Jimmy, that social worker would have been wrong." The amazing woman with whom Hauk had fallen in love, was a living testimony to the contrary. "You raised a wonderful daughter."

Star reached across the table to pat Jimmy's hand. "I'm glad you kept me."

"Me too, squirt." A tender smile floated on Jimmy's lips. "And thank you, Hauk. I'm glad you noticed."

Hauk glanced at the woman blushing by his side. So much for her father not seeing right through them.

* * *

Hauk cursed the narrow, winding road with its tight curves that forced him to keep both hands on the steering wheel. They had left her home hours ago, but deep in thought, Star seemed oblivious to his presence or her environment. "You're not ghosting me, are you?"

She blinked repeatedly. "What?"

At least he had gained her attention. "Were you daydreaming about me?"

A nice shade of red tinged her face.

If there were room alongside the road to stop, he would pull over without hesitation and resume where they had left off the previous night. "If you're not thinking about me, then what's on your mind?"

"My mother. Where does a teenage girl go to give birth if not a hospital?"

"Why?" The relevance escaped him. "It won't help us locate her."

Star absently swept a lock of hair off her shoulders, exposing the graceful curve of her neck. Dark bruises shaped like fingerprints marred her tender skin. Rage tightened his chest, but for her sake, Hauk fought to control it.

"Maybe she named my father on my real birth certificate. Maybe he knows where she disappeared to."

Hauk doubted that a man who didn't bother to be around his daughter while she was growing up would care about the whereabouts of the teenager he knocked up. Searching for her birth father a quarter of a century later sounded like a good example of a wild goose chase, but it wasn't like they had a better lead to investigate. "Why don't you call Scott and ask him to implement a search?"

She gaped in surprise. "Really? Isn't Scott too busy?"

"He's an expert in multitasking." His

researcher had no social life and lived for the excitement of a new search. "Go ahead. Call him."

After a long day on the road, Hauk was glad to moor the small Zodiac to his vessel and follow Star up the ladder.

"Skip, Star. Welcome back." Arnie greeted them from his chair at the helm. "Scott is waiting for you inside the cabin. How was the trip?"

"It was interesting. Join us. I'll explain inside." His hand on the small of Star's back, Hauk led her inside the cabin where Scott worked on his computer. "Where's Kyle?"

"On assignment. I tracked down the insurance rep who took over Adrian Humphrey's caseload twenty years ago." Scott lifted his gaze from the screen. "The guy relocated to Antigonish, and Kyle flew out early this afternoon to meet with him."

Appreciative of his crew's initiative, Hauk nodded in approval. "Any luck on the white pickup?"

"I spent a lot of time hacking into the DMV records, and I'm only halfway through—"

"Did you find something or not?" Tired after their long drive, Hauk paced the cabin, making no effort to mask his impatience.

"You're going to like it." Scott rummaged through the pile of paper littering his desk. "It's a total fluke I found it. I wasn't searching for it."

From her cot, Star chuckled, visibly amused by Scott's antics.

"Skip the trivia, would you?" The sooner Scott shared his discovery, the sooner Hauk would spend some quality time with Star, not that he had any idea how to achieve that feat in such close quarters.

"Eleanor Watson's ex-husband had a son from a previous marriage. A guy named Bruce Robert. He runs an auto body shop in town." Scott pulled a blue sticky note from a sheet of paper. "Ultimate Makeover Body Shop."

Hauk wouldn't have associated a name like *Ultimate Makeover* to an auto body shop. "Why exactly do we care about the ex-stepson or the body shop?"

His researcher stuck the note onto the corner of his computer screen. "Because Bruce Robert owns a white Dodge pickup. It may be a coincidence. Like I said, I'm barely halfway down the DMV list."

"You could have led with the truck, you know," Star chided nicely. "Do you have his picture by any chance?"

"Give me a sec." Scott's lanky fingers flew over the keyboard. "Here. This is the picture on his driver's licence. Recognize him? Was he the man behind the wheel?"

Star approached the computer screen. "Not sure, but he looks familiar somehow. I'm pretty sure I've seen him somewhere."

Intrigued, Hauk peeked over her shoulder. "Does his licence plate match the partial number provided by the nurse?"

"Not precisely." Numbers and letters were scribbled on a yellow sticky note, also attached to his screen. "F3V compared to P8V, but once you take the distance, the light reflection, and the moving truck into consideration, those numbers and letters could be easily mixed up."

Bruce's licence and his association to the Watsons raised Hauk's suspicion. "Let's place him at the top of the suspect list." Not that they had rounded up many suspects yet. "Do we know if he stayed in contact with his former stepmother Eleanor?"

"No idea, but I'll keep digging."

Chapter 13

Looming clouds obscured the night sky. Hauk stood at the helm of his vessel, scanning the lake. A hundred and twenty metres off the starboard bow, an anchor light shone at the top of the police vessel surrounded by red blinking buoys, a visual warning not to enter the forbidden perimeter.

"I tried to anchor closer but was told to back off." Arnie removed his baseball cap and ran his hand over his bald skull. "With their guns, they make me nervous."

"With any luck, heavy police presence will also make the assailant too nervous to attempt another night boarding. Where's Star?" Hauk had seen her leave the cabin when his discussion with Scott had switched to passwords and security measures.

"In the Zodiac." Arnie chuckled. "Where else?"

Where else indeed? Hauk's chances of convincing her to sleep inside tonight probably hovered around zero. "Star and I are going for a ride."

"Now?" An enigmatic smile swept over his helmsman face. "It's awfully late and dark, skip."

Darkness means privacy. "We'll be back in an hour or so."

Hauk ventured down the ladder then cautiously boarded the Zodiac. Still, the craft swayed when his feet touched the bottom.

A blanket covered Star's body. "Hauk?"

He sat near her pillow then brushed a tender kiss on her cheek. "Were you asleep?"

"Almost." Her quiet answer stretched into a yawn. "What are you doing here?"

"Spending time with you. Would you like to go for a ride?" If not, he would be content to hold her in his arms while she slept.

She rubbed her eyes. "Sure. Where are we going?"

"You'll see." He released the docking rope, turned on the spotlight, and fired up the engine.

The Zodiac glided on the calm water, away from the other boats. Their blinking red lights gradually faded to tiny sparkling dots. Hauk stopped the craft near a cove at the far end of the lake and turned the spotlight off.

The anchor lights shimmering across the surface of the water had transformed the lake into a celestial tapestry.

"It's beautiful, Hauk." Her melodious whisper carried her wonder in the quiet night.

"Not as beautiful as you." His covert caresses under the kitchen table an eternity ago had left him aching for her touch.

He wrapped her into his arms and tangled his fingers into her hair. Gently and sensuously, she caressed his bristly chin, brushing and teasing his lips in passing. He pulled her closer, relishing her warmth and soft curves. Shivers coursed through her body. She trailed a hand over his shirt, undoing buttons along the way. Their mouth met, and he spiraled into a dance with her tongue. They slid to the bottom of the craft. His shirt parted. Her tender caresses over his chest melted his remaining willpower. He slipped a hand under her tank top, and relishing the softness of her skin, he pushed the fabric up. She pressed closer. Her bare stomach pushed against his chest with every raspy breath she took. Lost in her arms, he stroked the skin along the waistband of her short. She arched into him. Entangled together, they rolled over. He pressed on her hip.

A yelp of pain echoed on the lake.

* * *

In the cabin of the vessel, Hauk lay motionless on his cot. The rain drummed against the roof and mingled with the regular breathing sounds of his sleeping crew. On the cot next to him, within reach but out of bounds for the night, Star slept.

A storm that came out of nowhere had saved him from wasting his time arguing with Star about spending the night in the Zodiac.

Hauk sighed, silently cursing how careless and insensitive he had been during their escapade.

In the middle of passion he had forgotten about her injuries, and because of him, she had buckled in agony. He had cradled her in his arms and kissed her cheek, tasting the salty residue of fresh tears. Despite her objections, he had reached inside the emergency kit and pulled out a flashlight to peek at her hip. The depth and extent of the bruising had shocked him. Her right hip had to have absorbed both the initial hit on the hood of the pickup and the landing on the pavement to have caused such damage.

It was a miracle she didn't fracture her hip, or any other bone in her body. Still, Hauk couldn't begin to imagine the amount of pain she had endured in silence since the incident.

He knew she had suffered injuries, maybe not to that degree, but ignorance wasn't an excuse. Knowing she was injured, he should have been more caring and less impetuous. *How can I expect her to trust me with her heart when I can't even take care of her body?*

The rhetorical question ran in a loop in his mind. And for the umpteenth time, he cursed the sudden downpour that had forced their hasty return to the vessel where he lacked the privacy to discuss their relationship.

* * *

Silent and motionless on her cot, Star listened to the sound of the raindrops thumping on the roof of the cabin.

As the day progressed, she had almost convinced herself that the events in the attic had been either a figment of her imagination or a misunderstanding. Hauk's impromptu invitation to go for a night ride had proven her wrong. The butterflies in her stomach had soared to unparalleled heights. She had found herself caught in a whirlwind of exquisite and forgotten sensations, until her cry of pain cut their evening short.

With one innocent gesture, he had exposed the throbbing pain she silently endured since the hit-and-run. Accident-prone, she had grown up fending off her father's protective tendencies. Blocking her pain and minimizing her injuries had become second nature, but alone with Hauk in the Zodiac, she failed to convince him that she looked far worse than she felt, or that his tender touch was a balm, not an aggravation to her injuries.

Physically and emotionally exhausted, she fell asleep thinking about him and woke up to the sound of Scott's fingers tapping on his keyboard.

All the cots around her were empty. "Where's everyone?"

Scott's pen clattered on the floor. He swiveled around in his chair. "Are you on some meds? Cause you sure slept through the commotion this morning."

After her attack, the doctor had prescribed pills to reduce the swelling. Drowsiness wasn't listed as a side effect, but maybe she reacted differently than most people. *Or maybe I was just exhausted.* "What commotion?"

"Kyle called." Scott picked up a pen and slid it behind his ear. "He talked to the guy who took over Adrian Humphrey's caseload. While the guy didn't recall anything peculiar, he kept Adrian's logbook and loaned it to Kyle."

Star assumed the police had conducted a thorough investigation. If the logbook had revealed any pertinent information, it seemed logical that they would have kept it as evidence. Still, there was a slight chance they might have missed something twenty years ago. "Has Kyle browsed through it yet?"

"He didn't say. He was at the airport waiting for his flight."

Standing between two cots, she stretched her stiff muscles. "Did Hauk go pick him up?"

"No idea." Scott shrugged. "He doesn't always keep me in the loop."

"I know the feeling." Hauk's loop didn't always include her either. In search of answers, she left the cabin and found Arnie at the stern, bent over the engine of one of the Zodiacs. "Problems?"

"Regular maintenance." He tossed a pair of pliers in a red toolbox. "How do you feel?"

"Fine." When it came to pain, denial felt better than reality. "Where's Hauk?"

"He's..." A rag that used to be green fell off the toolbox as Arnie rummaged through it. "He's snooping around Bruce Robert's property."

"Without me?" *Talk about being left out of the loop.* If Eleanor's former stepson was involved, Star wanted a piece of him.

Arnie wiped his forehead with the dirty rag. "Listen, girl, if that Robert guy is the one behind the attacks, taking you wouldn't have been a good idea."

"I guess not." Still, she hated feeling idle. "I—"

"Star." Scott dashed out of the cabin. "I found something."

The statement combined with his excitement caught her undivided attention. She closed the lid of the toolbox and sat on it. "I'm listening."

"Since your father's doctor already searched the hospital birth registries, I concentrated my search on alternative places where your mother could have given birth. Of course, we also have to consider the possibility that she may have given birth at home."

Her need to hear every single detail prevailed over her desire to rush him along, so Star bit her tongue.

"I located a women's shelter in Lakewood, so I called them. I figured someone might know what was available twenty-five years ago for pregnant teenagers." Youthful exuberance exuded from every pore of Scott's body. "Can you believe that the shelter has been in existence for over forty years?"

Hope surged in her chest. "Did my mother take refuge there?"

"The lady didn't know, but—" His emphasis on *but* didn't fall on deaf ears. "They never got around to weeding out the old medical records."

Galvanized by the possibility that her mother's records might still be there, Star jumped to her feet. "And how do I access those old records?"

"Only in person." Scott glanced at Arnie. "I'll go with you. I have the address."

"I appreciate the offer, I truly do, but I'm taking the Zodiac and going alone—unless one of you wants to give me a ride to shore." It would be unfair to ask Scott to accompany her. The researcher had more important things to do than shadow her every move. She extended a hand. "Address, please."

A wrench dropped onto the deck near Arnie's knee. "Hauk won't mind if you borrow a craft or the red car, but he won't like that you go alone. If I were you, I'd reconsider Scott's offer or wait for Hauk's return."

* * *

Hauk drove to a middle-class neighbourhood where quaint bungalows were surrounded by green lawns and colourful flowerbeds. Here and there, a tree planted near the curb of the road offered shade to the car parked directly under its branches.

No sidewalk ran on Bruce Robert's side of the street. No garage was attached to his house or hidden behind it. No white truck was parked in his asphalt driveway or anywhere in sight.

That was a waste of time. Disappointed but far from defeated, Hauk drove to Robert's auto shop located in the industrial district.

Ultimate Makeover Body Shop's bold, neon sign, visible from a block away, evoked images of shady strip clubs.

Hauk parked alongside a chain link fence and walked around the shop.

Judging by the number of damaged vehicles sitting on the lot, business was thriving. Hauk didn't see any white Dodge parked in the vicinity, only a lanky teenage boy hosing off a silver hatchback.

"Hi, there!" Hauk shouted over the sound of gushing water.

The teenager turned the water off. "Good morning, sir. Are you picking up your car?"

"Not exactly, young man, but a friend of mine recommended this shop." Improvisation was an art that Hauk had developed in college. "I have an old beater that needs some work done." It wasn't a lie. The only thing with more dents and scratches than his red sedan parked on shore was Star's body.

The teenager straightened up his back, gaining few inches in the process. "Best place in town, sir. They totally fixed my mom's car after she hit a lamppost."

"Glad to hear that." Not interested in learning how the mother managed such an exploit, Hauk glanced around. "I was told to talk to a guy with a white truck, but I guess he's not here."

"If you mean Mr. Robert, he came to work in the courtesy car this morning. I guess he left his truck at home."

Wrong guess. The truck wasn't anywhere near Robert's home. *I just checked.* "Does Mr. Robert often borrow the courtesy car?"

"No. It's mostly for clients." The teenager's voice cracked. "Want me to go get him for you?"

Erring on the side of caution, Hauk declined. "I'll find him. He's the one with a tattoo on his forearm, right?"

"Tattoo?" The teenager chuckled. "Mr. Robert doesn't have any tattoos."

So much for that theory. "I should have known my friend was pulling a fast one on me." Hauk lied to put the teenager at ease. "So, how do I recognize Mr. Robert?"

"Short man, dark hair, black pants, blue shirt." The teenager grinned. "And no tattoo."

Hauk plastered a smile on his face. "Thanks."

Through the open door leading inside the shop, Hauk caught a glimpse of Bruce Robert. The owner was bulkier than Star's assailant and a good six inches shorter.

Robert was Eleanor Watson's former stepson and he owned a white Dodge pickup that mysteriously vanished into thin air, but he wasn't the man who attacked Star at the Humphreys' house.

Annoyed by the physical discrepancies, Hauk checked his watch while walking back to his Jeep. If he hurried, he might catch Murphy before he left for his daily tee time at the Country Club.

A shadow crossed the doorway of the auto shop. Curious as to why someone had left the premises without coming in, Bruce Robert stepped outside in time to see Hauk Ludwig drive away in his Jeep.

"Hey, Dawson!" His secretary's nephew dropped the hose and rushed toward him. "Did you see a tall, blond man snooping around?"

The teenager nodded. "He was looking for you."

If Ludwig was looking for me, he would have entered the shop. "Did he say why?"

"To fix his car." Dawson's response contained a hint of sarcasm, like the answer should have been obvious.

Bruce resisted the temptation to smack some respect into the teenager's skull. "Did he say anything else?"

"He said his friend sent him." A smile spread across Dawson's freckled face. "And he thought you had a tattoo on your arm."

The reference to a tattoo acerbated Bruce's stomach ulcer.

* * *

"No wonder no one's ever stolen Hauk's

red car from the shore."

The car had lost part of its back bumper. The part still hanging scraped the road, giving the disturbing sensation of dragging a squealy roadkill. It also rode worse than a farm tractor on a bumpy dirt road after a torrential storm. The lack of suspension tortured her sore bottom, forcing Star to shift position every few minutes to alleviate the pain.

A gaping hole had replaced the radio, the air conditioning didn't work, the windows wouldn't roll down, and she had to rely on the small vents for fresh air.

"I should have heeded Arnie's suggestion and waited." *Not for Hauk, but for his Jeep.*

On the bridge, where sections of the rail had collapsed following the bus collision, cement blocks laced with yellow tape provided a temporary barrier between the road and premature death.

Star tightened her grip on the steering wheel, and the muscles along her arms constricted under the strain.

The newspaper had praised the deceased bus driver's heroic efforts for keeping the bus from falling down the ravine. The strong possibility that her presence on that bus had caused death, critical injuries, and suffering upset her. Deep down, she realized she wasn't responsible for someone else's actions, but it didn't alleviate her guilt.

Upon arriving in Lakewood, Star headed toward a neighbourhood overcrowded with decrepit apartment buildings and illicit shops. Some bystanders glanced in her direction, but no one appeared threatening.

Scott had scribbled *154 Hogan Street* on a piece of paper. The damaged street sign at the intersection said *–ogan St.*

Most houses didn't have numbers on their facade, but Star was confident that she was driving down the right street. Two blocks farther down, she spotted a cardboard sign taped to the window of a three-storey grey house.

Safe Haven. Welcome.

"That's it. I found it." There wasn't any parking spot in front of the shelter, so Star drove around the block looking for one. On an adjacent street, a SUV parked a metre or so in front of her zoomed into the traffic, cutting her off. Star hit the brake then eased into the vacant parking spot. "Thanks, idiot."

Reeling from the near miss, she marched to the shelter and knocked on the front door.

A plump matron with hazel-green eyes and an engaging smile welcomed her. "Hello, dear. Please come in."

Noisy children ran circles around Star.

"Children. Shush!" The matron sent them scuttling down the hallway. "You have to excuse them. They're always curious when someone new arrives."

"They're adorable." Star smiled at the children before turning her attention back on the women who appeared to be into her sixties. "May I have a word with you in private, please?"

"Follow me." The matron led Star into a large kitchen furnished with two tables. "Would you like something to eat while we chat? You look hungry."

Her stomach rumbled, but Star refused to deprive someone else of a meal. "I wouldn't mind a cup of coffee."

"Have a seat. I've been running this shelter for thirty years." Kindness and compassion flowed from the woman who placed a cup of coffee on the table then sat opposite Star. "You're safe, dear. He can't touch you here."

Star would have dropped the cup if she had already picked it up. "No... it's not... it was a traffic accident." *That wasn't accidental.* "I know I look beaten, but I'm not here to seek shelter. I'm searching for my mother." Star showed the close-up of her mother to the matron. "She ran away when she was pregnant with me."

The matron closely examined the photo. "And you think she came here?"

"I don't know. Does she look familiar? Her name was Stella or Ella Fisher." Hope, more than hunger, made Star's empty stomach flip. "It would have been some twenty-four years ago."

"That was a long time ago, dear. Lots of women have come and gone since then. My memory isn't—" Lines creased the matron's forehead. "A very polite man phoned this morning. He was looking for a birth record."

"Yes, mine." Start was glad that Scott had made such an impression. "Do you have it?"

The matron returned the picture and stood. "Grab your cup and follow me. I don't usually allow outsiders in the house, but you do look like you need help, one way or another."

They went down a narrow staircase then into the hallway of a well-lit basement. A dozen empty chairs were lined up against the left wall. They walked by an open door.

Star peeked inside. The room was equipped with an examination table, an office desk, cupboards and shelves, filled with all the amenities of a modern medical clinic. "Do you have doctors on call?"

"On call and on regular schedule. When women arrive here, with or without children, they often suffer from all sorts of ailments." The matron closed the door, which was labelled *Clinic.* "Most of our women endured a lot of physical, mental, and emotional abuse before seeking help. It's not easy to leave an abusive relationship, as you may know."

Star had a strong feeling that the bruises visible on her body conveyed a different story than that of an accident, but there wasn't much she could say to change the matron's opinion. "Do women still give birth here?"

"Not if the doctor can avoid it. We've only had one clinic birth in the last five years." The matron shuddered. "The woman was afraid her partner was stalking the hospital, so she didn't tell anyone she was in labor until she was fully dilated. She, and I, were lucky a doctor was on the premises, or else I would have been the one catching that baby. Back when your mother was pregnant, we had a midwife and an obstetrician on call. If she delivered you here, your birth would have been recorded."

Toward the end of the hallway, the matron opened a door marked *Storage*, flipped the light switch, then gestured for Star to step in. The room was crowded with columns of cardboard boxes. "The boxes are labeled by years, which correspond with the year the women sought refuge here. Unfortunately, over time, the boxes were moved around, so they're no longer piled in order. I wish I could help you, but I have a full house."

"Thank you." A question crossed Star's mind as the matron walked away. "One more thing, could my mother have used a false name?"

The matron paused in the doorway. "Sometimes they do use a different name while they stay with us, but if they see a doctor, the name on their records will match the name on their health cards. I hope you find her."

Chapter 14

Undaunted by the sheer number of boxes facing her, Star drank her coffee while searching for the box with the right year. After reorganizing some piles, she finally spotted the box she wanted. A slightly crushed box at the bottom of the tallest column.

"Of course it's at the bottom. Where else would it be?"

She emptied her cup, pondering how to get the top box down without causing a major tumbling. Her gaze wandered around the room. In the corner by the door, a stepladder was visible from behind a box.

"That will work." Her cup set aside, she grabbed the ladder and placed it in front of the column.

The stepladder gave her the extra few inches she needed to get the top box safely down. Lowering the others became easier as she worked her way down the pile. Finally, she grabbed the bottom box. It was heavy, which gave her hope that one of the files inside belonged to her mother.

Star pried the taped box open and pulled a folder at random. The tab wasn't labelled, which she found odd, so she looked at the pages inside. And sighed. "Why did I think it would be easy?"

The woman's first name was Tanya, and she stayed at the shelter from January 10th to June 23rd of that year. However, Tanya's last name, date of birth, and provincial health care number were all blacked out. Any personal information that could have helped identifying Tanya's were redacted, but it still contained a fair amount of medical information.

Halfway through the list of fractures that Tanya suffered at the hand of her partner, Star closed the folder. "Mandible fracture?" Sickened by the violence, Star set the folder aside and pulled another one from the box.

Her long search yielded mixed results. The medical records indicated fourteen women were or might have been pregnant while at the shelter that year, six of them gave birth at the clinic, and none of them were named Stella.

Nonetheless, Star noted all their details.

* * *

Upon leaving the shelter, Star called her father to update him on her search and ask if he remembered the address of her mother's apartment.

"What exactly are you hoping to accomplish by visiting it?" Jimmy's response suggested that he disapproved but still remembered.

"I'm hoping to glean a detail that will help me narrow down the list." *Or trigger a memory buried deep inside my mind.* "What do I have to lose?"

His heavy sigh spoke volume. "It's in a shady area of town. I'm texting it now. Be careful."

"I will." Her phone beeped. "Thanks."

According to her phone, the apartment was only two blocks away.

Her gaze travelled up and down the street where children played on the sidewalk and old ladies strolled by with shopping bags.

"It'll be faster to walk than drive and search for another parking spot." Star left her car where she had parked it, and ventured into the neighbourhood on foot.

Around the next corner, a sleazy motel advertised rooms by the hour. Men with shabby clothes, unkempt hair, and scruffy beards were gathered near its entrance. Star accelerated her pace. A hand grabbed her arm from behind. She drove her elbow into her assailant's midriff, spun around, and slammed her knee between his legs.

Cheers and jeers rose from the crowd of onlookers.

Scrunched up in pain, the man—or boy, rather—hobbled toward his buddies.

Star glared at them, more enraged than a shark smelling blood. To her relief, their interest shifted toward a different section of the street.

* * *

Dusty pulled up his jeans, smirking. The hooker had been in top form. He hadn't wasted his money renting the room on the second floor for a change.

Intrigued by the commotion coming from the window, he opened the discoloured curtains and looked onto the street below.

Behind him, the hooker ran her hand up and down his bare back. "You're tensing up again, Dust. Need some more love?"

He pushed her down on the bed and threw some bills at her. "Go take a shower. I'll be back."

By some miracle, his prey had materialized on his doorstep. He would be damned if he didn't finish the ugly bitchling once and for all.

* * *

Kyle's plane landed early, allowing him

to make a stop at the insurance company in Lakewood.

Eager to return to the lake, he took a shortcut through downtown, but construction forced him to make a second detour through an underprivileged neighbourhood. At every intersection, onlookers eyed his SUV with a mixture of envy and curiosity.

An old lady jaywalking sluggishly across the street forced him to stop. While he waited for her to reach the other side, Kyle scanned his surroundings for potential signs of trouble.

A small red car with a trailing back bumper caught his attention, and what was left of his good mood evaporated.

The boss and Arnie only used the red car to run short errands. Hauk's wreck shouldn't be in Lakewood.

Kyle parked behind it and got out of his vehicle.

His boss was nowhere in the vicinity. Kyle looked into the wreck through the driver side window. The seat was positioned forward, too close to the steering wheel for someone as tall as the boss or as bulky as Arnie.

It had either been stolen or driven by a person of small stature.

"No one in his right mind would steal that piece of junk from the lake, but—" The possibility that a slender someone sat behind the wheel and drove into this neighbourhood churned Kyle's stomach. "For your sake, kid, it better be a stolen car."

He pulled a gun from the glove compartment and went looking for her.

* * *

"Do I have a sign on my forehead that says *Attack Me*?" Star muttered under her breath. Sore from her encounter with the boy, she hunted down the landlord of her mother's former apartment building.

The landlord, a gruff man reeking of tobacco and alcohol, didn't know the names of his current tenants, didn't give a damn about old ones, and slammed the door in her face to prove his point.

"Well, that was a waste of time." Still, there had to have been places in the neighbourhood that her mother frequented.

Desperation led Star to a maroon brick church on the outside chance that Stella had sought redemption, peace, or forgiveness. The elderly priest who had ministered to the community for over thirty-five years exuded trust and discretion, so Star explained her search.

After listening to her story, he asked to see her mother's picture.

"She reminds me of a young woman who stayed at the shelter a long time ago. Her name was... let me think here... I want to say

Lisa, but Ella sounds more familiar." On his lips, the name *Ella* sounded like a prayer. "She went into premature labor during my sermon. It was on Thanksgiving long weekend, not that she had anything to be thankful for." The priest bowed his head. "She was consumed with grief after delivering a stillborn baby boy. She died a few years later. Drug overdose. Her body was found in a dumpster nearby."

* * *

"She's where?" Hauk returned to the boat around suppertime only to learn that no one had heard from Star since she left for Lakewood too many hours ago.

His five-minute conversation with Murphy had stretched into an all-afternoon discussion when retired inspector Kenneth had joined them. Bruce Robert's name was never mentioned in the original investigation, and they had no reason to believe that Robert might have been involved.

"How could you let her go?" Wrecked with fear and guilt, Hauk glared at Arnie, Scott, and all the inanimate objects on the deck while dialling her number. His call went directly to her voicemail. "She's not answering. What's the phone number of that shelter?"

"On it." Scott dashed inside the cabin only to return a few minutes later, looking utterly dejected. "I called the shelter. Star went there but she left early this afternoon."

"What did she do? Get lost between the front door and the car?" Hauk took a deep breath. Venting his frustration on his crew served no purpose. "Have you heard from Kyle? Has he landed yet?"

"I tried calling him too." Scott slumped against the doorway of the cabin. "And got his voicemail."

Why do they bother carrying cell phones if they don't turn the darn things on? "Keep trying their phones and give me the address of that shelter."

* * *

Hidden behind a dumpster at the entrance of Bloody Lane, Dusty kept his gaze on the large wooden door adorned with a cross. He had almost caught up with the ugly bitchling when she entered that church.

The urge to barge inside and kill her and the old priest on the steps of the altar surged inside Dusty's soul, but the wrath he would incur from the street gangs proved to be a powerful deterrent. For reasons that Dusty couldn't fathom, the street thugs showed a fearful reverence for the priest despite his efforts to put an end to their activities.

The door of the church swung open.

Dusty's heart rate accelerated and sweat dripped from his hands. He wiped them on the sides of his jeans and reached for his gun.

* * *

"Star... Star..." The light breeze carried her name to the steps of the church.

Star paused on the last concrete stair and glanced around. Seeing no one, she shook her head. Not only was she hungry and tired, but she was also imagining things.

Anxious to get back to her car before nightfall, she hesitated between a shortcut through a deserted alley or the longer route around the block. In the end, she opted for the detour, a safer choice in this neighbourhood.

Farther down the sidewalk, a teen wearing a black and grey bandana over his head sat on the front step of an apartment building. He jumped to his feet and blocked her path. "What do we have here?"

The vehicles parked bumper to bumper along the sidewalk blocked Star's direct access to the street. "Get out of my way."

Arms crossed over his chest, he took a step forward and sneered. "Make me."

With no passersby in the vicinity, Star walked back toward the church, the safest alternative to a confrontation.

A scrawny teen wearing a dirty, sleeveless shirt materialized from the shadow of a staircase. "Hello, kitty, kitty."

Star looked over her shoulder. The bandana teen had followed her. Trapped between the two thugs, she dashed into the deserted alley. Steps resonated on the pavement behind her.

Halfway down the alley, a bare-chested teen emerged from a door. "Are you lost, baby?"

Corned by the trio, Star slipped her hand in the front pocket of her cargo shorts and wrapped her fingers around her pocketknife. "What do you want?"

The bandana teen licked his lips moving his hand over his groin. "We'll let you guess."

Jimmy often said that the best defence was a good offence. Hoping her father was right, she lunged at the sleeveless teen, grabbed his bare arm, and twisted it behind his back. A howl of pain rewarded her efforts.

She flicked her knife open, encircled his bony chest with her arm, and pressed the blade against his throat. "Back off."

Warm liquid splattered on her feet, an unwelcomed gift from the teen in her grip.

"Gutsy kitten." Bandana teen rubbed his hands together. "Time for some fun."

To scare them away, she pushed the blade until blood trickled down her captive's dirty shirt. "I won't say it again. Back off, or I kill him."

The teen in her clutches quivered with fear.

"Go ahead." Bandana teen pulled out a hunting knife. "You kill him, I'll kill you slowly, so slowly you'll beg to die."

* * *

Kyle entered the alley and froze.

Two thugs flanked Star, and a third one, his face ashen, trembled in her grip.

Fearing for all their safety, Kyle drew his gun. "If you don't scatter, I'll put a slug in all your brainless skulls."

His warning, issued in a deep deadpan voice, bore the desired effect. The two thugs turned to face him. When they saw the weapon pointed directly at them, they hightailed.

Kyle slowly approached the remaining duo. "Let him go, kid," he commanded calmly. "He's not worth a night in jail. Not when I don't have enough money to bail you out."

The haunted look in her eyes faded away. She lowered her knife and took a step back.

Relieved to have avoided a tragedy, Kyle grabbed the teen by his bloody shirt. "If I ever see you again, I will be the one slicing your throat. Got it?" He then shoved the teen in the same direction his cowardly friends had disappeared.

Satisfied that they were no longer in immediate danger, Kyle tucked the flare gun into his waistband then pried the knife from Star's cold grip. "What the hell were you thinking venturing here alone? Didn't you hear me when I yelled at you? You could have been killed."

"I took a stupid risk." Her empty hand dropped to her side. "Not sure how or why you're here, but you saved my life. Thank you."

The sincerity in her quavering voice dissipated his anger and obliterated his remaining misconceptions about her. He didn't deserve her gratitude, not after so badly misjudging her. Through no fault of her own, Star physically resembled the seemingly innocent blonde girl that Kyle had introduced to Macey—the girl who later assaulted his best friend.

Kyle owed the courageous woman standing on wobbly feet in front of him a long, overdue apology.

* * *

From behind the dumpster, Dusty smirked at the irony that she would die in the same alley as the nanny did.

After the nanny escaped in the river with the ugly bitchling, Dusty had canvassed the streets where he had previously approached her for sex. It was her fault that he remembered her. If she hadn't kept turning him down, he would probably have forgotten her face. Luck had struck when he stumbled onto her crossing the alley. The light of recognition in her eyes sealed her fate. The satisfying revenge he enjoyed forcefully taking what she had denied him ended when she overdosed on the shot he gave her. Short of a better resting place, he had chucked her body in the closest dumpster.

The trip down memory lane pumped blood below his waist.

The ambush taking place in the alley added a fascinating spin to the ugly bitchling's demise. The thugs would play with her, and once they discarded her, Dusty would finish her off, assuming she was still alive. With any luck, they would do his dirty work for him.

The cocky thugs had her cornered, but they underestimated her. Dusty smirked again. A tiny part of him admired her pluck, but he doubted she had the guts to kill her hostage. The thug with a bandana called her bluff.

A warning resounded in the alley, and Ludwig's diver stepped out of the shadows.

How dare he interrupts my fun. Under his breath, Dusty muttered every swear word that his drunken father ever taught him.

The diver tucked his weapon away and took hers. Immobile by his side, the ugly bitchling offered the perfect target.

Dusty pulled the trigger.

Chapter 15

The presence of Kyle's SUV in the vicinity of the red sedan baffled Hauk. Either Scott had succeeded in reaching Kyle and he was searching for Star, or they were both missing.

After another failed attempt to reach either one of them, Hauk canvassed the nearby streets.

A block away, two teens bolted out of an alley, shortly followed by a third wearing a bloody shirt. As he ran by Hauk, the third one cursed a blonde kitten with a knife.

The blood and the description ran chills down Hauk's back. The resemblance between the blonde kitten and the blonde spitfire who had once scared him with a knife was too striking to ignore.

Hauk hurried toward the alley from which they had fled and stopped dead at the entrance.

Alone in the darkening alley, Kyle wrapped his arms around Star. A pang of jealousy struck Hauk in the guts. He—

A gunshot pierced the air. Star slumped against Kyle.

"Star!" Each running stride toward her thrust an invisible knife deeper into Hauk's heart. He glimpsed a man fleeing toward the opposite end of the alley. "Stop! Help!"

"Boss, she's alive." Blood spilled through Kyle's fingers as he ran them over Star's head. "The bullet grazed her skull, but missed."

Relieved, Hauk pulled her into his arms. "Turn on your phone, Kyle, and call for an ambulance."

"Stop shouting." She growled against his chest. "My head hurts."

"I'm not—" Fear and exasperation had amplified his voice, so Hauk strived to regain control of his emotions. "I didn't mean to shout. I was just scared." He pulled a clean handkerchief from his pocket and pressed it against the wound. "You'll be okay."

Sirens announced the arrival of emergency services.

* * *

Hauk climbed aboard his vessel on the heels of his two divers.

"They're back, Scott." Arnie yelled from the helm.

The researched rushed out of the cabin. "Is everyone okay?" He stared at Star who retreated to her favourite bench. "What happened to your head?"

A large bandage, impossible to miss, covered her forehead. "It's a long story. I made a list on my phone of all the women who might be my mother. Can I send you the list once I recharge my phone?"

"We can do it now if you want to come inside and plug..." Scott's enthusiasm suddenly dampened. "It's okay if you want to rest. We can do it later."

"Not you too." She bolted to her feet, visibly annoyed, and nudged Scott toward the cabin. "I'm fine. Let's do this."

Seconds later, Kyle disappeared around the cabin without saying a word.

"What happened, skip?" His helmsman joined Hauk on deck. "That's a pretty large bandage on her head for someone who's fine."

During the ride back, Star had shed no light on what had transpired between her and Kyle in the alley, but she opened up about the shelter, so Hauk shared what he learned and what he saw in the alley.

Arnie's eyes bulged out of his skull. "She was shot? Shouldn't she be at the hospital?"

His helmsman's reaction mimicked Hauk's initial reaction back in the alley. "According to the paramedic, it's a flesh wound and he couldn't force her to go to the hospital if Star didn't want to go." Hauk exhaled sharply. "She's more stubborn than—"

Arnie chuckled. "Don't let her overhear you, or you'll be the one needing a huge bandage."

"Point taken." It wasn't funny, but it somewhat rang true. "Star was still being treated by the paramedic when the police showed up. The officer who took my statement called the alley *Bloody Lane*. Apparently, that's where the two gangs in town like to settle their differences, but the three thugs who ambushed Star had already fled the scene by the time I heard the detonation." The anger and helplessness that Hauk felt in the alley resurfaced. "I even glimpsed the shooter, Arnie. Star or Kyle, or both, were targeted. There was nobody else to shoot at in that alley."

Arnie leaned forward against the railing. "Did the police officer consider the possibility it was related to the precious attempts on their lives?"

"He didn't rule it out and he said he would look for the bullet." Hauk left shortly after giving his statement, so whether the officer found the bullet or not was unknown. "In the meantime, stay vigilant at the helm."

"Always do, skip."

Hauk went looking for Kyle.

Slumped on deck, his back to the cabin wall, Kyle stared at the water, holding a green notebook.

Hauk sat beside him. "Tell me your flight east wasn't a waste of money."

"It wasn't." His diver handed the book over. "This logbook contains Adrian Humphrey's caseload. According to his former colleague, Humphrey wasn't working on any noteworthy investigations at the time of his death, but he was spending lots of time in the archives room."

"In the archives room?" No one wasted time searching the archives unless they were looking for something specific. "What was he searching for?"

"That's just it, boss. I don't think Humphrey was searching for anything, at least not at first." His diver's enigmatic response made little sense. "According to the colleague, Humphrey liked reading about old claims and was fascinated by the ingenuity of his predecessors when it came to investigate them."

In a way, Hauk recognized the entertainment value of reading about old cases. "He wasn't searching, but I'm guessing he found something interesting?"

"He sure did." The smug look on Kyle's face denoted results. "It's all in that little green book."

Hauk flipped through the pages, but the dates, names, places, and events didn't provide him with a single clue. "I'm listening, Kyle."

"If you look closely, on the backs of some pages, Humphrey scribbled numbers and letters that seemed unrelated to his cases. After I landed this morning, I stopped by the insurance company in Lakewood and showed the annotations to the secretary. She'd spent hours last week searching the archives for a document and she'd stumbled on those annotations by accident. They are references to old policies issued by a small insurance company amalgamated in the late sixties."

"That's promising." In the morning, Hauk would give Murphy another call to check if the police had looked into those policies. "Anything else?"

Kyle's smile widened. "The secretary gave me a tour of the archives room, but her boss interrupted while I peeked at the files. Anyway, care to guess which name I saw written in there?"

Only one name popped into Hauk's mind. "Watson?"

* * *

Hauk lay on his cot in the cabin. To his great distress, the gentle rocking of the boat and the soft slapping of the water against the hull didn't quiet his mind.

Did Adrian Humphrey uncover a secret worth killing for? Could it be related to Mary Watson's death? Did he somehow find out she was murdered? But then why kill his family first? Unless... He opened his eyes and scanned the cabin illuminated by the dim light emanating from the computer screen. "Scott?"

The cup of coffee in the young man's hand tilted dangerously. "Could you all stop startling me?"

"Sorry." After a glance toward the cot on which Star peacefully slept, he joined Scott. A birth certificate and an autopsy report were displayed side by side on Scott's screen. "Star's mother?"

"No. That woman's daughter drowned in her bath when she was a toddler. Lack of supervision. Some women shouldn't have children."

Agreed. "Listen. I was thinking about Adrian Humphrey. The murder of his family could be seen as an act of retribution for something he did or failed to do." This was an angle they hadn't explored yet. "Any indication that Adrian ever blackmailed the Watsons?"

"From what I gathered, Adrian Humphrey was a straight arrow." Scott rubbed his face with both hands. "Frankly, I doubt it."

"Appearances can be deceiving." Hauk had learned that lesson the hard way. "Could you access the financial records of every member of the Watson family including Bruce Robert around the time of the murders?"

"Legally, no."

"It doesn't need to stand up in court." Hauk tapped his researcher's shoulder. "And go to bed before you make mistakes. Good night.”

Dispensing with his own advice, he left the cabin.

Hauk sat on Star’s favourite bench and closed his eyes. The cool breeze caressed his bare chest, a torturous reminder of her hands roaming over his skin. As much as his body yearned for her touch, his mind couldn’t reconcile the sensual evening they had shared in the Zodiac to the tender embrace he had witnessed in the alley between her and Kyle.

* * *

Tiptoeing down a hallway toward the bathroom, a little blonde girl played with a rabbit-shaped button of her nightgown. She stopped in the doorway and peeked inside. Her gaze wandered to the cupboard above the toilet.

“Don’t look,” Star begged. “Stop.”

The left door of the cupboard slid open. Red blood dripped from the shelf onto the floor. The heads of a woman and two young children stared back with empty eyes. Horrified, the child screamed.

Terror swelled inside Star’s chest.

High above the little girl’s head, a blade shone under the lone light bulb hanging from the ceiling. A callous hand swept the knife through the air, and a bird soared to life.

Star bolted upright on her cot, gasping and shaking. The cool air burned her throat, her muscles ached, and her head pounded as loud as the thumping of her heart.

On the cot next to her, Kyle slept, seemingly undisturbed by her nightmare. And slouched in his computer chair, Scott snored like a freight train. She sneaked out without glancing at Hauk's cot. The door closed behind her without a sound.

In the wee hours of the night, the light breeze carried the subtle scent of the forest surrounding the lake. Hands on the railing, she listened to the eerie wails of the loons. Their beautiful calls soothed her senses and calmed her agitated mind.

A metre below, the empty Zodiac swayed gently, beckoning her to come and rest. She counted the rungs climbing down. One, two, three—

A beam of light shone in her eyes. Startled and blinded, she lost her grip and tumbled into the Zodiac.

"Star? Are you okay?"

Through the bright blinking dots dancing in front of her eyes, she made out Hauk's silhouette leaning over the railing. "Yes." *I didn't hurt anything that wasn't already sore.* "Light."

"Sorry." The beam of light moved toward the sky. "I thought I heard an intruder. What are you doing up?"

"Nightmare." Anticipating that he would follow her into the craft, she retreated to the far end.

Seconds later, Hauk stepped inside and sat near the engine. The flashlight rested on his lap, illuminating the hull of his vessel. "Did you recall anything new?"

"I saw the bird tattoo again." Knees bent and feet tucked underneath her, she faced him.

Hauk made no attempt to close the distance between them, his guarded expression speaking volume.

"I understand why you're mad at me, Hauk. Crossing that alley was reckless." She should have taken her chances on the sidewalk instead of backing into the alley. In hindsight, going to Lakewood alone had also been stupid.

"Reckless, yes, but I'm not—"

"Let me finish, please." The incident in the alley changed her perspective. "The three teens who attacked me only had knives, not guns. Someone else was lurking in the shadows, waiting to shoot. If I'm his intended target like you suggest, then I need to leave."

"Leave?" The flashlight bounced to the bottom of the craft. "Why?"

"You're asking why?" *Didn't you listen to what I just said?* Exasperated, she growled. "Every attack I sustain places the people around me in danger. The bus driver is dead because of me. Kyle almost drowned, and he could easily have been hit tonight.”

“Kyle can take care of himself,” Hauk snapped.

“I can’t have the death of those around me on my conscience.” The killer might not care about collateral damage, but she did. “This is my fight and I will fight him on my own terms.”

“Like you fought in the alley?”

The unfair retort pierced her heart. In the alley, surrender had not been an option. If Kyle hadn’t shown up, she would have fought until her last breath. Hauk had no right to belittle her actions. “Get out, Ludwig.”

The order chilled the air between them.

“I’m sorry, I didn’t mean—”

Tears spilled down her cheeks. “Out!”

* * *

The sun rose over the lake and white clouds hung weightlessly under a light blue sky, but Kyle paid no attention to the beautiful sunrise. He walked along the railing, searching the water for the annoying ducks.

“In the Zodiac.” Hauk’s low grumbly voice originated from the helm.

Baffled by his boss’s response, his bad mood, and Arnie’s absence from his post,

Kyle stared at Hauk with a blank expression. "The ducks are in the Zodiac?"

His boss's forehead crinkled. "What ducks?"

"The quacking ducks that woke me up before sunrise. I'm contemplating using them for target practice." The feathered creatures encroached on his sleep. "I have two dates tonight, and I can't be tired."

"She's leaving." Hauk gripped the armrests. "She won't be here tonight."

"Which one?" When or how his boss became privy to his social life was a mystery that Kyle wasn't inclined to elucidate. "Please tell me Sylvia didn't cancel on me."

"Who's Sylvia?"

"Sylvia's the nurse, and Jaclyn's the secretary." *I shouldn't be explaining the intricacies of my love life, and Hauk shouldn't be interested by it.* "I'm taking Jaclyn out for dinner to thank her for helping me in the archives. Then I'm taking Sylvia out for—I'm sure you can guess."

"How about Star?"

"What about the kid? Was I supposed to take her somewhere?" As much as Kyle racked his brain, he couldn't think of anything important he might have forgotten. Unsettled by Hauk's peculiar expression, Kyle rocked back and forth on his heels. "Is there something wrong, boss?" An alarm rang into his mind. "No. Definitely not. I'm not babysitting the kid tonight." His boss would need to find someone else. "We're talking about Sylvia, boss. It's her only night off this week. Ask Scott or Arnie or—" Hauk's laughter echoed over the lake, confounding him further. "Am I off the hook?"

"Your mother never warned you about dating two women at the same time?" Hauk teased.

"Yes, but that short trip into the archives room cost me dinner." A duck quacked nearby, setting Kyle's nerves on fire.

"You can rest assured that we appreciate the obvious sacrifice." Hauk leaned back in Arnie's chair. "Enjoy your evening."

Kyle stretched his neck above the railing but he couldn't see any ducks. "I will, but who's leaving?"

"No one... if I can help it." His boss's cryptic response didn't answer the question. "What really happened in the alley, Kyle? Why didn't you take Star out of there as soon as the teenagers fled?"

Understanding dawned on Kyle. His boss was snappy because he had kept Star in the alley and allowed the attacker to take a shot at her. "The alley wasn't even dark when those thugs ambushed her." Kyle felt obligated to first defend her actions. "How was Star supposed to know she would be in danger?"

"I don't blame her, Kyle. I just want the truth."

He joined his boss at the helm. "Good, because she did nothing wrong. She handled them like a tigress." The memory brought a smile to his face. "My arrival only expedited their departure. I may even have saved *them* from a bad outcome, but after they ran, she… she probably doesn't want anyone to know that, but she looked like she was going to faint. I hugged her to reassure her. That's when he shot her. I knew we needed to get out of there, but it never occurred to me that we—that she was in immediate danger. I'm sorry. I wish I'd acted sooner."

"How did you find her?"

"A fluke. An extraordinary fluke." Kyle leaned against the panel controls and recounted his lucky detour.

* * *

Hauk relinquished the chair at the helm to go sit at the top of the ladder above the Zodiac.

In a strange twist of fate, Star's misfortune in the alley had earned her Kyle's admiration and respect, but Hauk had misinterpreted the interaction between them. Like an angry lover, he had lashed out at her with an unwarranted remark, demeaning her actions. He would laugh at the irony if not for the fact that he deeply hurt her.

Her long eyelashes fluttered. "How long have you been staring at me?" she asked groggily.

"A while." The morning rays highlighted her golden curls. It saddened him to see the bandage over her forehead tainting the perfect picture.

"It's early, Ludwig." She cast her blanket aside. "Are you in a hurry to drive me to town and get rid of me?"

Her fiery nature drew a smile to his lips. No woman had ever enchanted him so much as to cloud his mind so completely. "You're not going anywhere."

The fury burning in her eyes intensified as she crawled on her knees across the Zodiac. "This isn't a negotiation."

"Glad we agree, havfrue." He jumped aboard. The craft rocked against the hull and threw her into his arms. "I'm sorry for what I said last night. I wasn't angry at you for crossing the alley. I was angry at myself for not being there and I was scared. Scared to lose you. For the record, I am so very proud of the way you stood up to those thugs."

She studied him through two narrow slits. "Really?"

"Yes. Very proud." A blonde curl stuck to the bloody bandage, and he gently untangled it. "I'm sorry I acted like an overly protective lover."

Her expression saddened. "You are overprotective, Hauk, and I can't live in a cage. I would get restless, and reckless. I'm just not the docile girl you imagine I am."

Chuckles rose deep from within his chest. "If there's an adjective that doesn't apply to you, it's docile. You're impulsive, rebellious, stubborn—"

Fine lines creased her skin below the bandage and her brows slowly knitted together.

"Did I forget to mention adorable, intelligent—"

"Nice try." She rolled her eyes. "But you were right about one thing last night. I need to fight better and smarter than I did in that alley."

"You have good instincts, havfrue, and you're a formidable fighter, but every hero has a sidekick." The sky had no limits, and as much as Hauk would like to shield her from every danger, her spirited nature deserved to soar above the clouds. "You can be Superman, I'll be your Lois."

Her clear laughter bridged the misunderstanding between them.

Heartened by her reaction, he rubbed her nose against hers. "You, me, the crew, we make a fantastic team, so would you stay and let us fight with you?"

Her gaze softened. "Only if you feed me breakfast."

Chapter 16

Star couldn't tell how long Scott had been pacing the deck any more than she could read his expression, but his gaze appeared focused on her, and her alone.

"Scott?" His scrutiny stirred suspicious feelings inside her mind. "Were you waiting for me? Is something wrong?"

"No... yes..." He sat on the bench. "Maybe..."

Hauk stoked the small of her back. "I'm going to get coffee. Would you like one?"

"A large mug, please." In light of Scott's evasive answer, she needed something strong to kick start her brain. "So, Scott, *no* to waiting for me, *yes* to something wrong, and *maybe* to... what? Going inside the cabin and talk?"

"No, not inside the cabin." His shoulders dropped a notch. "Kyle is trying to sleep and he threatened to silence anything that quacks like a duck. According to him, my keyboard makes a good imitation of a duck, not that I think—"

"Stop dawdling like a duck, Scott." She leaned against the railway, her patience wafting away with the breeze. "If you found something, spit it out."

"I found something, but it's what I didn't find that is more revealing." He lowered a stack of papers onto his lap. "You gave me a list of fourteen women who could be your mother. Among them, six gave birth at the shelter. I tracked down their children. One child drowned and the other five are accounted for. I can tell you with certainty that you were not born in that shelter."

"Okay." It wasn't what Star expected to hear, but it still eliminated candidates. "Did you look at the other eight women who might have been pregnant in case they gave birth somewhere else?"

"One wasn't pregnant. Two miscarried early in their pregnancy. Four gave birth at the hospital." The researcher flipped through a few pages. "One baby boy and three baby girls. None of them are you. That brings me to the last woman. Lise. Do you remember what you wrote beside her name?"

All the details that Star noted were imprinted in her brain. "She suffered from gestational diabetes, but there was no mention of labor or birth in her file."

"I can't say I'm surprised." Scott fidgeted with the papers. "Lise went into premature labor and was admitted to the Lakewood Hospital on October 10th. She—"

"October 10th? That's around Thanksgiving weekend." The date rang a church bell in Star's ears. "Lise, not Lisa, was the name of the young woman that the priest remembered." The befuddled look on Scott's face prompted Star to explain further. "After I visited the shelter, I entered a nearby church. The priest had preached there a long, very long time, so I showed him my mother's photo. She reminded him of a young woman who gave birth to a stillborn baby boy around Thanksgiving and overdosed a few years later. He thought her name might have been Lisa or Ella. He might have run into Ella at some point and confused both women. Like Jimmy likes to say, his memory is probably running on a floppy disk, not a flash drive."

Scott choked on his chuckles, and the tension emanating from his body evaporated in the morning sun. "I like your father."

"Yeah, he's an interesting character." Sometimes, Jimmy's sense of humour left to be desired, but Star still appreciated some of his colourful comparisons. "So, why are you interested in Lise?"

"Because your priest was right about her. The police initially believed that Lise was a drug addict and a sex worker—street name Ella—who was assaulted by a john prior to her death. A full autopsy was requested. The coroner ran a tox screen and noted all her injuries. I'll spare you the gruesome details, but somewhere on that list is a single needle mark. Right there." Scott touched the back of his neck. "Lise died of a drug overdose, but the coroner didn't find any evidence that she was a drug addict. In his opinion, the brutal assault would have left her barely conscious and unlikely able to jab a needle anywhere on her body, let alone at the back of her neck, so he deemed her death suspicious. The police opened an investigation. They didn't have any lead, so it didn't take long for the case to get cold. Now it's frozen solid, but I may have knocked off a big chunk of ice."

"You solved Lise's murder while searching for my mother?" It wasn't the lucky twist that Star had hoped for, but she was glad her list yielded important information. "Have you contacted the police yet?"

"There's more to her death, Star. Her body was found in a dumpster in an alley, the alley known as Bloody Lane." He took a long, noisy breath. "In the evening of July 28th, the day after the Humphrey murders."

Dazed from the coincidence, Star gripped the railing behind her with both hands. "You can't be thinking she's my mother, Scott. You said it yourself, Ella was her street name. My mother's name was Stella Fisher, not Lise."

"I need to show you Lise's birth and death certificates." Scott patted the seat beside him. "But first, please sit."

His request released wasps inside Star's stomach, each stinging more than the previous one. She plopped on the bench. "My mother changed her name to Lise, didn't she?"

"Not exactly." Scott handed her two documents. "Look at her full name."

She stared at the names. *Stella Lise Fisher. Lise Stella Fisher.* Same birthday. *My mother's birthday.* "She switched her given names around. I didn't even know her middle name was Lise." There were so many things that Star didn't know about her mother. *So many things that I will never know now that she is dead.* "The monster caught up with her after Jimmy rescued me, didn't he? And he killed her in the same alley he tried to kill me." The irony wasn't lost on her. Nonetheless, the timeline added up in her mind, except for two details. "The priest seemed so sure she'd lost her baby boy. How come Jimmy was never notified of her death?"

"There was no next of kin listed in the police report or anywhere else I could find. If someone was aware she had an older brother, they didn't or couldn't locate him. Now, about the priest, his memory wasn't saved on a floppy disk." Scott placed another certificate on her lap. "This is baby Noah's Stillbirth Certificate. His mother is listed as Lise Fisher and his father is unknown. You told me your father's doctor searched for your birth certificate. Maybe he stumbled on Noah's, but he wasn't looking for a baby boy born to a Lise Fisher, he was searching for a baby girl born to a Stella Fisher, except that baby girl never existed. I believe Stella, Lise, and Ella are one woman, one courageous woman and devoted nanny, who gave her life to save yours. Star, you're—"

"Don't say it." A tear fell onto the Stillbirth Certificate, blurring Lise's name. Star longed for a deep dive, for the cold embrace of the water to numb the feelings in which she was drowning.

* * *

Transfixed, Hauk listened from the doorway of the cabin with two cups of coffee. The revelations didn't shock him as much as they rattled Star.

Her sudden departure left Scott's visibly perplexed.

Hauk joined him. "You did good, Scott."

"Did I?" His young researcher picked up the papers that Star dropped on deck. "I could have blurted it out, but I tried to be sensitive. She didn't let me finish." Scott didn't always wear his feelings on his sleeve, but the way he presented the facts showed how much he cared about Star. "I didn't mean to hurt her."

"You didn't hurt her." *The monster who hurt her isn't onboard. He's roaming the streets. Free like the bird tattooed near his wrist.* Once again, Hauk fought to keep his anger and frustration at bay. "She didn't

235

need to hear more, Scott. Her nightmares told her the truth a long time ago. Now she needs time to reconcile who she is with who she was."

A splash prompted Hauk to scan the lake. Moments later, he glimpsed her streamlined silhouette moving fluidly through the water and shrinking in the reflection of the sun.

* * *

Star swam, pushing through the pain in her body, the ache in heart, and the grief of losing the child she once was and the fear of losing the woman she became. Through it all, she kept on swimming until exhaustion claimed every muscle in her body and every tendril in her mind. Only then did she flip on her back and whip kicked her way back to the Zodiac.

The craft was deserted, but amid her clothes, someone had left a dry towel. The small gesture brought tears to her eyes. She wrapped her battered body in the large towel, concealing her wet bra and panties, picked up her shorts and t-shirt, and climbed onboard.

Hauk rested on a bench. A wide brim fishing hat concealed his eyes, but not the twitching of his mouth. "Wanna talk?"

236

"No." By now, the crew were undoubtedly aware of Scott's discovery. Soon or later, she would need to face the elephant in the room. "If Lise is Jimmy's sister, and I'm not her daughter, that means he's not my uncle, and I cannot accept that."

"You were never his niece, havfrue." Hauk tipped his hat up and looked her straight in the eyes. "You are his daughter, and that will never change regardless of who gave birth to you. His love for you isn't a DNA algorithm, it reaches beyond the stars."

Tears pooled in her eyes again, but this time there was no water to wash them away. "I don't want to be who you think I am."

"I think you are the most wonderful woman I've ever met and I want to spend the rest of my life with you." The love reflected in his face soothed her aching heart. "Maybe you're not the missing twin who was attacked by a dog. Maybe Vanessa drowned despite Ella's efforts to save her. It's not like you share anything in common with that rambunctious twin, right? You were probably just a little stray that Ella found on the corner of a street at night and took in."

"A stray?" Staggering between laughter, tears, and the desire to strangle him, Star slumped against him. "That wasn't funny. If I'm Vanessa, I may have seen the monster who murderer my family, but I don't remember anything."

"No child should ever endure the ordeal that Vanessa survived that night. Confronted with incomprehensible violence, her young mind coped the only way it could. It blocked those horrific memories." He slipped a hand behind her back and held her close. "It's a defence mechanism, havfrue. It buries those memories deep inside your subconscious where they can't hurt you, but they never get erased. There's a reason Vanessa visits you in your nightmares, she's trying to make you remember."

Star leaned her head against his shoulder, wishing she could forget but knowing she needed to remember. "How did... how could she survive falling in the water? Shouldn't I be afraid of the water if I'd almost drowned?"

"Ella grew up by a lake. She would have been a good swimmer, just like you. Maybe she kept you afloat and you felt safe in her arms." He spoke softly in her ears. "Or maybe Ella threw the nightgown in the water as a diversion and escaped without crossing the water. We'll never know those details, they died with Ella, but her suspicious death leads me to believe that the killer did everything he could to tie up all the loose ends."

"If you're right—" A part of her couldn't deny the logic behind his assumption. "Why didn't he come after me back then? Why wait twenty years?"

"We know that Jimmy had already rescued you by the time death caught up with Ella." Hauk's chest rose and fell in a comforting rhythm. "At the time, Ella lived in an apartment near Bloody Lane, in the kind of neighbourhood that attracts lowlifes like the monster. Maybe he hunted Ella down or maybe he believed she drowned only for their paths to cross the next day. One way or another, he realized Ella survived, which raised the possibility that you did too. Maybe he looked for you but didn't have enough information to find you, or maybe—that's my favourite scenario— maybe Ella told him you drowned to stop him from looking for you. Maybe he assumed you were dead or maybe he waited for you to resurface. For twenty years, you lived a quiet life with Jimmy far away from Lakewood. Your paths never crossed—until now."

"But I don't remember him." The horror movie playing in her head at night never showed the monster's face. "How could he remember me? I'm a grown-up woman who looks nothing like the four-year-old twin in the Humphreys' family picture, and don't say my scar. I'm not the only child who was ever mauled by a dog."

"The scar alone might not have raised his suspicion, but you also share Ella's last name. Fisher. That may have caught his attention. Then we found Mary's remains and discovered that her descendants, Amy and two of her children, were murdered. What might have started as a weird coincidence unraveled into a real threat for the killer. Whether you remember him or not is irrelevant." Hauk's lips brushed her cheek. "You're a loose end that he can't afford not to tie, and it's all my fault. If I hadn't convinced you to join my crew, he may never have found you."

Sooner or later, her fate would have come full circle, without or without Hauk's involvement. "For twenty years, there was an invisible sword hanging over my head. All you did was brought it to light before it stuck me dead." No one was to blame, only the monster. "I'm having a hard time reconciling Vanessa's life with mine. It feels so unimaginable, so twisted, but I also believe you're right about the killer believing that I'm the missing twin who survived." Her stomach grumbled. "I'm hungry. Let's go eat."

She wasn't just hungry, she was starving for revenge and justice.

* * *

"I can't believe you missed." Bruce had always been able to rely on his friend, but lately Dusty had become less reliable. "Were you even aiming at her?"

"It's not my fault she moved at the last moment." Dusty threw the cigarette on the concrete floor and squashed it under his

240

boot. "The ugly bitchling has more lives than a cat."

"She was in the house when I threatened her father. She can't be allowed to remember me." Spending the rest of his existence in jail for causing Adrian Humphrey's death wasn't part of Bruce's retirement package. "I don't care if you have to shadow her day and night. Do I make myself clear?"

"Relax, I have a plan." Dusty pulled a plastic bag from a shelf above the workbench in his garage. "After I fled the alley, I ran into one of the street thugs who threatened her, and I borrowed his knife." Inside the bag was a hunting knife smeared with dark maroon stains. "His prints are on it, so I might as well seek revenge in his name."

Hopeful that his friend hadn't lost his flair after all, Bruce tossed the hammer onto the workbench and examined his handiwork.

Taking the afternoon off had paid off. At this rate, his pickup would look like new in less than a week. And any trace of the collision with the bus would vanish under a new coat of white paint.

* * *

In a private lounge at the Country Club, Hauk recounted his findings as he laid out the corroborating documents on the table

241

that he shared with Star and Kenneth. "My researcher couldn't prove that Stella Lise Fisher was the Humphreys' new nanny, but everything that unfolded from the moment Jimmy Fisher took custody of that little girl with a fresh scar on her cheek couldn't be explained any other way."

The retired inspector switched back and forth between perusing the documents and scrutinizing the woman seated across the table, his silence only broken by the rattling of Star's spoon in her cup.

Sensing the mounting tension in her body, Hauk stroked her thigh under the table. Star lowered the spoon on a napkin, grabbed the cup with both hands, and took a long sip.

Kenneth's gaze settled on her. "We searched high and low for the missing twin and her nanny. The possibility you might be Vanessa is quite extraordinary."

Star stilled, her cup freezing centimetres from her lips. "Does that mean you think I am her, or I'm not her?"

The retired inspector smiled, warming his expression with compassion and kindness. "You never forget the missing children you couldn't reunite with their family, Miss Fisher, but you also never lose hope that one day someone will be able to finish their stories and close their files. Happy endings after twenty years are rare, but the possibility that I'm staring at the little girl who still haunts me at night is overwhelming, in an amazing way. Would you agree to a mouth swab so we can compare your DNA to the hair found on Vanessa's nightgown?"

Star nodded.

"Unfortunately, I don't carry any swab kit with me." Kenneth scribbled in a notepad. "If you could go to the police station today, they will do the test right away. Just give them this." He ripped out the sheet he wrote on and gave it to Star. "It'll take a few days before the results come in."

Pleased that the retired inspector took the evidence regarding Star's identity seriously, Hauk aimed for a second concession. "What about the logbook? Any chance we could look at those old insurance policies?"

"Adrian Humphrey's logbook was investigated. At the time, no connections were found with the murder of his family, but then we didn't have the information you collected." Kenneth's chair screeched on the floor. "I'm heading to the police station right now to talk to whoever is in charge of investigating Mary Watson's remains."

"His name is Pratt. Detective Pratt." Hauk didn't recall a first name. "I came to you with this information, not because I don't trust Pratt, but because you have first-hand knowledge of what happened to the Humphreys."

"That's fair. When you show up for the swab test, please bring all these documents with you." With his hand, Kenneth encompassed the tabletop. "By the time I am done briefing Pratt, he will want to talk to you."

* * *

Eager to leave the police station after the mouth swab and long interview with Detective Pratt, Star pressed the elevator button.

The detective's no-nonsense attitude and pragmatic approach had put her at ease. He reviewed all the evidence with her and Hauk, didn't dismiss any possibilities, and promised them that no stone would remain unturned.

The elevator doors parted.

"Could we stop somewhere to eat?" Star took a step forward. "I'm starv—"

A man getting out bumped into her, throwing her off balance.

Strong arms steadied her from behind. "Careful, havfrue."

The man eyed her, triggering memories of a different encounter, then walked away mumbling an apology.

Seeking the images floating at the edge of her consciousness, Start spun around and stared back and forth between the corridor and the closing doors of the elevator. His face slowly appeared from the shadows protecting her mind. "He was there. That's where I saw him."

"Star?" Hauk pressed one hand on her shoulder, and with the back of the other, he tilted her head up, forcing her to meet his eyes. "Who are you talking about?"

"I knew he looked familiar when Scott showed me his driver's licence." She couldn't contain her nervous excitement. For once her mind graced her with a straight answer. "Remember the day you forced me to visit Kyle at the hospital?"

"How could I forget the day you were ran over by a truck?" He pressed the elevator button again. "If I hadn't *forced* you to—"

"Not so loud." The doors parted. She grabbed his arm and dragged him inside the empty elevator. "After I saw Kyle, I rode the elevator down to the lobby. On my way out, I bumped into a man. He gasped in horror when he saw my face. I couldn't understand why he looked so appalled. Lots of people stare at my scar, but never to that extent. That man was Bruce Robert, but I mistook the look in his eyes. It wasn't revulsion. It was recognition."

Chapter 17

Hauk chose a popular seafood restaurant. There was safety in numbers, or so said the expression. At any rate, a large crowd surrounded the area around the table that he shared with Star.

Shrimp and scallops disappeared from her plate at a steady pace. "Do you think Kyle will be able to convince the secretary to give him access to the archives room again?"

"Kyle can be very convincing when it comes to women." Hauk laughed at her dubious expression. "And I'm happy to know you're immune to his charm, or I'd be fighting him off right now."

"No need to worry." Dark brown eyes gazed at him above the lone blue and white carnation displayed in a smoky glass on the table. "Kyle made sure he kept that charm hidden from me."

"I'll admit that Kyle is sometimes rough on the outside." Hauk intertwined his fingers with hers over the blue cotton tablecloth. "But deep down, he's a decent guy."

"I know he is." A bashful smile danced on her lips. "We worked out our differences."

"I'm glad." With his thumb, he stroked the sensitive spot on the inside of her wrist. "Since we're still in town, what would you say if we stop by Bruce's auto shop later tonight to peek at his inventory?"

Her fork stilled between her plate and her open mouth. "Isn't that risky?"

"Not if we wait until nightfall." Besides, knowing her, it would have been only a matter of time before she made the same suggestion. "I know you want to search for the truck, havfrue, and I understand your motivation. So, I'd rather join you than wage a losing battle against you."

She squeezed his hand. "Thank you."

* * *

Bored out of his mind, Dusty drummed his fingers against the steering wheel. Of all the restaurants in town, Ludwig had chosen the one reputed as much for its seafood as for its snail's pace service.

Ludwig's bad taste had forced Dusty to switch parking spots twice in the last hour to avoid undue attention. He was now relegated to the end of the street, his view of the restaurant hindered by a group of teenagers hanging out on the sidewalk.

It took him all day to track the pair down. Dusty couldn't afford to lose sight of them again. Twenty years ago, he had underestimated the nanny who messed up his plan, but this time he would ensure the ugly bitchling was dead before walking away.

Craving a snack or a cigarette, he searched the glove compartment where he stumbled on a tracking device.

I was looking for you last week. While Dusty couldn't remember what he wanted to use it for back then, the tracker solved his immediate concerns.

He got out of the car and strolled down the street toward the back of the restaurant where Ludwig's grey Jeep was parked under a tall willow tree. Its drooping branches didn't only provide shade, they obscured Dusty's silhouette from bystanders as he attached the tracker to the bumper of the Jeep.

* * *

Star's gaze travelled up and down the street. It was deserted with not even a stray cat in sight.

Hauk parked under a streetlight near the auto shop. Less than three metres away, an opening in the chain-link fence provided them with a convenient point of entry into the auto lot. The large gap in the fence alleviated her fear of running into a guard dog as the animal would have undoubtedly escaped.

Together, they searched the outdoor lot where she counted five white pickups but no Dodge.

Disappointed by their lack of success, she followed Hauk toward the auto shop building.

* * *

The tracking chip allowed Dusty to follow the Jeep from a safe distance, and he cursed himself for not thinking about it sooner.

All the hours he spent with his gaze glued onto that Jeep could have been put to better use. He could have picked up a girl, or two, to entertain him while he waited for Ludwig to be on the move again.

As Ludwig's destination became apparent, Dusty dug his nails into the leather steering wheel. "What the—" The curse died on his lips at the realization they had given him the perfect opportunity to get rid of them.

He slipped on his mask and gloves before entering the lot through an opening in the fence. That fence should have been fixed long ago to stop interlopers from trespassing, but tonight Dusty was glad that his friend didn't deem the repairs a priority.

On the lookout for the meddling couple, he slowly canvassed the lot. A beam of light reflecting faintly off a window of Bruce's shop gave away their location.

Dusty hid behind a trailer to observe them.

The breeze whistling between the parked vehicles covered their words but not their gestures. With his hand, Ludwig appeared to order the ugly bitchling to stay put.

Once Ludwig ventured around the building and disappeared, Dusty approached her from behind.

If he successfully caught her off guard and slit her throat before she screamed, he would flee without killing Ludwig. The fingerprints on the knife dropped near her lifeless body would lead to one of the street thugs who assaulted her, a crime that Ludwig and the other diver would be able to confirm.

Dusty smirked at the irony that they would absolve his participation in her slaying.

* * *

With Hauk gone looking for an unlocked entry into the shop, Star peeked through a different window. Two trucks were inside. One dark, the other—

The breeze carried a strong, pungent, musky scent to her nose. Sensing a foul presence behind her, she shoved her elbow backwards. It connected with someone's midsection and spawned a gasp from the intruder.

She spun around. A masked assailant lurched at her with a knife. She ducked and slammed her fist into his forearm. The blow propelled his hand into the window. Glass shattered, and he tumbled forward.

A loud alarm went off, muffling her attacker's yelling and her call for help. He staggered on his feet and gripped the side of the window. Adrenaline flooded her bloodstream, bottling up her fear. She thrust her shoulder into his side, trapping his arm in the broken window frame. Howling like a wounded animal, he smacked her across the face. The force of the blow threw her to the pavement.

Sirens blared in the night.

"Star!" Hauk ran around the corner of the building.

The assailant took a step in her direction. Sprawled on her back, she pushed away from him with her heels and hands. He glanced behind her then bolted in the opposite direction.

Hauk scooped her into his arms. "Are you all right?"

"No, but we need to get out of here."

The police arrived before they had a chance to flee the scene.

* * *

Recounting attacks to police officers had become second nature, a second nature that Star would rather live without.

The officer who took her statement looked like he recently stepped out of police school. "That's not a very detailed description of your assailant, Miss Fisher."

"The guy wore a dark ski mask over his face, a dark shirt, and jeans. Medium build. Above six feet tall." Surely, the officer didn't want her to invent a description just to make his job easier.

"I see." He scribbled something on a notepad. "And, again, how did you set off the alarm?"

"I didn't." Twice already, she had explained the attack. If the officer waited for her to change her story, they would be at it all night. "*The assailant* set the alarm off when *he* broke the window." If she weren't so damned angry, she would laugh at the irony that the assailant himself had triggered the alarm that alerted the police.

"And what were you and Mr. Ludwig doing trespassing on private property?"

The question, which she should have anticipated, threw her for a loop. *Keep it simple. And plausible.* "We were driving down the road when something... when something zoomed in front of the Jeep." Improvisation had never been her forte. "It looked like a fox, or maybe a raccoon."

"I thought I'd hit it so I stopped," Hauk continued. "Star wanted to call animal control, but I convinced her to look for the animal first in case we were mistaken."

"You looked for an injured wild animal in the dark?" The officer had stopped writing to stare at them in dismay. "Do you realize how foolish and dangerous that was?"

Star nodded.

"Hey, Jerry." His patrol partner, a tough-looking officer with a chiseled face, walked toward them holding a bag. "I found a knife under a broken window. Possible fingerprints and dried blood on it. There's also lots of glass fragments on the floor, some with fresh blood on them. The fire department is on its way."

Sirens announced their imminent arrival.

A paramedic examined Star's and Hauk's arms for bleeding cuts, no doubt to confirm their story that the blood on the glass fragments didn't belong to them. "No injuries. They're clear."

An hour later, the officers released them.

Star held onto Hauk's arm walking back to the Jeep. "He wore gloves, Hauk. If the police find prints on the knife, they won't be his."

"But it'll be his blood on the window." He unlocked the passenger door of the Jeep. "Did you see a tattoo on his arm?"

"He wore long sleeves." Even if her assailant had gone sleeveless, she might not have noticed his tattoo in the dim light of the lot. "But he smelled like the same guy."

He leaned against the open door. "Are you sure?"

"Yes, but it doesn't mean it was the same guy." *Just that both attackers smelled awful.* Physically and mentally exhausted, she slumped into the passenger seat. "Thank you for coming to my rescue."

"Always. Would you like a long, hot bath tonight?"

The prospect of a long bath appealed to her sore muscles. "That would be wonderful, but last I checked, you haven't installed one onboard yet."

* * *

Hauk glanced at the strong woman sitting in the passenger seat. The sword hanging over her head had struck again and missed again. Still, she deserved better than to be at the mercy of a past she couldn't change. All he wanted at this moment in time was to pamper her, to make her feel special and safe.

Ninety minutes away from Lakewood, a century-old resort surrounded by square kilometres of protected forest operated away from the public eye. Its misleading name didn't appear on booking sites, but those who could afford its nightly rate knew its name. *Old Cottage.*

An eye on the road ahead and the other on the rearview mirror, Hauk drove toward Old Cottage, making sudden changes of direction when the same vehicle tailed him for too long.

Two and a half hours later, the headlights of his Jeep illuminated a black sign posted near a dirt road. The words *Old Road Dead End* were painted in uneven yellow letters.

Confident no one had followed him, Hauk turned onto the narrow dirt road and cautiously navigated the next winding kilometres until he reached a crowded parking lot flooded with filtered green lights.

Star bolted upright in her seat. "What is this place?"

"Welcome to Old Cottage, havfrue." His Jeep looked out of place parked between a red Audi sedan and a black BMW SUV, but Hauk couldn't find a spot on the outskirt of the lot. "I'm hoping there's a room available for us."

"A room? Here?" She unbuckled her seatbelt, visibly aghast. "Can you even afford valet parking here?"

"No, which is why I parked myself," he quipped to avoid acknowledging she was right about the cost. "Let's go, shall we?"

A cobblestone path led them to a magnificent five-storey mansion with a white, stone façade illuminated by strings of white and green lights laced between protruding balconies.

"That's not a cottage." Her lovely eyes grew wider and wider. "It's a... a..."

"It's the former summer residence of a very rich man whose descendants couldn't afford to maintain so they transformed it into an exclusive resort," he explained as they entered the luxurious lobby.

She pulled on his arm, stopping his progress toward the front desk. "I don't need a bath that badly, Hauk. Besides, I could probably install a tub on your boat for less money than it'll cost to take a bath here."

"I'm sure you could, but that's not the point." He brushed a tender kiss on hers lips to silence any further objections. "We can stay one night." With any luck, they would be able to afford a short honeymoon as well.

Astonished by the thought that sped uncensored through his mind, he stared at the woman who turned his world on its head, and smiled.

"Why are you looking at me like that?" Fine lines creased the new bandage that the paramedic had applied on her forehead. "Am I bleeding again?"

"All is fine." A bright and wonderful future awaited them, and Hauk would be damned if he let anyone ruin their lives. "Come."

At the front desk, the helpful young man who had once solved Hauk's technical issues welcomed them with a bow of his head. "It's good to see you again, Mr. Ludwig, Mademoiselle. What can I do for you tonight?"

"Good evening, Ash." Coming here had been a gamble, but Hauk hoped he wouldn't need a plan B. "I'm afraid I didn't make a reservation. Any chance you have an empty room for the night?"

"Let me check..." The name *Ashravya* along with the title *Manager on Duty* was written on the nametag pinned to his burgundy jacket. "I have a suite on the fourth floor. Would that suit your needs?"

One unspoken rule was in effect on the resort. *If you have to ask, you can't afford it.* Hauk didn't need to ask about the rate of that suite to know he couldn't afford it, but he owed Star a restful night. "That would be perfect."

"Credit card, please?" Ash swept his credit card then handed it back along with two coded cards. "Suite 4008. Have a pleasant night."

"Thanks." Hauk draped an arm behind Star's back and led her toward an open elevator located near the restaurant.

They stepped in, but as soon as the door closed, she distanced herself from him. Puzzled by her reaction, he racked his brain for something he might have said or done in the last few minutes to upset her. "You're not mad at me for spending money on you, are you?"

"Yes, but no." She crossed her arms over her chest, adding another obstacle between them.

More confused than ever, he scrutinized her face for a clearer answer. "What's really bothering you?"

"Why did you bring me *here*?" The emphasis on the *here* and the indignation in her voice stopped him from moving closer to her. "I realize you have a past, Hauk, we both do, but if you think I'm flattered that you're bringing me to your secret lair, think again."

"My what?"

The elevator door opened, temporarily ending the discussion.

His mind reeling, he gestured for her to go first then followed in silence until they reached Suite 4008.

Understanding dawned on him as he unlocked the door. "You think that—" He burst out laughing at the comical misunderstanding, only to regret it when Star elbowed her way into the suite. "It wasn't funny and I'm sorry, but would you give me a chance to explain?"

"Explain what? That you're *not* a regular guest? *Ash* knew your name." Her outrage would be justified, but only if she had correctly interpreted his exchange with the manager. "How often do you come here? On second thought, I don't want to know. I'm going to take a long bath."

Stubborn woman. One day she would be the death of him, and yet Hauk knew he would enjoy every second of it. "You're right, I am a regular guest, but I've only ever brought one woman here." His admission stopped Star in her tracks. "Her name is Hilda. She's my great-aunt, the one who generously funds my salvage operations. She's a smart, headstrong, and kind-hearted woman, just like you, and I love her with all my heart."

Star leaned against the doorframe of the bathroom. "Your aunt Hilda sounds like a wonderful woman." The fire burning in her eyes died down. "Should I ask why you both come here?"

"After every successful salvage operation, Aunt Hilda insists I give a press conference here before I donate my artifacts to the museums. She never explained her attachment to Old Cottage, but I know it's important to her, so I oblige." Relieved to feel the tension between them subside, Hauk joined Star. "Ash has organized my last two... no... my last three conferences, so I hope he remembers me. Aunt Hilda tipped him very generously."

Star nibbled down on her bottom lips. "Why did you really bring me here, Hauk?"

Despite his good intentions, he had inadvertently sent the wrong signals, making her suspect ulterior motives. "The resort is private and secure, beyond the monster's reach. He can't touch you here, Star. You can spend hours in the bathroom, or curl up on the couch with a book, or go to bed and close your eyes, or anything else your heart desires without looking over your shoulder for his shadow, sniffing the air for his scent, or pricking your ears for a sound that doesn't belong." Hauk stroked the cheek along the ridges of the accidental scar that stamped her fate. "You deserve to feel safe and carefree, if only for one night. I wasn't planning on seducing you tonight... Actually, I'm kind of flattered that you thought I brought you here for that reason. Does that mean I could stand a chance?"

She rolled her eyes and slapped him on the chest. "You should quit while you're ahead. I'm going to take a bath. Alone."

Chapter 18

Hauk browsed the room service menu for something sweet to eat. Half an hour later, a large fruit platter was delivered to the suite.

The woman who had playfully and quietly slammed the door in his face, was still in the bathroom, but the sound of flowing or ruffling water had long stopped.

Despite the assurance he gave her that she was safe, worry began to feast on unwarranted fears and the urge of checking on her swelled inside his chest.

I promised her she was safe. If he barged in there, Star would chew his head off and call him overprotective again. How to keep a loved one safe without acting like an overbearing fool was a juggling act that Hauk had yet to master.

Using the arrival of the platter as an excuse, he knocked on the door. "Star? Are you almost done?" When she didn't answer, he cracked the door open. "I have a surprise for you."

Steam and heat wafted through the opening, obscuring his view of the bathroom. As he stepped in, his gaze wandered around the opulent room.

Droplets of water slithered down the walls of the empty shower stall, and bubbles foamed up to the rim of a clawfoot bathtub.

"Star?" Fearing she had drowned from exhaustion, he set the platter on the vanity before dipping his hand into the warm water, and accidentally rubbing her thigh.

A tidal wave washed over the tub. Drenched from head to toe, he stared in admiration at the exquisite creature emerging from a thick mist of white bubbles.

* * *

"Are you trying to give me a heart attack?" Mad at Hauk for startling her, Star sank back into the warm water. "And stopping staring like I'm a bowl of popcorn ready to be gobbled up."

His grin only grew bigger and sillier. "I should have ordered popcorn." He knelt by the tub and dipped his hand in the water again. "Do you always sink to the bottom of the tub when you take a bath?"

"I'm a diver, Hauk. I enjoy being underwater." The caresses he bestowed on her arm awoke the butterflies sleeping in her belly. "Is there a reason you're interrupting my bath?"

His gaze skimmed over the bubbles. "I was hoping you might need my back-washing services."

"You're too late." Amid the bubbles, she wiggled her toes. "I took a cleansing shower before soaking in the tub."

"That's disappointing." Looking anything but disappointed, he took off his wet shirt then unzipped his cargo shorts.

Confused by his actions, she arched an eye. "What exactly are you doing?"

"I'm soaked so I'm going to take a shower while you turn into a prune." His shorts slid down muscular thighs and heaped at his feet. He then kicked his clothes toward the vanity where they bunched next to hers.

In her line of work, Star had seen divers of all ages and body shapes wear anything from long johns to G-strings that left nothing to the imagination. Not much fazed her.

Nonetheless, she enjoyed watching the happy faces on his boxers dance with every step Hauk took toward the shower. "Let me know if you need someone to wash your back, I'll call the front desk. I'm sure Ash can send someone if I tip well."

Hauk's laughter rose in the bathroom, and she basked in the newfound intimacy they shared.

* * *

From the frosted shower panels, Hauk glimpsed moving shadows. By the time he stepped out, the tub was empty and their clothes drooped from its rim. One of the two royal blue bathrobes hanging from the hooks on the wall had disappeared, the platter was gone, and Star was nowhere in sight.

After quickly drying himself, he donned the remaining downy robe and went looking for her.

In the bedroom, his bare feet sank into the plush beige carpet. The velvety burgundy curtains were closed, and the room bathed in the yellowish glow of an elegant Victorian-style table lamp.

Propped against fluffy pillows, Star picked a segment of mandarin from the platter on the bed.

"I see you've started without me," he teased, glad that she enjoyed the midnight treat. "I asked for chocolate dip, but they didn't have any."

Amused by her weak imitation of feigned disappointment, he joined her and took a pineapple chunk from the platter. She snuggled against him, her cheeks flushed and her hair smelling like a field of wild strawberries sprinkled with a hint of vanilla.

"This is delicious." She teased his lips with a slice of kiwi that ended up in her mouth at the last second.

Hauk kissed her in retaliation, tenderly at first then more passionately as he savoured the sweet tangy flavour lingering in her mouth. Their playful fruit game continued in comfortable silence until only juice remained at the bottom of the platter.

The platter set aside on the closest night table, Hauk trailed his hand down the graceful curve of her neck to her bare shoulder, peppering her skin with kisses along the way. She ventured a small hand down the opening of his robe and teased his chest with feathery light caresses. Enchanted by her response, he parted her robe, exposing the swell of a breast and an old, ragged, and rather alluring scar that extended farther beneath the fabric.

Reminded of the night in the Zodiac when he had inadvertently discovered another one of her painful injuries, Hauk gently skimmed a finger over the scar. "I worked once with a Québécois from La Tuque who affectionately called his wife *mon trésor*. It literally translates into *my treasure*. Since your body resembles a treasure map, I may just start calling you, *mon trésor*."

Quiet laughter shook his treasure map. "I know men tend to be proud of their scars, but they rarely see them attractive on a woman."

"That's a bad double standard." Unfortunately, Hauk knew not only men but also women who judged people without ever looking beneath the surface. "So, are you going to tell me how you got that battle scar?

Or did it happen when you fell off that tree you weren't supposed to climb?"

"I'm sure I didn't walk away unscathed from that tree. I have lots of cuts that healed over time but that I can't explain." She traced invisible lines within the V of his robe. "Do you remember me telling you about Jimmy being stabbed during the river dump ambush?"

Hauk hadn't forgotten the reason why she almost severed his air hose. "If I recall correctly, you weren't aware of the drugs stashed in the trunk until Jimmy was attacked."

"Correct, except Jimmy wasn't the only one who was injured. The drug dealer slashed me twice before I fought him off. He got me on the upper chest first, then on the lower left." She rubbed her abdomen. "I was lucky that one didn't damage any internal organs."

Learning that she almost lost her life in the ambush added another dimension to her underwater response, but she had possessed enough mental discipline to override her survival instincts at the last second—and spared his life. "Your courage and resilience never cease to amaze me, havfrue, but you need to stop meeting shady characters in dark places," Hauk quipped, grateful for second chances. "What happened to the dealer? Was he ever arrested?"

"He tried to flee, but he didn't go far. I heard he made a deal in exchange for a reduced sentence only to plead guilty to all charges after he lost two fingers in prison." She sighed softly. "I didn't have to testify against him. He's just another piranha bitten into silence by a shark who poses no direct threat to me. Unlike the monster."

He cradled her head in the crook of his shoulder and held her tight. "Feel free to close your eyes and sleep. You're safe in my arms and you will always be. I love you, havfrue."

"I love you, too," she whispered, unknowingly branding her name all over his heart.

* * *

Persistent knocks on the back door pulled Bruce away from the television set. Annoyed at being disturbed after midnight after spending most of the evening on the phone with the police, he marched across the kitchen and yanked the door open.

Contempt rose in his throat at the sight of the man cradling a bandaged arm sullied with blood. "Are you crazy coming here?"

Dusty pushed his way in and slammed the door with his foot. "I need your help."

Irritated to be dragged into whatever landed his friend in this predicament, Bruce grudgingly pulled out a chair. "Sit at the table and don't make a mess." He retrieved a first aid kit from the closet then unwrapped the bloody bandage. "Are you going to tell me what happened or do I have to guess?"

Shards of glass were imbedded in Dusty's skin. "The ugly bitchling."

Puzzled as to how the girl impaled Dusty with a salvo of action figure's size daggers, Bruce pressed for details. "What did she do to you?"

Dusty's jaw clenched. "She fought back."

What a novel idea! "You're trying to kill her, Du—" The word *Dummy* almost escaped Bruce's lips. "Did you expect she wouldn't fight back while you kill her?"

His friend growled. "She ain't dead."

"What?" Bruce was tempted to stab Dusty with the tweezer he pulled out of the kit. "She and Ludwig broke into my auto shop tonight. They're suspecting me. *Me.*"

"I know." Dusty winced when the tweezer touched his arm. "I was there."

"You were on my lot?" Fury roared inside Bruce's chest. "Of course you were. That's my darn window embedded in your arm, isn't it? Give me details. All the details."

"Come down. It's not like the cops saw me."

Bruce hung on every word coming out of his friend's mouth, and more than once he resisted the urge to thrust the shards deeper instead of removing them.

"The cops phoned me, Dusty. I didn't press charges of trespassing against them because I didn't want the police to look for my truck." *I should have guessed you were somehow involved.* "They found the knife."

His friend shrugged. "Prints aren't mine. That was the beauty of it."

Using a magnifying glass, Bruce examined Dusty's bloody arm for any remaining fragments. "How about the blood on the window?"

"Our old records got erased. My DNA isn't in the system." Dusty yanked his arm. "Enough prodding. I'm good."

Their old records weren't erased, they were sealed, but trying to explain the difference to his friend was a waste of Bruce's time. "If you'd killed Ludwig first, he wouldn't have saved the girl. Why didn't you?"

"What part of *I was trying to frame the street thug* don't you get?" Dusty fished out a gauze roll from the first aid kit. "Ludwig wasn't in the alley when the bitchling was ambushed. The thug would have targeted her first, not some guy he had no beef with. Trust me. I know how those thugs think."

His longtime friend had always derived a perverse pleasure from killing, but somehow he hesitated to eliminate Ludwig. Bruce didn't buy the half-cocked excuse any more than he trusted Dusty's judgment. The term *liability* crossed Bruce's mind.

Once the girl had been dealt with, he would permanently terminate his association with Dusty.

* * *

Star fought against the strong current.

A small body thrashed in her arms. Tiny feet kicked the water and little fists pounded her chest.

Cold water seeped through her clothes. Her grip on the child loosened.

"Mommy."

The child's scream echoed with her own, and terror swelled inside her mind.

"Mommmmmy!"

Water burned her throat and dragged her under. The child scratched and clawed to hold on to—

A sudden weight pushed against her chest, expelling the air from her lungs. Her eyes flew open. She abruptly bolted upright.

"It's over, havfrue."

"Hauk?" In the dark, Star sought the path to his voice.

"I'm here." Gentle arms lowered her back against the mattress, her head sank into the soft pillow, and his lips grazed her cheek.

"Don't let me drown." Muffled by the frantic beating of her heart, her voice sounded scratchy and disengaged to her own ears.

"You're safe, havfrue."

Shaken by the nightmare, she clutched at his bathrobe with tight fists. Her bare breasts pushed against his chest with each raspy breath she took. Sometime during her imaginary struggle in the water, her belt had come untied, unwrapping the bathrobe from her body. As she forced herself to relax, she loosened her grip and let her hands trailed down his chest.

His sudden sideways shift gave rise to another wave of panic. Desperate to hold on to reality, she encircled his waist. "Don't leave."

"I'm not going anywhere." He delicately brushed a lock of hair from her temple. "I promise."

She closed her eyes leaning her cheek against his shoulder.

"Would you like to talk about the nightmare?"

"Not now." The images slowly faded. She would revisit them once she dealt with the raw emotions they triggered. "Hold me. Please."

He tightened his embrace and speckled her lips with light kisses. Feeling loved and safe in his arms, she parted her lips in a silent invitation to delve deeper. A fresh, ocean-breeze scent, unique to Hauk, permeated her senses. His hand skimmed over her imperfect breast then trailed down her bruised hip. Shivers coursed along her skin. She stirred against him in a futile attempt to appease the scorching heat slowly engulfing her entire being.

"We're playing with fire, havfrue, and you're overestimating my willpower.

Besides, I don't carry any protection with me. My past isn't as colourful as you think." The husky warning whispered in her ear registered through her hazy mind. "Truth be told, my life was rather dull until I met you."

"Mine was too, until I met you." Against all odds, she had survived, unaware she lived on borrowed time. Her life was a fragile gift that could be stolen or destroyed in the blink of an eye. Tonight she longed to live in this unfettered moment, regardless of the consequences. "In my nightmare, I was tossed in the frigid water at the mercy of the river. Right now, all I want, all I need, is the warmth of a burning fire."

* * *

Hauk would have loved to extend their stay at Old Cottage, not that his wallet would have approved, but an early morning call from Detective Pratt prompted them to depart shortly after breakfast. By the time they returned to the lake, they had yet to wrap their heads around what had transpired at the police station.

Back on his vessel, Hauk gathered his crew inside the cabin.

"Last night, Star and I snooped around Robert's auto shop where she was attacked, again, by a man wearing gloves." Hauk proceeded to recount the events in great details, only omitting the amazing night he shared with her. "Detective Pratt called me early this morning with bizarre news. The prints on the knife are a match to one of the juvenile delinquents who attacked Star in the alley. The police arrested him in the middle of the night, and after being confronted with the evidence, namely the knife, he confessed."

"What?" Kyle wrapped a towel around his neck. "I'm not sure those back-alley juvies could hit the water if they fell off a frickin boat, but if the knife-yielding teen had the presence of mind to wear gloves, one would think he would have erased his prints. Besides, as soon as they saw my flare gun, they all skedaddled faster than their shadows. If you ask me, none of them had the balls to drive all the way from Lakewood to get even with Star."

Hauk had raised the same objections, in a less colourful language. "Yes, but the teen told the police he became obsessed with Star after his botched ambush."

"It makes no sense that he confessed to a crime he didn't commit." The sun shone on Arnie's baldhead through the porthole. "We're missing something."

"They checked his arms." Star sat on her cot, hugging her knees against her chest. "He didn't sport any scratches to account for the blood on the broken window. The police think he's covering up for one of his buddies."

"The police are wrong. I'd bet my father's watch that none of his buddies are responsible." Kyle took a swig of his water bottle, his watch in full display on his wrist. "Will they at least run a DNA match with the blood on the glass?"

That question was also raised during their conversation with Pratt, but the answer hadn't impressed Hauk. It still didn't impress him. "They will, but the police need a sample to compare it with. As surprising as it may sound, most of those teens don't have criminal records. The one who was arrested insists that he is guilty, and he refuses to provide a sample."

"I think I know why he may have confessed." The casters on Scott's chair squealed wheeling on the floor. "Last night, during a fight in Lakewood, two men were stabbed, and one is in critical condition at the hospital. If the teen in police custody was involved in the stabbing, his guilty plea to Star's assault in Robert's lot gave him a perfect alibi for the time of the stabbing."

The idea that the teen might serve a few months behind bars for a summary offence and get away with attempted murder while Star's real attacker ran free outraged Hauk. "No one is going to make a mocking of the justice system. Kyle, tell me your dinner with that secretary wasn't a waste of time."

His diver paced the cabin. "To make a long story short, Jaclyn leads an uneventful life and longs for some excitement. She promised to sneak me into the archives room tonight if I bring a friend with me."

His helmsman whistled. "That girl has dangerous fantasies."

"Lucky for her, I'm not a creep." Kyle's wink at Star who rolled her eyes at him.

The friendly moment between his divers didn't escape Hauk. "Which friend?"

Kyle paused by the computer table. "I'm taking Scott with me."

"Me?" Scott's eyes widened in horror. "Why me? I don't want to be stuck in a dark office with a thrill-seeking girl."

"She doesn't bite... that I know of." Kyle slapped Scott with his towel. "Besides, I need you to make sense of those files."

Hauk also questioned the girl's definition of thrill, but they couldn't afford to waste the opportunity to look at those files. "Scott will go with you, right Scott?"

"Sure, boss." The researcher sank in his chair. "It's not like I had other plans for tonight."

"Hopefully, your sacrifice won't be in vain." Hauk appreciated Scott's cooperation, even if it was under duress. "In the meantime, did you find anything on Bruce Robert?"

"I'm having trouble accessing old financial records," his researcher muttered unhappily. "But I uncovered a few interesting tidbits, though it might be as irrelevant as the type of fish swimming under the boat."

"No fishing." Hauk resisted the temptation to grab Kyle's towel and smack Scott with it.

"Six months after the Humphrey murders, Bruce Robert bought a house and opened his auto body shop, but as far as I can tell, he never applied for a mortgage or a commercial loan."

"No loans of any kind?" Those tidbits left an illegal taste in Hauk's mouth. "Where did he get the money? His father?"

"That's where it gets interesting." Scott's enthusiasm resurfaced. "I dug into the society pages again. When Bruce was five years old, his father, Frederick Robert, divorced Bruce's mother to marry his pregnant mistress, Eleanor Watson."

"Who raised Bruce?" Star asked. "Eleanor or the ex-wife?"

"The ex-wife, and she sued her ex-husband on numerous occasions for failure to pay child support. In court, Frederick argued that his new wife, Eleanor, held all the money and properties, making him insolvent." Scott shrugged his bony shoulders. "Apparently, the judge agreed."

"Nice guy." Star's sarcastic remark rang true. "Though it may explain why Frederick Robert embezzled those millions of dollars. He needed the money to run away with his future third wife."

Hauk pinched his chin. "If Frederick never provided for his son, he makes an unlikely candidate to finance Bruce's house or business venture."

"I agree, boss, except for a short article I found about Eleanor and Frederick attending the ribbon cutting ceremony of the auto shop." Scott turned his laptop toward Hauk. "There's even a picture."

The close-up picture, taken during the summer, showed Bruce standing between an older version of himself and a woman in a flowery dress.

Hauk's mind reeled with scenarios, each less probable than the others. "You're telling me that Eleanor somehow contributed to the financing of her stepson's auto shop?"

"I'm saying she held the scissors and cut the ribbon." Scott shifted in his chair to meet Hauk's gaze. "I didn't find any record of a financial transaction."

Another red flag flapped in Hauk's ears. That was one more coincidence among too many. "Keep digging, and take Wowsy with you tonight. It may come in handy."

Chapter 19

Parked in the bushes near the launch ramp, Dusty welcomed the darkening sky, the heavy winds, and the whitecaps over the lake.

The forecast called for a severe thunderstorm over the area. If he successfully timed the detonation with a lightning strike, the storm would take the blame for the explosion.

He stepped into the back of his van, leaving one door open so he could hear any threats before they materialize.

Two full scuba tanks were already strapped to his vest, but only one was connected to the regulator. He rigged a detonator to the spare tank then activated his remote. A red light blinked on the detonator, confirming he acquired the signal.

He placed the remote in a corner so he wouldn't accidently flip the switch while he put on his diving gear.

The noise of an engine reached his ears. He peeked through the bushes.

The male diver and a younger guy disembarked on shore. They tied their Zodiac to a tree and left in the green SUV.

Good timing and good riddance. Having three sets of eyes onboard instead of five lowered Dusty's chances of getting caught.

* * *

Amid the howling wind and Arnie's snoring, Hauk concentrated on Star's harsh breathing. He lay a mere metre away from her, and yet, he felt powerless to alleviate the emotional effects of those resurging memories on her sleeping mind.

A gust of air disturbed his blanket, jolting Hauk.

If not for the opening and closing of the cabin door, he would have missed her departure. He followed her outside.

Star sat on her favourite bench, hugging her knees.

He joined her. "It's raining, havfrue."

"I like rain, and I like diving in currents." She heaved a long sigh. "It's feeling powerless while the river drags me down that I find disturbing. I still cannot fathom how Vanessa and Stella survived. My latest nightmares focus on their ordeal, but not on how they escaped the river."

"Your mind needs to unravel all those forgotten memories. Give it time." Longing for her touch, for the feel of her bare skin, he wrapped her in his arms. "I think we need a new boat."

"New boat?" Her curiosity sounded unleashed. "Why?"

"A boat with two cabins, so you and I can enjoy some privacy onboard." His crew already suspected their relationship. "What do you say? Would you like to go boat shopping with me?"

"I'd like that." Her sultry whisper caressed his neck. "I'd like that a lot."

The rain poured down on them, recreating the steamy shower they had shared at the resort before breakfast. Seeking her lips, he leaned toward her. The boat lurched sideway. Caught off balance, he slipped off the wet vinyl bench and landed on deck with a painful thud.

* * *

Inside the cabin, Star examined Hauk's left wrist.

He didn't complain about pain, but his wrist had swelled too big for the strap of his watch, and he flinched at the slightest touch.

When the boat tossed him off the bench, he broke his fall with his hand. Star was no doctor, and she didn't have x-ray vision, but she suspected a broken bone.

A thunderstorm was looming on the horizon, but it hadn't unleashed its fury yet. She still had time to take him to shore. "I'm taking you to the hospital, Hauk, and before you argue, let me remind you that you would drag me there kicking and screaming if the roles were reserved."

Arnie hiccupped a chuckle. "I'll get you some painkillers for the road, but we're out of anti-inflammatories, and I can't get the ice machine to work, so off you go."

* * *

Star waved Arnie off then steered the Zodiac away from the vessel. Knowing the helmsman, it wouldn't surprise her if he stayed on deck watching them until they reached the shore.

The wind intensified.

Thankful for the spotlight illuminating the course ahead, she headed toward the launch ramp, taking the waves head-on. Unlike her father who often teased her about her pirate sea legs, choppy water had never made her feel seasick.

A sizzling bolt zigzagged in the distance, highlighting their predicament.

Star silently counted the seconds. *One, two, three, four five, six, seven, eight, nine, ten—*

A crack of thunder pierced her ears.

Light travelled faster than sound, roughly one kilometre for every three-second delay, and lighting could strike several kilometres outside the thunderstorm clouds.

At ten seconds, they were about three kilometres from the centre of the storm, but very much within its danger zone. "Hang on," she shouted over Mother Nature's uproar as she pushed the engine to its speed limit.

Hauk sat in front of her, partially shielding her from the gusty rain pricking her face.

Lightning struck again, illuminating the launch ramp and surrounding area, and five seconds later, thunder boomed.

We need to get off the water before we get fried. In normal times, Star would come to shore off the right side of the ramp where the slope wasn't as steep and the grainy terrain didn't grow any bushes, making it easy to pull the Zodiac out of the water.

Tonight, she plowed toward the left of the ramp where the trees concealed a narrow trail leading to the parking pad. The spotlight shone on the large tree guarding the footpath.

The tree grew even larger by the second as the distance between it and the Zodiac shrank in a flash.

"Brace yourself," she shouted, veering and killing the engine within a metre of the tree.

The momentum carried the Zodiac sideways toward the shoreline. She grabbed the rope and jumped off a fraction of second before the Zodiac bumped against the tree.

"You're one top gun pilot," Hauk praised loudly. "That was one heck of a landing."

"I know," she quipped, proud of herself. After pulling the Zodiac as close to the path as possible, she tied the rope to the tree. "How's the wrist?"

"Let's just say the painkillers haven't kicked in yet." He disembarked on his own and stepped away from the water. "You can drive the Jeep."

The storm unleashed more cracking lightning bolts over the lake, electrifying the air around her.

Mesmerized by the loud and electrifying light show, Star gazed at the water. An explosion rocked the night and debris flew in the air, sinking her heart in the pit of her stomach.

Hauk's vessel was engulfed in a ball of fire.

Dazed from the horrific scene, she gaped in shock at the lake, unable to move.

The police vessel sprang to life. Beams of light illuminated the water, and crafts were dispatched toward Hauk's vessel.

"Move up, havfrue." Hauk forced her up the path.

Out of nowhere, an engine roared and sputtered. Seconds later, a vehicle darted out of the bushes onto the access road and sped away.

His good arm wrapped around her waist, Hauk walked her to the Jeep and helped her onto the passenger seat.

Drenched from head to toes, cold inside and out, she shivered.

He draped a blanket over her. "Hold on. I'm cranking the heat up."

Her door closed then his opened. He slipped behind the wheel. The engine came alive, and the vents blew air in the vehicle, air that quickly warmed up.

Through the curtain of rain, she watched the police crafts patrol the water around Hauk's vessel.

He took her hand into his and squeezed hard. "Arnie was on deck when we left. There's a chance he was ejected when the boat exploded."

Hope flickered in her chest. If Vanessa survived, anything was indeed possible. "Arnie is good swimmer, right?"

"Arnie never boasts, but he was on the Irish National Swim Team when he was a young man. So, yes, he was and still is an excellent swimmer." Hauk leaned his shoulder against hers. "He's just not as fast as he used to be."

"Arnie is Irish?" Learning that there was leprechaun luck running in Arnie's veins gave her some unexpected comfort.

"He was born in Nova Scotia to a Canadian father and an Irish mother. Back then, he held dual citizenship. Not sure if he still does."

An ambulance arrived and parked next to the launch ramp. The paramedics pulled out a gurney. Minutes later, a police craft came ashore. A tall and muscular officer wearing a black jacket with *Police* written in white letters, gestured for the medics to approach.

"Stay inside and keep warm. I'll be back." Hauk rushed outside.

* * *

At the sight of the man moaning on the gurney, Hauk expelled a long sigh of relief. "Those guys will take good care of you, Arnie. I'll see you at the hospital."

The female medic turned toward the officer who seemed in charge. "Can we take him?"

The officer sent the ambulance off with a nod, but then he pointed in Hauk's direction. "You're Captain Hauk Ludwig, aren't you? May I have a few words with you and the lady before you leave?"

Unsure what the officer meant by *lady*, Hauk looked left, right, and above his shoulder, only to roll his eyes at the *lady* who sneaked up on him. *Of course you didn't stay in the Jeep. Why am I even surprised?* "I'm guessing he means you, Star."

"Arnie will recover, right?" Her voice was shaky, but some colours had returned to her face.

"I'm no doctor, ma'am, but he was conscious and not missing any body parts when we pulled him out of the water. He said he was the only one onboard." The officer held on to his radio. "Can you confirm so we can stop looking for survivors?"

"Yes, Arnie was the only one onboard." Learning that Arnie had given a coherent answer reassured Hauk. "My other guys are in town."

"Everyone is accounted for." The officer spoke into his radio. "Call off the search."

Eager to get to the hospital, Hauk led Star toward the Jeep.

"We're not done, Mr. Ludwig" The officer followed them. "But I wouldn't mind taking your statements from inside your vehicle. I'm old-fashioned and like to use a pen and a notebook, which is not that convenient in the rain."

"Sure." Once they reached the Jeep, Hauk sat at the back with Star to demonstrate their full cooperation. "What would you like to know?"

The officer turned on the dome light then pulled out a pen and a coiled notepad from inside his jacket. "To start, can you tell me why you were on shore during a thunderstorm in the middle of the night, and not on your vessel?"

"We were on our way to the hospital." Hauk extended his arms between the front seats, showing his wrist. "I slipped on deck."

The officer arched a thick brow. "That looks painful. I'll make it fast so you can join your guy at the hospital. Was your vessel equipped with a lightning protection system?"

Lightning had struck around the same time that his boat exploded, but Hauk was pleased that the officer questioned the chain of events. "Yes, the system was working, and no, we didn't notice anything strange or suspicious, but something blew up my boat and almost killed my helmsman. I doubt it was the storm, and your detective Pratt will likely agree."

"I'm aware of Pratt's investigation." The officer tucked the notepad back into his jacket. "I'm sure Detective Pratt will be in touch."

"Wait." Star gripped the headrest in front of her. "When we near the Jeep, right after the explosion, I heard a vehicle. It came out of the bushes and just zoomed out of here. I couldn't begin to give you a description, but it sputtered. Its muffler was damaged."

"Anything else?" The officer glanced back and forth between them. "Mr. Ludwig?"

"My attention was mostly on Star, but now that I think back, I did see a vehicle speed away." Amazed that Star remembered the vehicle considering her state of mind at the time, Hauk racked his brain for more details. Had it been a white truck, he liked to believe he would have done a double take. "It wasn't a car... it was something bigger like a van, a SUV, or maybe even a truck. Its colour is a blur, but it was dark, not light."

* * *

Star dozed on and off by Arnie's bedside in his semi-private hospital room.

Through the undressed window, the sun shed its weak morning light into the room, but it had yet to wake him or the elderly gentleman in the next bed.

Back at the lake, she didn't notice Arnie's lacerations and burns on his face and arms, but here, she couldn't unsee them anymore than she could overlook the cast on his right leg which was elevated above his heart to help reduce swelling and pain.

He was connected to a monitor, and an intravenous line ran from his left hand to a bag hooked to a pole. His vital signs were normal. In time, he would recover, but his life should never have been in danger in the first place.

"How is he?" If Hauk hadn't spoken, Star wouldn't have realized he entered the room.

"We talked a little bit. He was holding on to the railing, watching us, when he was suddenly thrown overboard by the explosion. He's sure it wasn't lightning, but then a nurse came in and he asked for pain medication. She pumped something in his IV and he fell asleep. On her way out, she told me that visiting hours were over." The nurse hadn't come back yet, so Star waited to be officially kicked out before leaving Arnie's bedside. "You were gone a long time. How's your wrist? What did the doctor say?"

His arm, supported by an elevation sling, was across his chest and his fingertips touched his shoulder. There was a bulge underneath the fabric, but Star couldn't tell if his wrist was immobilized by a cast, a splint, or a bandage.

Hauk leaned against the window. "Badly sprained. It'll be in a splint for a while, but not as long as Arnie's leg will be in a cast, and I get to remove mine when I shower. I'm good to go if you are, but you're driving. I wouldn't pass a drug test right now."

Driving served her purpose. Hauk wouldn't be able to stop her until she reached her destination—assuming her bladder held that long. "Let me go to the bathroom first."

* * *

The radio, tuned to the local station, spilled country songs into the garage while Bruce worked on restoring his truck to its original beauty.

"I timed it perfectly with the lighting. You should have seen it blow up. All the debris flying in the air and landing in the lake." Dusty hadn't stopped bragging for the last ten minutes. "It was spectacular."

The song ended.

"Shut up." Bruce turned the volume up. "I want to hear the news."

I'm your host, Sunny Bluesky, with the morning news.

"Like that's his real name," Dusty mumbled under his breath.

Tragedy struck a research team searching the bottom of Henstridge Lake for buried treasure. Late last night, their vessel exploded after being hit by lightning.

"See!" Dusty gloated again. "I did it."

An ambulance was dispatched to the lake. One man was pulled out of the water alive. He was taken to the hospital where his condition is reported as stable. The fate of the other crew members is unknown, but the search for survivors was called off. According to our source, the police are expected to switch from rescue mode to recovery mode later today.

"Someone survived?" Bruce turned the radio off. "You said they were all dead."

"It's just the bald old guy. Relax. When I heard the ambulance approaching, I pulled off to the side of the road, killed my lights, and waited. Nobody saw me. When the ambulance drove back, I followed it to the hospital. No other ambulance was dispatched. Like the radio just said, he's the only survivor."

* * *

Star drove out of town, passing a few motels along the way. When Hauk didn't react, she glanced at him. He was fast asleep in the passenger seat.

I don't know what drugs they're giving out at the hospital, but they sure do the trick.

The longer Hauk stayed asleep, the longer she could delay telling him since she doubted he would approve of her idea.

It started to rain, and her thoughts grew darker.

No one believed the explosion to be an accident, not even Arnie. If this was another attempt on her life, and she believed it was, the monster had escalated drastically.

"Star?" Hauk stirred in his seat. "Where are we?"

"We're on our way to Jimmy's cabin. Before you argue, I need you to listen. The explosion wasn't an accident, and whoever drove the suspicious vehicle that dashed out had to be involved, or else he wouldn't have fled the scene. If you hadn't sprained your wrist, we would all have been asleep in the cabin when it blew up. None of us would have survived, which is what angers me the most. Whoever set up the explosion doesn't care how many people die as long as I'm one of them. It's the bus accident all over again." Innocent people shouldn't die because of her. "You can't keep me safe from a monster who burns down a house to kill a cockroach, but you and the crew can keep looking for him. I'm counting on you all to help the police catch him. In the meantime, I need to go into hiding. No one followed me. I'll be safe at the cabin."

Silence engulfed the Jeep.

For kilometres on end, the only sound she heard was the sweeping of the wipers across the windshield. Then the rain stopped. "Are you going to say something?"

"I... I wish you were wrong. I wish I'd done a better job at protecting you. I wish I could come up with a better idea. I wish..."

He sighed. "I wish we could just run away
and live happily ever after."

"Me too, but the monster recaptured my
scent." She wouldn't be safe until the
monster was apprehended. Or slain. "I just
have no idea how to tell Jimmy the truth."

Chapter 20

After his morning chat with Bruce, Dusty joined the crowd of nosy onlookers that had congregated near the launch ramp.

The forbidden perimeter on Henstridge Lake was extended to include the area where the lost research vessel was anchored. Police officers aboard Zodiacs collected floating debris while divers dragged the lakebed.

Shortly before four o'clock, an officer stepped on shore. "Good afternoon, everyone. Here's a brief media update. We've opened an investigation to determine the cause of the explosion, but at this early stage, we cannot share any details. However, I can confirm the rumour that we pulled a survivor out of the water and that he was transported to the hospital."

"Any casualties?" someone yelled.

"Not at this time. Thank you for coming. That will be all for today." The officer retreated to his cruiser.

The ambiguous answer left Dusty perplexed. It could mean no bodies had been recovered yet, but it could also mean no one else died except for the old man who might not survive his injuries. *That's not good.*

The crowd began to disperse.

Dusty wandered off the makeshift parking, deep in thought.

The bitchling, the captain, and the old man had to have been onboard. Dusty would have seen them disembark, unless they did so while he was underwater attaching the explosive. *No, they couldn't have disembarked then.* After swimming back to shore, Dusty had surveyed the parking area. If there had been a second Zodiac on shore, he would have seen it. Besides, he vividly recalled Ludwig's Jeep parked underneath a big tree with a half-broken branch, next to a red beater. *Both vehicles were there. Ludwig and the bitchling had to have been onboard.*

The police hadn't recovered their bodies yet. It was the only acceptable explanation.

Hoping karma had hit back during the storm and struck the roof of the Jeep, Dusty looked back over his shoulder at the big tree. The half-broken branch was still half-attached, but the Jeep was gone.

* * *

"Jimmy!" Star searched the cabin. "Jimmy?"

There were no signs of forced entry or struggle. Nothing had been touched in her two bedrooms since the last time she was here.

Jimmy's room on the other hand was uncharacteristically neat. His bed was made. A laundry basket containing folded clothes rested in front of the closet. The photo frames on top of the dresser had been rearranged, prompting her to run a finger over the surface.

She didn't pick up any dust. "This is weird."

Her father hated household chores. Star had never stepped in his bedroom without tripping on a sock, a shirt, or whatever else he took off and left on the floor until laundry day.

"I suppose that rules out burglars, because no one in their right mind would break in only to pick up after Jimmy."

The screen door screeched then banged against the frame. "It's just me."

Glad to hear Hauk's voice, she rushed to meet him in the kitchen. "So? Did you see anything suspicious?"

He peeked inside the refrigerator. "There are fresh veggies. The milk isn't expired. Jimmy can't be far." Once the door closed on its own, Hauk leaned his shoulder against it. "To answer your question, his truck is nowhere on the property, but the garage wasn't locked. Is that unusual?"

"Fixing the lock is on his to-do list." It had been for years. Tackling that list while she was in hiding wouldn't be a bad idea. It would keep her busy. "The house is clean and empty. It shouldn't be that clean and it shouldn't be empty after nightfall." The apprehension she had felt during the entire drive was no longer about telling him the truth. It had switched from fearing for his emotional health to fearing for his life. "Something isn't right."

"Did it occur to you that maybe he's taking advantage of your absence to spend a night in town? That maybe he has a social life you know nothing about? You realize your father isn't a monk, right?" Hauk appeared oblivious to the dubious looks that she threw at him. "I know you're afraid to call him, havfrue, to let details slip over the phone, but would you at least let me contact him before imaging the worst?"

"Sure." Somehow she couldn't picture Jimmy on a bar stool engaged in a sultry conversation with a gorgeous redhead, but the police wouldn't take her seriously if she were to report Jimmy missing without trying to reach him first. "Go ahead."

Hauk used his phone to call Jimmy. "Hey, Jimmy. How are— Yes, Star is fine. She's with me. We're coming for a visit— No, you don't need to rush home— You don't owe me an explanation— It's fine if you're not there when we arrive. Star knows where the towels are." Hauk was a better liar than she would have been. "You, too. Good night."

"So?" From the sound of it, her father was fine, but she wanted details. "Where is he?"

"He's... he's busy wrapping up a case." His steel-blue eyes twinkled with amusement. "He'll be back in the morning."

"At midnight?" Her father was an early bird, not a night owl. "Jimmy never works that late. Where was he? What are you *not* telling me?"

"He didn't say, but I heard muted voices, and soft giggles, in the background. It was probably a television. So..." He wiggled his eyebrows. "Would you get us towels and help me in the shower with my splint?"

"Good deflection, Ludwig." *I was so wrong about you. You are a very lousy liar.* On second thought, she might not want to know the kind of case that Jimmy was wrapping—or unwrapping.

* * *

The morning rays shone through the kitchen window and onto the table where Star sipped on a cup of coffee.

She convinced Hauk to get up at dawn so Jimmy wouldn't catch them in bed together. As it turned out, they could have enjoyed a few more hours of sleep. Her father had yet to come home.

"Remember, this is my old laptop. It's slow, way slower than the one that is resting in pieces, not peace, at the bottom of the lake." She had logged in for him, but now she waited for him to type in the name of a website using only one hand. "Are you trying to get to your insurance website?"

"No, I will call them in person later this morning. And yes, you will get a new computer." Boats appeared on the screen. Hauk pointed at a blue boat on the lower left corner. "What do you think of this one?"

"I like the colour, but it looks big." Star leaned her head against his shoulder to get a better view. "Where are the specs?"

"Coming..." Upon clicking on the picture of the boat, he scrolled down to its characteristics. "Here."

A characteristic instantly caught her eyes. "A hot tub? Okay, I'll admit it would be very nice to soak in a tub every night, but you're buying a research vessel, not a cruise ship. A tub, hot or cold, is a waste of space and money."

"*I am not* buying a research vessel, havfrue." He kissed the top of her head. "*We are buying* it together."

The back door opened as the words sank in.

Her father walked in, smiling. "That's what I call a great surprise."

"Jimmy." Glad to see him safe and sound, Star welcomed him with a huge hug. "I missed you."

"Missed you too, squirt." He looked her up and own with inquisitive eyes. "I don't see any new bruises, but are you all right?"

"Let's just say a lot happened, but first why don't you take a seat at the table? I'll bring you a coffee." Her father would need one to hear what she had to say, and she would need a second cup to say it. *Today would be a good day to start drinking something stronger.*

"Nice to see you again, Jimmy." Hauk got up to shake Jimmy's hand.

"Morning, Hauk. What's with the sling? Any bad chance it's part of the reason you're both here?" Her father took the seat that Star had occupied a few moments ago. "And why are you looking at boats?"

Jimmy appeared to have connected the dots, but it didn't sound like the news of the explosion had reached his ears yet.

"It's a long story." Star placed a steaming mug of coffee in front of him. "Careful, it's hot."

"Thanks, squirt." He wrapped his hands around his mug. "I'm listening."

Unable to stand still, Star paced the kitchen while Hauk recounted the events leading up to them fleeing here. Her father stared back and forth between them, his expression sobering up with each new detail that Hauk unveiled.

"That's about it." Hauk closed the lid of her laptop, as if to physically bring finality to the story. "We're not one hundred percent sure of Star's real identity, but she isn't your sister's daughter."

"I... I've always suspected there was something different, something special about you, squirt." Jimmy approached her, stopping her in her tracks in the middle of the kitchen. "You never resembled Ella, or anyone else on the Fisher side. I assumed you looked like your birth father, but deep down I think I've always known you weren't my niece, but it doesn't matter. You are my daughter, and you will always be my daughter." He wrapped her in his arms. "And I love you with all my heart. I'm just so sorry I took you from your rightful family."

"Please don't be sorry." She hugged him back with all her might. "You're my father, the one who protected me for twenty years." Tears streamed down her cheek. "If not for you, I would have died with Stella. She saved my life."

"For many years, too many years, I was angry at Ella for neglecting you, for staying behind, but learning she sacrificed her life to save yours brings me closure." Jimmy stoked her back, holding her close. "She now rests in peace with her little boy, and I will forever be grateful for the wonderful gift she gave me. You."

Hauk couldn't have anticipated a better outcome. His fondness for the man that he longed to call his father-in-law would have reached a new high if he wasn't already totally fond of the man who raised such an amazing woman.

Back at the table, Jimmy sipped on his cup of coffee. "There's something I don't understand. Why didn't Ella report the murders right away?"

This was an excellent question, one for which Hauk wished he could provide a logical answer. "When you picked up Star, did Ella say anything that could help identify the man terrifying her?"

Jimmy shook his head sadly. "You have no idea how much I regret not paying more attention to her incoherent babblings. Ella was afraid of him, that much I remember, and I got the feeling she knew him."

A deluge of questions crossed Hauk's mind. *Did Ella know him, or did she recognize him from somewhere? A known acquaintance or a familiar stranger? Could he have been a john? A tenant from the same apartment building? A thug she occasionally met on her way to church? Or maybe someone she met at the Humphreys? She'd only worked for the Humphreys a few days. The likelihood she met the killer in their house was slim but not impossible.*

Could it explain why she was afraid to go to the police?

"Hauk?" The woman who stood behind him placed her hands on his shoulders. "I can hear the wheels spinning in your head."

"I'm thinking of the places from where Ella might have known her killer. I'll get Scott on it. In the meantime..." Hauk reached behind his chair and pulled onto his lap the only woman who had ever been able to read his mind. "It is imperative that you stay out of sight. No one can know you're hiding here. I'll be back in a week at the latest."

Jimmy leaned forward. "Don't worry, Hauk, I'll keep her out of trouble."

"Trouble finds her no matter where she hides, Jimmy." Amused by her feigned indignation, Hauk kissed the adorable pout on her lips. "Just stay safe, havfrue. You mean everything to me."

* * *

Dusty shook the portable receiver, but no amount of shaking got the blinking dot to appear on the small screen. He had lost the tracking signal of the Jeep.

The radio frequency tracking device didn't use Bluetooth or GPS, making it that much more difficult for anyone to detect, but its range was limited to sixty kilometres.

Someone either discovered the device and disabled it, or the Jeep is out of range. Both scenarios equally enraged Dusty.

In need of a diversion, he cruised the streets in search of his favourite hookers. At sunset, he spotted Vixen on the corner.

His blood pumping down, he stopped at the green light and lowered the window. "Get in."

She sat in his dirty passenger seat. "The usual?" Her miniskirt bunched up at her crotch. "Why is there a blinking light? You're not recording me, are you?"

"What light?" He followed her gaze to the middle console where he had put down the receiver. A red dot blinked at the edge of the screen. "Get out!"

The timing sucked, but now that he reacquired the signal, Dusty had to check who drove the Jeep around.

He followed the signal and ended up across the street from the hospital.

The Jeep was parked in a visitor space underneath a lamppost. The driver's door opened.

Dusty held his breath.

A tall silhouette stepped out, looked up, then walked toward the entrance.

Upon recognizing Ludwig's face, Dusty cursed like a drunken sailor on shore leave. The captain still was alive, but the ugly bitchling was nowhere in sight.

* * *

With its purple doors and red bricks, the two-storey motel had to be the ugliest building that Hauk had ever seen, but it was conveniently located within a block of the police station.

He entered a suite on the second floor and frowned. The carpet was littered with cartons of takeout. "Did a bomb also explode in here? Or do they clean only once a week?"

"Glad to have you back, boss." Propped against a pillow, Kyle decreased the volume of the television. "Arnie told us about the lucky broken wrist that saved all your lives, but he didn't mention the fashionable sling. Where's the kid?"

"First, it's a sprain, not a break. Second, Arnie didn't know about the sling until I visited him an hour ago." Hauk was glad to have stopped by the hospital before coming here. Seeing his helmsman awake and alert had lessened his worries. "He told me you two took turns visiting him. In case you wonder, he did appreciate it."

Seated at a round table near the window, Scott peeked over his laptop. "We gathered that much."

"Good. And third, Star went home. Her father will protect her while we unearth the truth. So, did you accomplish anything productive during my absence?"

The smug smile on his researcher's face boded well. "The evening we spent in that archives room was worth every second, but I'll admit that reading the legal lingo was a challenge. I thought only lawyers took five pages to say one sentence, but that was before I met insurance guys. I had to call a girl I know. She's finishing law school. She's... not important. As I was saying, we found a life insurance policy issued for Mary Watson the day she got married. Her husband was named the beneficiary."

That was standard practice as far as Hauk knew. "But she never officially died. Was the payout ever made?"

"Within weeks of her disappearance, Banker Watson presented a claim, but without a death certificate, it was rejected. The insurance company informed him they wouldn't pay until the expiration of the seven-year presumption of death clause."

Watson didn't wait before getting a new wife, so Hauk had trouble picturing him waiting years for anything. "Are you telling me he waited seven years?"

"No." Scott shrugged. "He never collected the money."

Confused, Hauk sat at the foot of the bed. "What do you mean by *never*? Watson was a banker, and bankers don't forget about money paid or money owed."

"Ten thousand dollars was a lot of money back then." Kyle added a second pillow behind his back. "It must have hurt giving it up, but I guess it wasn't worth claiming it if it meant landing in jail."

"Jail?" His crew had unearthed something, but Hauk was at a loss to understand the ramifications. "Would you two start making sense, please?"

"I need my notes." Papers fell to the floor as Scott searched the table for the right paper. "Here it is. Back in 1912, after being fired for misconduct, a disgruntled bank employee alleged that Banker Watson fabricated his wife's lover story, killed her, and then disposed of her body in the lake in order to steal her fortune." The allegations rang true. "The employee had already been fired from two other institutions, and on each previous occasion, he'd attempted to blackmail his former employer into rehiring him." Scott lifted his gaze from his papers. "In light of the employee's past, and lack of evidence, the police questioned his credibility and deemed the accusations insubstantial."

"It's unfortunate the employee lacked moral character." Still, Hauk wished that the police had dug deeper. "Please continue."

"The investigation should have ended there, but it didn't. An adjustor for the insurance company heard of the allegations." Scott returned the paper to the stash on the table. "I'm guessing something didn't sit well with him because he attached a note to the policy recommending further investigation before any payment was made."

"You think the banker didn't claim the money because he was afraid a second investigation might reveal evidence that were missed the first time around?" Hauk understood unnecessary risks. "I'm not disagreeing, but what makes you think that Adrian Humphrey found that note?"

"It was attached in full view." Kyle tossed the remote control in the air. "Humphrey wouldn't have missed it, and it wouldn't have taken him long to suspect that his wife's grandmother was murdered, not that it explained the killing of his own family."

Scott pressed his hands together. "According to the disgruntled employee's allegations, Banker Watson was after Mary's fortune, so I extended my search. The banker married rich. The money and properties belonged to his wife Mary, not him. Logically, the estate should have passed down to Mary's son, not to the banker's second son."

Kyle swung his feet over the side of the bed and stood. "Scott's girl in law school, her dad is a lawyer. He agreed to look up Mary's will, if he can find it. It may be irrelevant, but we're curious to know if or why Watson cheated his first son out of his inheritance."

Relevant or not, Hauk agreed that it begged for answers. "Great job, you two."

Chapter 21

Star welcomed the isolation her home offered, though there had been times growing up when she wished for neighbours so she could have playmates.

The few families living around the lake were concentrated at the other end. If she squinted hard enough, she could make out their colourful red or orange roofs amid the green leaves. And in the winter, she could see the smoke rising from their chimneys over the treetops.

Her new diving suit, a custom drysuit she ordered from the dive shop months ago, had finally arrived. Jimmy picked it up, and she spent the week testing it in the lake.

After surfacing near the floating dock, she glanced toward the cabin and was surprised to see an empty lawn chair in the shade of the boathouse.

Jimmy should have been watching her, not pacing in front of the kitchen window with his phone against his ear. In the last few days, he had received many secretive calls, and Star ached to know who, or what, had captured his attention.

She tossed her fins on the dock before climbing the swaying ladder. By the time she shed her drysuit and entered the kitchen, any hope of eavesdropping on his conversation died.

Jimmy sat at the table, seemingly deep in thought. "Is it serious between you and Hauk?"

The sudden inquiry surprised her. "I think so."

"You think so?" Jimmy scratched his chin. "Aren't you talking to him every morning, afternoon, and evening since his departure?"

Heat rushed into her face. How Jimmy managed to be privy to her conversations when she couldn't even figure out the identity of his mysterious caller was another mystery she couldn't elucidate. "Hauk asked me to stay with him on his new boat."

Hands flat on the table, Jimmy studied her. "Do you love him?"

She acknowledged the question with a timid nod. After spending years hiding her heartache, it felt strange to admit she had finally found someone who truly loved her back.

"So what's the problem, squirt?"

Deep down, she worried about Jimmy's welfare if he lived alone, not that she could tell him without hurting his pride. "If I leave, you'll need another associate, and..."

"Are you hesitating because of me?"

Of course I am. "Well..."

He took her hand in his and forced her to sit beside him. "Listen, I raised you to fly toward your own destiny. I'd be an old fool to stand between you and the man that your heart has chosen as travel companion."

He was the best father that she could have dreamed of having. "Are you sure you'll be okay if I leave?"

"Yes, squirt. You and Hauk have my blessing. Next time he calls, put the poor, love-struck guy out of his misery and tell him you accept, okay?"

Love swelled inside her heart. She rose to give him a hug. "Thank you."

"I love you." He kissed her forehead. "Now, there's something I need to tell you."

* * *

Dusty stepped into the garage, holding an injured fox by the back of its neck.

The truck was gone, but the words *Find Her* were written in white paint on the wooden workbench. Infuriated by the message, Dusty slammed the door.

His dog growled at the end of its chain.

Dusty tossed the fox on the ground. When the limping animal reached the edge of the woods, he unchained his dog. "Go catch it, Fang."

While Fang fetched its food, Dusty entered his old, dilapidated house. The air

311

felt hot and sticky, and he cursed the broken air-conditioning that hadn't functioned in years.

Fisher. The name evoked scorn and hatred. Dozens and dozens of Fishers lived in the region, but no Star Fisher.

The online phone lookup proved as useless as the old telephone directory he kept in a kitchen drawer.

He sat at the table with a cold beer. The newspaper that he had shown to Bruce rested underneath a dirty plate. Had Dusty not seen her picture, they would never have known she survived.

"There was an article attached to that picture." He took the newspaper, read the article again, and smirked.

Ludwig had recruited the ugly bitchling at the Northern Ballard Institute.

* * *

Star had no idea that Jimmy had thought of retiring from the investigation business since the ambush cost him his diving career. "I can't believe you only kept our family venture alive because of me. Why didn't you tell me?"

His shoulders rose slightly. "I didn't want you to land on some company's payroll and be miserable."

While she appreciated his thoughtfulness, she wished he had been honest with her. "And how will you afford to live?" His meek savings were far from sufficient to ensure him a comfortable life, unless he hid money from her. Lots of money.

"Maggie and I were talking—"

"Maggie? Who's Maggie?" The name Maggie didn't ring a bell. On the other hand, Star knew a Margaret who lived at the end of the lake. "Are we talking about Josh's mother?"

Last summer, Josh, a twelve-year-old devil, drove his mother's car down the family boat ramp, and the investigation landed on Star's plate.

"Josh's father died during a hunting accident two years ago." Jimmy had mentioned the hunting accident at one point, but Star didn't recall the details. "During the winter, the boy started misbehaving again, and his behaviour has grown worse since he finished school. Josh is seeking attention, and Maggie struggles between raising him and managing the daily operation of the retirement village that she and her late husband owned. So I stepped in. I take Josh fishing and hiking. I play handyman at the village." The enthusiasm in his voice was unmistakable. "Last week, she offered me the manager position."

"And?" Star was happy for him. "Are you hesitating because of me?"

He chuckled. "Very funny, squirt."

"So why the long face when I came in?" She sincerely hoped that Maggie didn't withdraw her offer.

"It's Josh." A long sigh deflated Jimmy's chest. "He pulled another prank on his mom. Maggie took him to the retirement village this morning. While she dealt with a tenant, she left him alone in her office. From the drawer of her desk, Josh gathered all the spare keys to all the rooms, brought them home in his backpack, and threw them in the lake."

Laughter bubbled inside Star's throat. "Not funny, I know."

"Maggie isn't laughing, but it is kind of funny. Anyway, Maggie is wondering if you could possibly dive and retrieve them."

Surprised by the request, Star stared at him. "Does she know I'm here? Did you tell her?"

"Well..."

Understanding dawned on Star. "You were with her when Hauk called you the night we arrived." *That was what Hauk wasn't telling me.* "She was the case you were *wrapping up.*"

"Well..." Heat rose to his face. "I wouldn't put it quite like that."

In all her years, Star had never seen him so flustered. "And when were you going to tell me about her?"

"Eventually."

"Sure," she teased.

"Squirt, you can count on Maggie's discretion, and her neighbours are gone for the week."

"Sounds good to me." Star welcomed the diversion. The challenge would occupy her body and mind for a few hours. "But we need to make a stop by the dive shop to refill my bottles."

"I'll go right now while you prep your equipment."

* * *

Fourteen minutes was all it took Dusty to break and enter the Northern Ballard Institute, look at the divers' personal files, and leave without triggering any alarms.

There was only one Fisher, a S. Fisher, and a PO Box address in a town he had never heard of. According to the newspaper article, the ugly bitchling was called Star. It stood to reason that S. Fisher was Star Fisher.

Before embarking on a wild-goose chase, Dusty browsed the internet for dive shops in the area. If anyone knew where Fisher lived, it would be the local dive shop's employees.

He found two shops and dialed the first one.

"Under Water, how may I help you?" The cheerful female voice sounded young and fresh, like Dusty liked them.

"I have a purchase order for a Star Fisher." It had taken Dusty a few minutes to come up with a believable story. "She requested home delivery but the guy who took the order wrote your shop address instead of Fisher's. Any chance you can help me?"

"Are you sure she requested home delivery? Star usually picks her orders here. Mind you I haven't seen her lately, but her father Jimmy came earlier to refill her scuba tanks." The *her* in *her* scuba tanks didn't escape Dusty. "Hold on, sir, I'll check if we have her address on file."

Thrilled that he succeeded to locate the bitchling on his first attempt, Dusty waited impatiently for the information that would seal her fate.

"Sir, we only have her postal address on file. I'm sorry."

"Don't be. I assumed my guy wrote the address wrong, but now I'm thinking he checked the home delivery box by mistake. He's new and not good at his job yet." Dusty feigned a chuckle to cover the alleged mix-up. "You said her father just refilled her tanks. Is he also a diving enthusiast?"

"He stopped diving a few years back, but he's still a regular client. If you ship Star's order to us, I'll make sure she gets it."

If the father no longer dove, the tanks he refilled weren't meant for his personal use. The information warranted a trip north.

* * *

Hauk had just finished talking to Star when Kyle barged into the motel room following his meeting with the law student and her father.

"Boss, you'll love this." Kyle slammed the door and kicked his shoes. "And if you ask me, she suspected the bastard big time."

The shoes landed against the leg of Scott's table. "I hope you're talking about Mary Watson."

"Of course I am. I didn't go meet that lawyer for nothing." Kyle glanced at Scott who ate pizza at his desk. "The daughter is cute. She's—"

"Focus, would you?" Sometimes Hauk wanted to shake the two men. "You can fill in Scott later."

His diver sat on the bed closest to the window. "After the birth of her son, Mary changed her will in the boy's favour and gave guardianship of her estate to her parents until Samuel turned twenty-one."

"She disinherited her husband?" *Nothing like a scorned woman.* It pained Hauk to remember he had also known such women.

The pizza in Scott's hand dripped sauce down his hand. "Watson should have killed her while she was pregnant."

317

"Wrong," Kyle corrected. "If she'd died before producing a child, her fortune would have gone back to her parents."

"So what went wrong?" Despite her lack of success, Hauk applauded Mary's efforts to protect her son. "How did the banker end up with her fortune?"

"Very simple, boss. With his wife missing but not dead, he kept managing Mary's affairs until she was declared deceased seven years later. During those long seven years, he slowly transferred Mary's fortune to his new wife. By the time Mary was *officially* dead, and her will was unsealed, there was hardly any money left in her name to give to her son. The grandparents ended up with Samuel who was robbed of his inheritance."

This was a vicious takeover, but Hauk had to admit that it was brilliantly orchestrated. Still, a detail gnawed at him. "Scott, how did the banker legally remarry if his first wife Mary wasn't legally dead?"

"I recall reading something about it. Give me a sec." The researched dug through his notes tucked under the pizza box. "He was granted a divorce based on the allegations of his wife's infidelity."

The irony that the banker had more than likely fabricated those allegations didn't escape Hauk. "He kept managing Mary's affairs after the divorce, and the grandparents never opposed him?"

Scott shrugged. "The grandparents might not have been aware of the content of Mary's will until it was read seven years later. By then, it would have been too late to save Mary's fortune. Or maybe they didn't fight the banker because they thought the lover was real and they were ashamed of their daughter's behaviour."

"If you ask me, boss, the bastard planned his wife's murder to the last detail." No love was lost in Kyle's voice for the conniving banker. "With no statute of limitations on murder, if Adrian could prove Mary Watson was killed by her husband the night of her disappearance, it might give Amy Humphrey and her children a claim on Mary's fortune, which Eleanor Watson shouldn't have inherited because it never belonged to her father Erwin in the first place."

"And that could give Eleanor Watson a financial reason to kill, or arrange the killings of Mary's descendants," Scott continued. "We already suspect that her former stepson Bruce is involved. We have a strong motive, but we haven't connected all the dots yet. In the meantime, there's a big red target painted on Star's back. Do we know for sure that she's the surviving twin? Because whoever is trying to kill her seems convinced she is Vanessa, Mary's great-granddaughter, unless... unless we're barking at the wrong tree, in the wrong forest, in the wrong province, in the wrong—"

"Relax, Scott. You're doing great. You're both doing great." His crew went above and beyond the call of duty, and Hauk couldn't be prouder of the way they handled themselves and the situation. "The DNA results haven't come back yet, but if Star isn't Vanessa, we have an even greater mystery to solve, so let's not go there yet. For your theory about Eleanor's motive to stand on two legs, we need to prove that she knew her grandfather killed his first wife."

"But she bribed you to bury the discovery of the wreck," Scott argued. "She had to know we'd find Mary's remains."

"Yes, Eleanor bribed me." Hauk didn't dispute that fact. "But the reasons behind her actions are speculation. We need concrete evidence to tie Eleanor to the murders. This morning I saw Bruce driving his white truck. It looked fine to me."

Visibly frustrated, Kyle pulled a new shirt from a shopping bag and changed. "He had plenty of time to fix it."

The same thought had crossed Hauk's mind. "I know, Kyle, I—"

"Boss!" Scott's excitement electrified the air. "Don't ask how I found out, but Bruce Robert has a juvenile record."

* * *

To Dusty's growing frustration, the damn postal address didn't help narrowing down where the bitchling lived.

Stopped at a gas station, he racked his brain for a way to inquire about the Fishers without raising suspicion.

In a grassy field bordered by the remnants of a rusty barbed wire fence, three unsupervised boys poked sticks into burrows.

Hoping one of them heard of the Fishers, Dusty walked to the fence and leaned against a rotten post to light up a cigarette. "You'll get the gopher angry, boys, and it'll chomp your arm off."

The boys exchanged dubious looks only to ignore his advice.

Dusty blew smoke rings in the air. "Can one of you tell me where old Jimmy Fisher lives?"

The chubby kid wearing a red shirt and blue shorts lifted his head. "Why? You lost?"

"Just want to know how dumb you all are." The boys were cocky, reminding Dusty of his younger self. Insulting them should prevent them from telling their parents that they talked to a stranger.

"I ain't dumb." The boy whipped his stick in the air. "Fisher lives by the lake."

"The lake?" Dusty pointed randomly in one direction. "And you gonna tell me I'm supposed to take that road down?"

The freckled boy picked his nose and laughed. "That's the road to the cemetery."

"You have to turn after the ice cream stand to get to the lake." The littlest one puffed out his chest. "Everybody knows that."

* * *

When the outboard motor refused to start, Star remoored the motorboat inside the boathouse. She had had trouble with it all week, but today it sputtered and died before she even cleared the dock.

"I took you apart in the spring and barely used you. You should still roar like a polar bear." Kneeling at the back of the boat, she locked the motor in the upright position then pulled on the latch to remove the cowling. To her surprise, the latch was jammed. "What's wrong with you?" She took a closer look and groaned. The cowling wasn't properly aligned. The seal was damaged and somehow it got caught in the latch. "How on earth did that even happen?"

Jimmy taught her how to maintain and service a boat engine before he taught her how to drive a car. No one else but them touched that motor, and Jimmy was as meticulous as she was. Someone else fiddled with it, and only one name crossed her mind.

Her aggravation growing by the second, she fetched her toolbox, brought it on board, and grabbed a flathead screwdriver. She wiggled it into the latch, ended up stripping the seal, but managed to slide the cowling off. At first sight, it didn't appear that water had infiltrated the motor. Still, she spotted something that didn't belong. A dead leaf.

"Breathe, Star. Breathe." She checked the fuel filter and frowned. It looked worse than the one she replaced in the spring. "That isn't possible." Her growing suspicion prompted her to unscrew the spark plugs. The first one looked almost new, but then she glared at the second one. "Jimmy!"

He rushed into the boathouse. "Squirt? Are you all right?"

"The engine won't start. Look at that old spark plug." Madder than a nesting Canada goose, Star tossed the corroded spark plug at him. "Want to guess where I found it? In place of the new one I replaced a few months back, and it's not even the same brand. Want me to throw the old fuel filter clogging the line at you too? You let Ralph borrow the boat, didn't you?"

"I..." The colour drained from Jimmy's face. "He only borrowed it for an hour or so."

"An hour sounds about right." Every time Jimmy lent something to his obnoxious friend, she ended up fixing it, to the point she refused to let Ralph borrow anything. That he took advantage of her absence, and her father's kinder disposition, enraged her. "That's about how long it would have taken him to remove the cowling, pilfer the parts he needed, leave behind a dead leaf, and damage the seal while quickly relatching the cowling improperly."

"I'm not sure what to say, squirt, aside from I'm sorry. I know Ralph doesn't always return what he borrows right away, but we've been friends since we were kids." His gaze was directed toward the spark plug in his hands. "I've never seen him steal parts before. I would have given him new ones if only he'd asked."

Of course you would have. Star sighed. For better or worse, Jimmy was a great friend and a great dad. "This is what we're going to do. You'll go to the store, get me a new fuel filter, new spark plugs." She might as well change both, but now she understood why the fuel tank was almost empty when Jimmy swore it was full, and why Ralph stole only one spark plug. If he had switched both with old ones, the motor wouldn't have started, and Jimmy would have noticed right away that something was wrong. The realization that Ralph knew exactly what he was doing worsened her terrible mood. "I also need a new cowl seal, and fuel because he nearly emptied the tank. Then when I'm done fixing that motor, I will send him a bill for parts and labor, and if he doesn't pay, I'll file a claim in small claims court."

"I agree, squirt. Ralph went too far this time. I'll deal with him. I promise." Jimmy's palpable disappointment and indignation marked a change in his attitude toward his friend. "In the meantime, I'll go to the store and get you what you need. Will you be okay alone?"

"I'll finish cleaning the motor, then while I wait for the parts, I'll go for a swim." She moved her toolbox from the back seat to the middle one, so she wouldn't accidentally knock it over. "I'll be fine. I promise you won't need to bail me out of jail for wringing Ralph's thick neck."

Chapter 22

The door of the houseboat creaked.

"I thought you were going to the store right away." Star tossed the incriminating used parts in her toolbox. "Did you forget anything?"

His steps grew closer.

Surprised by Jimmy's silence, she looked up and froze.

A tall stranger stood on dock, pointing a rifle at her. His long, emaciated face, thin lips, and eyes were filled with hatred. "Hands up or I shoot you like an animal."

A jackhammer pounded inside her chest. "Who are you?"

"Your worst nightmare, ugly bitchling." The cold gaze sent chills between her shoulder blades. "Get out."

She glanced around for a makeshift weapon. "What do you want with me? I can scream."

"Sure you can." A smirk distorted his mouth. "And I promise you will, but no one will hear you."

Jimmy? Where are you? "If I were you, I'd leave before my father finds you."

"Your old man won't be back for a while."

Tremors rippled under her skin. The stranger wouldn't know about Jimmy being gone unless he had been watching her—or he had already silenced Jimmy.

"Don't you love remote cabins? So private." His guttural laughter contorted his hideous expression. "Move."

The lust in his eyes gave her the distinct impression that the depraved predator wanted her alive.

"Come and get me, creep." If she could lure him inside the boat, she might be able to trip him into the water.

The breeze wafted in, carrying his scent, a pungent, musky odour, the same musky odour she had—

"I said *move*." He brandished the rifle, and his sleeve bunched up his forearm, exposing a tattoo partly hidden by a dirty bandage.

A small gasp that she couldn't control escaped her lips.

"I either kill you now and wait to finish off your old man, or you come with me, and I let him live." He sneered. "Your choice."

Allowing her to see his face denoted his ultimate intention of killing her. To survive, she needed to buy time.

"Please." She purposely let him hear the tremors in her voice to give him a false sense of superiority. "Don't shoot."

His nostrils flared. "Nice and easy."

As she disembarked, she knocked over her toolbox with her foot. Her tools clunked as they landed at the bottom of the boat.

"Get moving." He poked her in the shoulder with the barrel of his rifle. "We're going into the woods."

The deserted path through the woods presented no escape. The shorts and sandals she wore offered meager protection for her bare legs and feet from the low twigs and thorny bushes obstructing the trail.

A shot was fired into the bushes. She jolted.

He laughed at her instinctive reaction. "Walk faster before I change my mind and slaughter you here."

"Why..." The terror she experienced at night every time she relived the nightmare surfaced in broad daylight, feeding her survival instincts. "Why me?"

"You cheated fate," he scoffed. "You should have drowned. Now shut up and walk."

Her temper worsened with every step she took, with every new scratch tearing her skin. She loathed the monster for robbing her of her family and belittling her existence. Her breathing grew heavier from the anger and hatred boiling inside her.

A dark blue utility van with no markings waited in a clearing. The make and model automatically registered in her mind.

The monster opened the left back door. The inside of the van had been stripped, and an opaque partition separated the cargo area from the passenger cabin.

"Jump in or die here."

The metal floor was slippery, and she fell to her knees.

He threw a pair of handcuffs at her. "Cuff one hand in it."

Under the pressure of her own fingers, the cold metal closed around her left wrist.

"Attach the other end to a hook on the wall."

Last fall, Star had gutted the cargo area of a similar van and found the jack compartment hidden in the sidewall. As she slowly looked around, she searched her memory for which sidewall.

"Pick a hook, or a bullet."

Shaking from fear and anger, she chose a low anchor on the right side.

He slammed the door and plunged her into darkness.

* * *

At the police station, Hauk stared in awe at the DNA results laid out on the table.

Detective Pratt, who had taken over the Humphrey case, on top of the Model T investigation, sat in front of him. "I can see you weren't absolutely sure yourself."

More astounded than he cared to admit, Hauk took a deep breath. "It made perfect sense, but at the same time, it seemed unfathomable for the twin to have survived." The innocuous piece of paper proved beyond any shadow of a doubt that Vanessa had beaten the odds and grown into an amazing woman.

"Where is Miss Fisher?"

"With her father at their cabin by the lake." Hauk's cell phone vibrated in his pocket. The number on the screen drew a smile on his face. "It's Star. Do you mind if I answer?"

"Go ahead."

"What's up, havfrue? I'm with—"

"Her toolbox was knocked down." Jimmy screamed into the phone. "Her phone was at the bottom of the boat with her tools. She's gone, Hauk."

The blood chilled inside Hauk's veins. "What do you mean Star is gone?"

"I left her alone and he took her." Jimmy's voice broke down. "The monster found her."

Aghast, Hauk met Pratt's gaze. "Star was kidnapped."

* * *

Closing her mind to the darkness surrounding her, Star sought the peace she experienced when she dove alone at the bottom of a dark lake. Slowly, the fear that had threatened to consume her receded, allowing her to focus on her situation.

The loss of her sight enhanced her other senses. The muffler rattled. It was the same muffler she heard the night that Hauk's vessel exploded. That couldn't be a coincidence. The monster had to have been involved one way or another, but she refused to dwell on the reasons why he hadn't killed her yet. His decision to keep her alive gave her a chance to orchestrate his downfall or die trying.

I didn't survive falling in a river to die in an unmarked van. If only one of us escapes this situation alive, it will be me.

The handcuff cut through her skin with every bump on the dirt road. Tossed around like a puppet, Star bit back the gasps of pain swelling inside her throat. She wouldn't give him the satisfaction of knowing he was hurting her.

The tires hit the asphalt. Taking advantage of the smoother ride, she stretched her arm and skimmed the wall with her fingers until she felt the narrow groove surrounding the side panel. Then with her fingertips, she traced the indentation to the latch and turned it counterclockwise to access the jack compartment.

The van swayed. The panel slipped from her fingers and landed on her foot. Screeching in pain, she crouched down and rubbed her throbbing toe through the straps of her sandal. A warm, wet substance smeared her fingers.

Swell, now I'm bleeding. The blood and the aching pain further fuelled her determination. She probed the inside of the wall, swearing she would make him regret not killing her when he had a chance. Her hope of finding a lug wrench or a tire iron sank in the pit of her stomach. *It can't be empty. It just can't...*

Driving by desperation, she scraped the bottom of the compartment for a wire or a nail that she could use to pick the lock. While not an expert, she knew enough about locking mechanisms to recognize a strong lock from a cheap version. The handcuff around her wrist belonged to the second category.

Her fingernails scratched a rugged metallic object partly stuck at the juncture of the floor. Unsure what she found, but thinking it could come handy to defend herself, she yanked on it. A thick, heavy pipe broke free, and she fell backwards. The cuff dug into her upper hand and broke her fall in an agonizing shriek. Still, she held on to the pipe.

Once the pain subsided, she probed both ends of her newfound weapon and smiled. *A crowbar.*

* * *

Hauk's first reaction was to rush out of the police station and drive to the cabin, but Pratt stopped him.

"Listen, Ludwig, our only chance to find her alive is to find her kidnapper." The detective assumed she was still alive, and Hauk wanted to believe him. "If you want to help, just sit tight and give me a few minutes."

Hoping to shake the overwhelming feeling of powerlessness weighing on him, Hauk paced Pratt's office while the detective ordered roadblocks and coordinated search units with the local police.

"Now please sit back. I want you to look at some pictures." Pratt handed him a tablet. "All these guys have some sort of bird tattoos on their forearms."

"I already told you, Pratt. I didn't see the guy." Hauk's patience ran thin. "Star is the only one who saw his tattoo."

"I'm not asking you to identify him, Ludwig, but I'm thinking the killer shadowed her for a while if he was able to locate her at her cabin. You may have seen him without knowing you saw him, so I want you to tell me if any of them look familiar."

* * *

Angry, frustrated, and tired, Hauk stormed into his motel room after spending the evening at the police station. Without giving a second thought to the travelers who might be sleeping, he slammed the door. "In this country, criminals possess more rights than their victims."

Seated in front of his laptop, Scott rubbed his eyes. "Boss?"

Hauk sat on the closest bed and dropped his head into his hands. "Why did I let her out of my sight?"

"Sending her home sounded like the right thing to do at the time." Scott lowered the intensity of his screen. "Any updates?"

"The police suspended the search of the forest for the night. They'll resume at dawn and extend the search area."

According to Jimmy, the police had searched the woods and divers had swept the lake near the cabin. There were no signs of Star. She had vanished without a trace.

In the meantime, there was nothing to do but wait.

"Her father blames himself when he should blame me. I swore to protect her, Scott. She's the missing twin, the only witness to her family's massacre. I should have known that once the murderer became aware she survived, he would track her down to finish what he started."

"From where I sit, Hauk, this is good news." Never in his life had Scott called him by his first name. "If they haven't found her yet, it can only mean she's still alive."

Alive, but for how long? And what is he doing to her? Rage choked Hauk, but he couldn't let rage cloud his mind or judgment, not when Star counted on him to rescue her. "Pratt placed Bruce Robert under surveillance, and he's looking into his past for criminal connections, but he's not having better luck than you. Robert's juvenile record is sealed. If Pratt can't prove Robert is involved, he doesn't get access, which means he can't cross-reference for former accomplices."

"After you called from the station, Kyle and I bounced around some ideas. Star was shot in the same alley in which Ella was found dead. While it could be a coincidence, it could also mean that Star stepped into territory familiar to the killer. Now that got us thinking that maybe—"

Hauk stood and glanced around. *How did I miss Kyle's absence?* "Tell me Kyle isn't snooping around Bloody Lane alone at night?"

"He's not snooping..." Scott's hesitation twisted Hauk's insides. "He's touring the bars seeking information."

"Is he out of his mind?" A neighbour pounded on the wall in response to Hauk's shouting. "Sorry!"

"Kyle isn't careless, boss. He knows what's at stake. After he left, I started searching for old crimes committed in the area by young offenders."

Intrigued, looked at the screen over Scott's shoulder. "Are you telling me they mention names?"

"No, but the news articles may give me enough details to track down the victims, and victims rarely forget the names of their assailants."

"If you find anything, call me right away." If his researcher got him names or addresses, Haulk would personally visit the victims and probe their memories. "In the meantime, I'm going to join Kyle. Between the two of us, we'll cover more bars."

* * *

Star inserted the end of the crowbar into the loop of the handcuff attached to the wall, then using the hook as a pivot point, she pressed with all her strength.

No snap, no creak, or any other sound broke the silence, but one moment her hand hung in midair and the next it fell to her side. Free.

The element of surprise played in her favour. However, to successfully escape, her timing was crucial.

Crowbar in hand, she hobbled around her moving cage, seeking the best vantage point from which to clobber her way out.

Once she was ready to set her plan in motion, she sat near the door.

The time passed and the temperature rose. Thirsty and drowsy, Star fought to stay alert. She hadn't seen or heard anything to indicate the presence of an accomplice in the van. With any luck, the monster was growing as tired of driving as she was of waiting.

After what felt like an eternity, the van stopped and the engine died. The monster slammed his door, shaking the van.

Mentally following his progression alongside the vehicle, she steadied her breathing. Her body tensed in anticipation. *One chance. One chance to escape and live.*

The door handle rattled. Slowly, the door opened, and a faint ray of light emerged through the gap.

"Time for some fun in—"

She swung the crowbar. Hard. The blow struck. He recoiled clutching his arm. Energized by the small victory, she took another swing, and struck another hit. With every blow she landed on her retreating target, childhood visions of a bloody blade sweeping through the air resurged in her mind.

Covered in blood, her assailant crumpled to the ground and stopped twitching. At the sight and smell of blood, her stomach heaved. She dropped the crowbar and took wobbly steps toward the van until she reached the driver's side. A dog barked, startling her. Shivering, she peered over the hood. Attached to a post near the garage, a ferocious golden beast pulled on its chain, baring its teeth and growling.

Star jumped inside the van and reached for the ignition. The absence of a key sank her spirits. She tried hotwiring the ignition. The engine coughed. "Come on." Then it died. "Nooo..."

Staying in the van with no means of escape and no weapon wasn't safe, not when the monster could wake up at any moment, break the window, and haul her out.

Her fears bottled up, she ventured outside and approached the man lying motionless on his back. She needed a set of keys or a phone. Hoping he carried either or both, she searched him. His bloody eyes flew open. He grabbed her ankle. A deafening scream originating from deep inside her chest echoed in her mind.

Spurred by an overwhelming sense of desperation, she pounded and kicked him until he released her, then ran down a dirt road.

Her hope surged at the sound of an engine only to plummet at the sight of an oncoming white pickup truck.

With nowhere to hide, she dashed across the ditch and ventured farther and deeper into the woods. A crude path covered with dry leaves and leafy branches opened in front on her. Running for her life, she increased her stride.

A gunshot echoed in the woods and the ground vanished from under her feet.

* * *

After losing the black car tailing him, Bruce drove to Dusty's shack.

Now that his friend had solved their problem, the time had come to sever any remaining connections with the past.

Dusty's van was parked between the shack and the garage. One of its doors was open. As he neared, Bruce caught sight of a body lying within metres of the vehicle. He stopped his truck and rushed outside.

The sight of the man sprawled in the dirt and covered in blood sickened Bruce. He gripped his friend by the shirt and pulled him into a sitting position. "What happened to you?"

"The ugly bitchling," Dusty grunted.

"The girl did this?" Hours earlier, Bruce had received a text from Dusty saying he had taken care of the bitchling. Confused and increasingly suspicious, Bruce thrust his friend back to the ground. "I got a text saying you took care of her. Tell me it came from you."

"Yeah, I had her locked up in my van, but I wanted to play with her before I killed her."

Damn idiot. "Where the hell did she go?"

"She ran into the woods." Dusty reached for the rifle discarded in the dirt. "When I find her, she'll beg me to finish her off."

His deranged friend had become a crippling liability. Annoyed at himself for not dealing with Dusty any sooner, Bruce snatched the rifle and fired.

Startled by the shot, Dusty's beast barked.

"Shut up, Fang." Bruce took his shirt off and used it to wipe his prints from the butt of the rifle then placed it beside Dusty's body. "The police will think she shot you before fleeing... except it won't work if she isn't wearing gloves." Bruce added Dusty's prints to the butt of the rifle. "I regret to inform you that you killed yourself after the girl escaped."

The dog growled and rattled its chain. Foam drooled from its mouth. Dusty underfed Fang and trained it to hunt for food. As a result, the beast wasn't only vicious around food, it was also an undiscriminating hunter. It attacked, killed, and ate anything that moved.

Bruce wasn't equipped to venture in the woods and track the girl, but if he released Fang, the beast would catch her scent. Nobody would blame a starving dog for hunting its next meal, not even the police.

"This is your lucky day, Fang. There's a yummy prey loose in the woods."

Afraid the dog might attack him, Bruce took the crowbar lying on the ground to protect himself. Armed and ready to slug the dog, Bruce cautiously unchained the animal.

Fang dashed into the woods.

The hunt had begun. Between the deadly traps scattered in the woods and the beastly predator on her tail, Bruce downgraded the girl's chances of survival from slim to none.

He threw the crowbar into the back of the van and put his shirt back on.

If by any miracle the girl lived to recount her ordeal, she couldn't implicate him without Dusty's testimony. And if the girl's real identity was ever revealed, Eleanor Watson would have to deal with the consequences on her own.

Bruce no longer cared if his wicked former stepmother lost her fortune. The money stopped flowing his way after his no-good father cheated on her.

Chapter 23

Insects buzzed in Star's ears, leaves rustled, birds chirped, and the woody smell of green twigs mixed with the earthy scent of a musty cave assaulted her nose. She stirred and made a fist, digging her fingers into the damp soil.

As she felt the dirt accumulating under her fingernails, her eyes flew open.

High above, the sun shone bright in a cloudless, blue sky.

Her entire body ached but she didn't experience any sharp pain, suggesting she might not have broken any bones. All her senses also appeared intact, and they didn't register any threat.

Dreadfully anticipating a sudden agonizing pain and a wave of dizziness, she slowly sat. To her surprise and relief, neither materialized.

She was trapped in a deep pit. Around her, moss grew and roots emerged from the walls marked with shovel imprints. The killer didn't appear to lurk in the vicinity. She had either escaped him, or he had left her for dead in this hole.

Using the roots, she pulled herself up. A sharp, stabbing pain seared in her foot, and her ankle buckled under her weight. She landed on her sore butt, wincing. *This isn't a competition between Hauk and me to see who can break more bones.*

Still, she considered herself lucky. A fall from that height could have easily resulted in a concussion or in a broken neck.

Clenching her teeth, she took off her sandal and tightly wrapped her swelling ankle with strips of fabric she ripped from the bottom edge of her T-shirt. Once her foot was immobilized, the pain subsided to a manageable level. She cautiously stood.

About a metre and a half wide, the pit rose some two metres above her head. One side exposed more roots than the others. It wasn't the best place to be trapped but it was also not the worst.

It sure beats that underwater cave I explored two summers ago. A huge rock had shifted and blocked the entrance. With little oxygen left, she and her dive partner Karine had miraculously found a second exit.

Star grabbed onto the roots and put her good foot against the rough surface of the wall, but with nothing to hold on to, her sandal slipped. And she tumbled. Again.

What she needed was footholds. She dug in her pockets for her knife, only to remember she had put it into the toolbox along with her phone. *Just great.* This day wasn't getting any better. *Think, Star. Think.*

A rock could have worked to dig narrow indentations, except there wasn't a single one in the pit. She tried the twigs that had fallen with her, but they broke before leaving a mark worth mentioning. As a last resort, she used the cuff dangling from her wrist. It left an indentation, not deep enough for the tip of her sandals, but she might be able to grip it with her bare toes.

She made indentations slightly on the right, then on the left, going up as far as she could reach.

"Here goes my best chance." Her sandals tied to the loops of her shorts, so she wouldn't end up bare feet in the woods, she grasped exposed roots and curled her toes in the lowest left and right indentations. Careful to put as little weigh as possible on her injured ankle, she pushed up with her good foot, and as she pulled on the roots and gripped higher ones, she painstakingly climbed up from one indentation to the next.

Sweat dripped down her back.

Her gaze on the wall, she watched for the last indentation she made. When her hand levelled with it, she looked up to check if she needed to dig a few more. A shadow crept over her, and she froze.

At the edge of the pit, a beast snarled at her. Blood drooled around its mouth. It swept its paw toward her, chucking down dirt and soil.

Blinded and petrified, Star lost her grip.

After spending the night visiting bars until closing, Hauk slept a few hours then spent the day visiting victims of youth crimes, only to strike out on all counts.

No patron and no victim recalled a Bruce Robert hanging out with a tattooed man. Hauk believed the victims, but not all the patrons. Then again, some of them were so drunk, they wouldn't remember their own mothers.

Back at the motel, Hauk sat on the bed after taking a quick shower, debating if he should join Kyle again.

"Listen to this one, boss." Since Star's disappearance, Scott hadn't left the motel room or his computer except to go to the bathroom. "Two youths arrested by the neighbourhood watch after breaking and entering a suburban house. They ransacked the place and gutted the family cat."

Desperate for a lead, any lead, Hauk didn't care if he embarked on another wild-goose chase at nine o'clock at night. "Name and address, please."

"It's late. They may not appreciate a visit at this time of the evening."

"They can curse me all they want." Hauk donned a shirt and tucked it into his jeans. "As long as they answer, I don't care."

"Here you go." Scott handed him a sticky note. "Good luck."

Twenty minutes later, Hauk parked in front of a row of identical houses. Undeterred by the absence of light inside the victim's house, he knocked, rang the doorbell twice, and knocked again.

Suddenly, the light on the porch came on, an elderly man answered the door. "What do you want?"

"Sorry, sir, but I need your help." Afraid to overstay his welcome, Hauk quickly explained that the young offenders who tortured their family cat might be involved in the disappearance of a young woman.

"That was more than twenty-five years ago..." The elderly man rubbed the back of his head. "I don't know about a tattoo, but I remember their first names. Bruce and Dustin. My daughter was pregnant at the time, and she wanted to name her baby boy Bruce. Needless to say, my grandson isn't named Bruce. Now, if my wife was still alive, she would be able to give you more details, but I lost her to cancer last year. I sure hope you find that young lady alive."

Me too. "Thank you. I'm sorry for your wife and I apologize for the late-night visit."

The elderly man nodded then closed the door.

As Hauk headed back to his car, his cell phone rang. He answered on the sidewalk. "Ludwig."

"Boss, I'm in the back alley of The Drunken Cave. A tattooed guy known as Dusty was seen in Bruce's company. Does the name mean anything?"

The question raised Hauk's hope. "Yes, Kyle, it does. Where can we find this Dusty?"

"I couldn't get an address except for a vague reference to a shack in the woods. Someone's coming. I gotta go."

* * *

Tears pooled in Star's eyes. She was back at the bottom of the pit, hurt and dejected.

Above her head, the beast prowled along the edge, growling.

Terrified it might jump, she recoiled into a corner, shuddering, and touched her cheek.

Hauk had seen past her scar into her heart, and loved her. Tears that she could no longer contain spilled down her face. He made her believe that they could build a life together, that beyond her nightmarish past lay a bright and wonderful future.

Too weary and too injured to make a second attempt only to face the slobbering monster blocking her escape, she curled up into fetal position and sobbed in silence.

Hauk entered the police station and walked right into Pratt's office. "Working overnight?"

Pratt frowned. "Coffee is over there, Ludwig. Get me one while you're at it."

Unsure how to interpret the request, Hauk grabbed two Styrofoam cups and poured black coffee in both. "You want sugar and cream too?"

"Two each, please." The detective stared at him with an impassive expression. "What brings you here?"

"According to my diver, Bruce Robert was seen with a tattooed man known as Dusty at a bar called The Drunken Cave." Hauk placed the double double on Pratt's desk and kept the black one for himself. "I also paid a visit to an elderly gentleman whose house was burglarized and cat tortured more than twenty-five years ago by a couple of screwed up teens, Bruce and Dustin."

The detective took a swig from his cup. "Any last name on that Dusty-Dustin character?"

"No, but according to my diver's sources, Dusty lives in a shack in the middle of the woods. One evening, I followed Robert after he finished work, but he lost me in the countryside." Hauk hadn't been pleased with himself for losing Robert. "It can't be a coincidence."

Both sleeves rolled up to the elbow, Pratt drummed on his armrest with his fingers. "Early this morning, Robert left in his white truck. He ditched his tails on a deserted road in the middle of nowhere and reappeared later this afternoon. It's possible he hooked up with his accomplice, and it may be enough to get his juvenile record unsealed. Go home, Ludwig, and let me do my job."

Home without Star wasn't home. She had claimed his heart, his entire future, and he wouldn't stop searching for her. *Ever*.

* * *

Hauk entered the motel room. "Scott, the victim remembered—" The rest of his sentence died in his throat. "What happened?"

"Someone idn't lie my wessons." Kyle's swollen jaw made it hard for him to speak and harder for anyone else to understand him.

Bent over Kyle, Scott cleaned the blood on the diver's face with a washcloth. "I think he means someone didn't like his questions."

Hauk seethed. "I'm taking you to the hospital."

"No... I'm fi-fine... I on't ave noting... boken... I nee ice."

349

"Lay down." The ice machine was located down the hall, and Hauk was certain he had seen an ice bucket somewhere in the bathroom. "I'll get you some ice."

On his return, Hauk found the bathroom door closed and the water running. "Is Kyle alone in the shower?"

Scott cast a dubious look in Hauk's direction. "I certainly wasn't going with him."

Annoyed by Kyle's noncompliance, Hauk forced himself to take a deep breath. "Did Kyle mention the name Dusty when he came in?"

"Yes. Bruce Robert was seen with him, but none of the patrons seemed to know or recall Dusty's last name. However, Kyle did glean that Dusty inherited a shack from his dead mother."

How Kyle gleaned a dead mother but not a last name baffled Hauk. "If he inherited the property from his deceased mother, wouldn't the land be registered in his name?"

"To his real name, which may not be Dusty, and we don't know the mother's name."

"The last victim with the tortured cat, he remembered a Bruce with a Dustin, so let's assume his real name is Dustin, not Dusty." A map of the area, provided by the motel, lay on the coffee table. With his index finger, Hauk encircled an area southwest of town. "This is where Bruce lost me while I was tailing him. Dustin's shack has to be within the area. Any chance you can access the land registry?"

"Let me get a coffee and—"

"I'll get you a coffee. You start searching."

At the front desk, the young woman with a bouncy ponytail was more than happy to brew a fresh pot for Hauk.

Once he returned to the room, he found Kyle resting on a bed with ice over his chin.

"Sowwy, boss."

Clean and refreshed, his diver didn't look half as bad as he did fifteen minutes earlier. "You did great, Kyle. Now take a break. When Scott gets us an address, we'll go check it out."

Hauk sat near the window and waited in silence, a silence broken only by the sound of Scott's fingers typing over his keyboard.

"I found a Dustin Carver. He owns an acreage about thirty-five kilometres from where Robert took you for a spin."

"Scott, you stay here and call Detective Pratt. Kyle, you're with me. We're going to check the place out."

* * *

Warning signs bordered Dustin Carver's land.

351

Hauk drove up a dirt road, agreeing with every unsavoury term that Kyle muttered under his breath.

Half a dozen police cruisers and a dark blue van were parked in the proximity of a dilapidated house and a garage framed with crooked doors. Hauk parked near a cruiser, and he and Kyle exited the Jeep.

"Ludwig." Pratt walked toward them. "Your computer guy called me. He said you were on your way."

"Did you find Star?"

"No, but we have a dead, disfigured body." Pratt stopped them from approaching the corpse surrounded by yellow tape. "According to his driver's licence, his name is Dustin Carver. The body has a bird tattoo at the edge of a dirty bandage."

A pistol shot resonated in the air.

A police officer stood with his gun drawn near the entrance of the garage. At his feet lay the lifeless form of an animal. "The dog lunged at me, unprovoked."

The detective approached the dead animal, and Hauk followed suit. A silver collar circled its thick neck, and dried blood matted its fur around its muzzle.

"Bag the dog," Pratt ordered.

Mind reeling with questions, Hauk spun around to face the detective. "Why? You think the blood belongs to Star?"

"Carver was mauled by an animal, shortly before or after he was shot." Pratt gestured to one of his men to help with the carcass. "I'm thinking it's his blood."

"Dustin was shot?" Hauk had never seen Star armed with a gun, only a fiery temper. "By who?"

"Too early to tell, but there was a rifle by his side. The floor in the garage—" Pratt blocked Hauk's attempts to head toward the building in question. "I can't let you go in there, Ludwig. The floor is covered with white splatters and there's a message painted in white that says *Find Her.*"

"White... like in white paint... and white tru... truck?" Kyle articulated slowly.

"The pattern *suggests* someone spray painted a white vehicle." Pratt's emphasis on *suggests* reminded Hauk that the detective was still in the preliminary stage of the investigation. "We also found broken headlights with chips of green on them, discarded in the garbage."

"Star's bus... was gueen... green."

"We know, and we put out an APB on Robert. We—" Pratt's cell phone rang, and he quick answered, but neither his blank expression nor his cryptic answers, offered much of an explanation to Hauk. As he put his phone in his pocket, Pratt's gaze wandered to the woods surrounding them. "We have Robert in custody."

Hauk's heart somersaulted inside his chest. "Star?"

"Not with him, and Robert's not talking. Listen up, everyone." The detective's voice boomed. "I want those woods canvassed. *Now*."

Without waiting for Pratt's permission to join the search, Hauk tore through the woods.

"Star!" Every few seconds, he called her name. "Star!"

A heart-wrenching scream echoed from somewhere around him. He rushed toward the agonizing sounds only to stop dead in his tracks some twenty metres farther.

A tall, brawny officer restrained his wincing colleague whose boot was caught in a steel-jaw trap while a third officer attempted to pry open the jaws.

"Sir—" A dark-haired officer advanced toward Pratt. "The woods are littered with conibear traps and—" The warning was lost in a shriek when a rope encircled the officer's leg and swooped him off the ground to hang him upside down.

Detective Pratt barked orders about medical attention and safety precautions, prompting Hauk to pick up a long and thick broken branch.

He swept the branch through the vegetation obscuring the ground, clearing a safe path forward. Moments later, he triggered a steel-jaw trap. Startled by the snapping noise, Hauk jumped backward, his makeshift stick shortened by a few inches.

The possibility that Star escaped the monster only to fall prey to a trap churned his stomach. *Your underwater survival instincts better extend to the surface, havfrue.*

He pushed forward into the woods, no longer flinching every time his makeshift stick got chomped.

Farther ahead, twilight cast a dark shadow upon what appeared to be a hole amid the foliage. Hauk cautiously approached, watching for the edge, then peered into the manmade pit.

Something had been tossed at the bottom.

"Pratt!" Hauk grabbed a branch from a nearby tree, and cursing his sprained wrist, he lowered himself down using only one hand.

The branch broke. He hit the ground with a thud that reverberated up and down his bad arm. Groaning with pain, he scanned his surroundings. His eyes slowly grew accustomed to the obscurity, and a silhouette took shape.

"Star?"

Curled up in a corner, she lay motionless.

"Star!" Anguish tore his heart. He knelt by her side and touched her bare arm. Her skin was cold and clammy. *No... no...* Losing her wasn't an option.

His gaze travelled down her arm. At the sight of the handcuff, rage roared inside his chest. He encircled her slender wrist with his fingers. A weak pulse beat against his fingertips.

"I found you, havfrue." The nightmare was over. "Pratt! Get down here! She's alive!"

Star stirred, moaning. "You... you took your sweet time."

A tear of joy and gratitude ran down his cheek.

Chapter 24

Careful of the intravenous line that carried a clear fluid into her vein, Hauk delicately lifted Star's hand and pressed her palm to his lips. She sighed softly in response, a gentle balm to his tormented heart.

Twice she had fought to stay alive, and twice she overcame the odds against her.

"It's over, Star." A blonde curl stuck to her cheek, and he gently brushed the hair behind her ear. "He will never hurt you again."

Even bruised, she was still the most beautiful woman he had ever laid eyes on. Her eyelashes fluttered open for a moment. "Hauk?"

"I'm here." With the tip of his finger, he traced her lips. "You can rest."

She peacefully drifted back to sleep.

"How is she?" a low voice asked from behind him.

Glad to hear Jimmy, Hauk invited him to step inside the hospital room.

"She'll be fine." The nurse refused to tell him anything more substantial, and Hauk still hadn't had a chance to meet with the doctor. "They're giving her a mild sedative through the IV line. She slips in and out of consciousness."

"Hauk... did he hurt my little girl?"

If not for the older man staring intently at him, Hauk could almost have believed he imagined the quiet question. "I don't know the extent of her injuries. I just know she's alive."

Jimmy sat in an armchair near the bed and reached for Star's other hand. "It's all my fault. I should never have left her alone."

"It's the fault of whoever orchestrated the murder of her family, Jimmy." Star wouldn't have been any safer if Hauk hadn't asked her to join his crew. It would only have delayed the inevitable. Sooner or later, the monster would have realized she survived, and that moment would have sealed her fate. "Not yours, not mine, not Star's, not anyone else's, but we all saved her together."

Her father nodded. "He's dead, isn't he?"

"Yes, it's over." Someone slew the monster, and Hauk wished it had been him. "Star is safe from her past, and she's given us a future. I love her, Jimmy. I want to become her husband."

A smile softened Jimmy's weary face. "Are you asking for my permission?"

Hauk held Jimmy's gaze, let him see his sincerity. "You've raised an amazing woman, and you'll always be her father. I don't know if I'm the man that you imagined would share her life one day, but I truly love her, and I promise to cherish her until my last breath."

"You have my blessing, son."

Steps resonated in the hallway, culminating with the entrance of a man with salt and pepper hair and wearing a white lab coat. "Is one of you Miss Fisher's next of kin?"

"I guess I still am, but not for very long." Jimmy smiled at Hauk. "Is there something wrong?"

The doctor looked over his glasses at Jimmy. "May I have a word in private, please?"

Jimmy leaned back in his chair. "Whatever you have to say can be said here."

"As you wish..." Visibly displeased, the doctor consulted the tablet in his hands. "I performed a full physical examination. Miss Fisher bears a multitude of injuries, some more recent than others."

"We're more concerned about the last forty-eight hours." At the moment, Hauk needed reassurance she would recover, not a lecture on her previous injuries.

"Yes, Detective Pratt apprised me of the situation." The doctor's neutral tone concealed any opinions he might harbour toward the situation. "Miss Fisher suffers from severe dehydration, a broken ankle, and many infected cuts and scratches. Antibiotics and nutrients have been added to her IV bag. Aside from the bruises left by the handcuffs, she didn't show any signs of sexual or physical assault. All the other abrasions and lacerations she sustained are consistent with an uncomfortable stay in the woods and a tumble into a pit, not a beating. She will make a full recovery."

Full recovery. Relief washed over Hauk at the sound of those two little words.

"Now I must insist to speak privately with you, Mr. Fisher. My office. Now."

The doctor exited the room without allowing Jimmy the opportunity to deny his request a second time.

* * *

The doctor had already established that Star wasn't assaulted, so Hauk couldn't think of anything else that needed to be said in private.

Worried, he paced impatiently in front of the window.

A few minutes later, Jimmy returned.

His inscrutable expression sank a brick in Hauk's stomach. He stopped pacing and sat at the edge of her bed, near her bruised wrist. "Is something wrong?"

Jimmy stood on the other side of the bed caressing her cheek. "Star's blood test showed an... an unusual result."

Unusual sounded too much like a synonym for abnormal. Hauk took her hand into his. "Tell me she didn't escape the monster only to be struck by a life-threatening condition."

"It's certainly a condition." Jimmy hiccupped a few chuckles. "And it's definitely life-altering."

Confused by the mixed message, Hauk stared at Jimmy. "She's suffering from a *good* life-altering condition?"

"The doctor used a fancy word to describe her *good* condition." A wicked smile cracked Jimmy's face. "He called it *pregnancy*. Care to explain?"

As understanding dawned on him, Hauk grinned in astonishment. "No, not in detail, except to say I'm really happy." *And hopefully, Star will be too.*

Joy and happiness radiated from the soon-to-be grandpa. "Glad to hear that, son."

In awe of the tiny spark of life growing inside her, Hauk gently stroked Star's stomach. An ethereal smile blossomed on her sleepy face. "Star isn't going to lose the baby, is she?"

"No, this little one is as tough as her mother, and the sedative is harmless."

Neither Jimmy nor the doctor could know this early that the baby was a girl, but Hauk loved the idea of a little twinkling Star. "Did the doctor say anything else?"

"Without knowing if you were the father, the doctor didn't want to say anything in front of you."

Father. "Yes, I am the father." The word sounded heavenly when spoken aloud.

"The doctor will come back later to talk to you. He's hoping you'll be able to convince Star to stay here for a few days."

The existence and wellbeing of their child might just be enough to persuade Star to enjoy the hospitality. "I'll try but we both know how stubborn she—"

"Hauk?"

His heart leaped in his chest at the sound of her voice. "I'm here, havfrue."

Weak and injured, she looked as pale as the white pillow on which she lay her head. "Where am I? I feel... groggy."

"That would be the medication the doctor is giving you, squirt." Tears shone in Jimmy's eyes as he stroked her hair. "The monster is dead. You're safe. You're all safe."

"Not dead..." Small tremors shook her body. "He grabbed my ankle... White truck... I saw the white truck and ran into woods..." Her voice trailed and her eyelids slowly closed. "The dog... I fell..."

"You're safe, squirt. Go back to sleep." Jimmy kissed her forehead and sighed. "I hope these new nightmares won't haunt her like the old ones did."

Hauk couldn't agree more, but he had the strange feeling that these were memories, not nightmares. "It sounded like she was trying to tell us something."

"Listen, son, you look exhausted. Why don't you go rest for a few hours?"

"But Star." Hauk wanted to stay by her side, by their side.

"Star's sleeping. Go to your motel and come back refreshed. You don't need to worry about her. I won't leave her side." Jimmy moved from the bed to the armchair, making his point. "Besides, there's a big scary guy in uniform with an even bigger gun keeping watch at the door."

As much as Hauk wanted to stay, he acknowledged Jimmy's wisdom.

* * *

On his way to the motel, Hauk made an unscheduled stop by the police station.

"Another sleepless night, Pratt?"

The detective ran his fingers through his cropped hair but stopped short of buttoning his shirt, straightening his tie, or rolling down his sleeves.

"What brings you here, Ludwig?" Files, reports, and paper cups cluttered Pratt's desk. "The doctor already sent me his report."

"Star woke up, and she said a few words. I think she might have seen the white truck before she ran into the woods."

* * *

Propped up against her pillow, Star smiled at the man entering her room, the man she loved with all her heart.

"You're awake?" Hauk sat at the edge of her bed, cupped her face, and placed a tender kiss on her lips. "How do you feel?"

"Tired." His thumb traced soft circles on her cheek, and she leaned into the sweet sensation. "Jimmy told me you went back to the motel to rest. Did you get some sleep?"

"Yes. Scott shut off the alarm by accident. I'm sorry. I meant to come back sooner."

"You're not late." During Hauk's absence, Jimmy stayed in the room. He was still there, seated by the window, gazing fondly at them. "Detective Pratt hasn't arrived yet."

"Pratt?" Hauk's brows knitted together over his nose. "Why?"

"To debrief Miss Fisher." Pratt's answered from the doorway.

"Now?" Hauk glared at the detective. "Can't it wait?"

"Hauk." Star touched his face. "I'm the one who asked Jimmy to call the detective."

His steel-blue eyes gazed intently at her. "Are you sure you're ready?"

Touched by his concern, she ran her fingers along the worried creases on his forehead in a futile effort to smooth them. "Yes, I am." To put her past behind her, she needed to revisit it one more time. One last time. "Would you hold me?"

A smile softened his expression. "With pleasure."

Pratt showed her a copy of a driver's licence. "Do you recognize this man?"

Feeling safe in Hauk's arms, she took a hard look at his picture. "He's the man who kidnapped me at gunpoint from the boathouse. Is he really dead?"

"Yes. Once the coroner cleaned him up, enough of his face remained to identify him. To be sure, we traced an old dental record, and we matched his DNA to fibers and hair collected all over his house." Priority must have been given to the case if Pratt had obtained the DNA results so quickly. "He's dead and cold. His name was Dustin Carver, also known as Dusty Carver. Can you tell me exactly what happened, Miss Fisher?"

Heartened by the unconditional love and support she saw reflected in Hauk's and Jimmy's eyes, she recalled the events. "I was alone in the boathouse when he—when Carver showed up." Speaking his name aloud lessened the power he held on her memories. "He pointed a rifle at me. I could tell from the hatred on his face that he wanted to kill me, but at the same time, he wanted to keep me alive."

With his back against the wall, Pratt stood facing her bed. "Did he say anything?"

She tried recalling their short conversations. "Threats, nasty threats. He said I cheated fate when I didn't drown. We walked through the woods to a dark blue van. He handcuffed me to a hook in the cargo area and closed the door." Hauk stroked her arm, encouraging her to continue. "The muffler sputtered. It was the same van that sped away the night the boat exploded."

The pen in the detective's hand stilled over his notebook. "Are you sure?"

"Yes, absolutely."

Pratt scribbled some more. "How did you escape?"

"I searched the hidden compartment in the wall where the jack and tire iron are usually kept. It was empty, except for a crowbar stuck in there. I dislodged it and used it to break the cuff from the hook. Then I waited, and when he opened the door, I... I hit him. I hit him until he collapsed." The images played in her mind, and his blood spattered in front of her eyes. "I wasn't sure he was dead, but he was unconscious. I needed the van key to drive away, so I searched him. Then all of a sudden, he grabbed my ankle, so I kicked him repeatedly." At the time, it didn't occur to her that she had killed him. Carver had shed the blood of her family, and she had spilled his. Justice had been served. "I just wanted the key or a phone. I wasn't trying to kill him, but I'm glad he's dead."

"Carver was shot, Miss Fisher, not kicked to death."

"Shot? But I didn't shoot him." His death brought closure. To learn that his blood didn't stain her hands brought her an unexpected wave of relief. "It didn't even occur to me to take his rifle."

"We know you're not responsible for his death." If the detective believed her, it could only mean that he knew who killed Carver. "Please continue."

"I kicked him so he would let go of my ankle, but the dog kept barking." The beast reminded her of the dog that disfigured her. "I... I panicked and fled."

The detective arched a brow. "What dog, Miss Fisher?"

"The big golden dog attached to a chain near the garage." Nobody could have missed that dog.

"We killed a golden dog who attacked one of my men near the house. Are you sure it was chained?"

"Yes." In her mind, she could still see the dog pulling on its chain and growling. "But I was scared it would break loose. I was attacked by a dog as a child, and I'm afraid of dogs. I ran down the road, but then I saw a white truck coming toward me. It resembled the one that hit me, so I fled into the woods and fell into a pit. I tried to climb out, but there was that dog prowling at the edge. It was drooling blood." Shivers coursed through her body. "It frightened me so bad, I fell again."

"Miss Fisher, the dog near the garage and the dog at the pit, were they the same dog?"

"I don't know." Pratt's question about the animals baffled her, and with her aversion to dogs, she didn't care if they were from the same litter. "Why?"

"What did it look like, havfrue?" Hauk's soft whisper tickled her neck, a subtle invitation to remember.

"They were both golden. The one chained near the garage had a silver collar. It shone in the sun. I'm not sure about the one by the pit."

"That's interesting." The detective tapped his notebook with the tip of his pen. "The dog we shot was bloody around the muzzle and it wore a silver collar. When we ran the prints on the collar, they matched Robert's."

The caresses that Hauk bestowed on her arm stopped. "You think he unleashed the dog on Star?"

"One more contradiction to his confession."

Surprised and confused, she stared at the detective. "Robert confessed? To what?"

"With his fingerprints all over Carver's garage and traces of blood on his shirt, Bruce Robert admitted knowing Carver, claimed Carver took his own life before his arrival, and denied any involvement in your disappearance."

"No involvement?" Outrage rose inside her chest. "Carver was unconscious when I fled down the road and spotted Robert's white truck. Carver wouldn't have had time to regain consciousness and—" The gunshot resonated in her mind. "I heard a gunshot as I fell down the pit. If Carver killed himself, he didn't do it before Robert's arrival. Robert had plenty of time to get to Carver before that gunshot, and that's the only one I heard."

Hauk tightened his embrace. "Can you tell us more about Robert's confession?"

"Sure, and I'm counting on any of you to keep on pointing out any discrepancies." Pratt pulled a sheet of paper from his pocket. "Like I said, this is Bruce Robert's version of the events." The detective cleared his throat. "He grew up estranged from his father, but they reconnected when Bruce was a teenager. At that time, his father was married to his second wife, Eleanor Watson. Bruce remembered an evening during which his inebriated stepmother entertained him with stories of her grandfather, Old Watson. Apparently, Old Watson had gotten his wife Mary pregnant, and then conspired with his mistress, Eleanor's grandmother, to eliminate Mary. After Mary gave birth to his son Samuel, Old Watson killed her and staged her disappearance so he could embezzle her fortune. He then abandoned Samuel and lived happily with Eleanor's grandmother, who by then had become his second wife, until the crash of 1929. Fired over bad investments, Old Watson jumped from his office window, leaving behind a guilty note seeking forgiveness for Mary's murder."

That resembled what Hauk had told her, except for the guilty note.

"That guilty note, if it really exists, proves that my great-grandmother Mary was murdered by..." Star refused to call him her great-grandfather when there was nothing great, grand, or fatherly about Watson. "By Old Watson. I'm not sure how I feel about that murderous blood flowing in my veins."

"I see you've been made aware of the DNA results." The detective smiled. "Unfortunately, we only have Robert's word that the note ever existed, but your birth father, Adrian Humphrey, found an old insurance policy containing allegations that Mary Watson was murdered. According to Robert, Adrian approached Eleanor and her husband Frederick Robert for permission to sweep the portion of the lake facing their residence. Afraid to lose their fortune if Humphrey proved that Old Watson killed his first wife, they refused. Adrian persisted, claiming his wife Amy wanted a decent burial for her grandmother. Distrustful of the Humphreys' intentions, Frederick Robert sent his older son Bruce to intimidate Adrian and Amy into forgetting about the family secret. The blonde twin with a scar, that would be you, opened the door when Bruce Robert knocked."

"There were two monsters, and I let one of them come into my house?" No wonder Bruce recognized her when Star bumped into him coming out of the elevator.

"After Adrian and Amy refused to yield, Frederick Robert paid his son's troubled friend, Dustin Carver, lots of money to scare them to death. Bruce claimed he was shocked to learn that Dustin followed the directive to the letter."

"Considering they gutted a cat for fun, Pratt, I find it hard to believe that he was shocked." Hauk's voice was laced with the same indignation that she felt.

"You're not the only one. Again, according to Bruce, Dustin bragged about how he staged the father's car accident, how he sneaked into the house and caught the mother by surprise, how each child stepped inside the bathroom one after the other, like docile little lambs at the slaughterhouse, how the..." Pratt glanced at her. "How the twin with the scar hesitated—"

Star doubted those were the words Bruce had used, but she appreciated Pratt's efforts to spare her feelings.

"—and how the nanny scooped the twin up before Dustin had a chance to kill either of them. Dustin recognized the nanny before she fled with the child toward the river. The nanny lived in the same neighbourhood that Dustin cruised for sex. When their bodies didn't resurface, Dustin sought the nanny out in case she survived, and he killed her."

Jimmy, who had listened without flinching, gave her a bittersweet smile. "Ella saved you, squirt. When it came right down to it, she made the right choices at the right times. Whatever else she did doesn't matter."

The woman that Star had always believed to be her mother was the one who had, indeed, given her a second life. For a few fateful hours, Ella had been her mother.

Pratt flipped to the next page. "Bruce claimed he only received a modest sum of money in exchange for his silence."

"The money financed his auto shop garage and his house. It wasn't a modest sum," Hauk said with conviction. "You can ask my young guy, Scott. He dug up a few interesting facts on Bruce Robert."

"I will, Ludwig." Pratt scribbled on the sheet of paper. "According to Bruce, he and Dustin forgot about the murders until the discovery of the Model T."

Star huffed. *How can anyone forget about killing someone?*

"Worried the police would reopen the Humphrey case if Mary Watson's body was discovered, Dustin boarded your boat at night and sabotaged the equipment with the hope of thwarting your recovery efforts."

Except, Dustin Carver didn't do his homework. He didn't watch her closely enough to know that she kept her gear in a different location.

"After his failed attempt, Dustin recognized you, Miss Fisher, as the missing twin. He enlisted Bruce's help to eliminate you before you could identify him."

"I only remember the knife he held over my head." Her mind had buried the memory so deep that she had forgotten what the monsters looked like. "I don't know if I even looked at him."

"You'll never have to look at him again, squirt." Jimmy approached her bed and took her hand. "It's over. You're safe."

The detective sat in the chair vacated by Jimmy. "Bruce said he refused to partake in your demise. When Dustin asked to borrow his truck, Bruce lent him the keys. He insisted he had no idea that Dustin would try to kill you until his vehicle was returned all smashed up."

"Sure, just like purple fish fly over the moon every night. I bumped into Bruce Robert that day at the hospital. He stood by the elevator and looked at me strangely. I know he recognized me. I could see it in his eyes." She struggled to keep her temper at bay. "I didn't see the driver when I got hit, and I know I can't place Robert behind the wheel, but he wasn't far away."

Pratt smiled. "We have a witness that places Dustin Carver across town at the time of your hit-and-run. With only Bruce left in the vicinity of the hospital, it is reasonable to assume he was indeed driving."

"A reliable witness?" Hauk asked, visibly surprised

"A prostitute, but we believe her. She also overheard part of an incriminating conversation between Dustin and Bruce. Her testimony combined with yours, Miss Fisher, puts a big dent in Bruce's confession."

Only a dent? Star would rather see a hole the size of the Atlantic Ocean.

"Bruce claims he regrets fixing the truck and not going to the police with the evidence, but with Dustin growing increasingly unstable and dangerous, he feared for his own life. When he received Dustin's message about your abduction, Bruce did what he should have done two decades earlier. He listened to his conscience and—"

Conscience? The monsters had no conscience.

"—he drove to the shack with the intent of stopping the bloodshed. Upon his arrival, he found Carver dead. He called your name, but—"

"He sure didn't shout very loud," she blurted out. Not that she would have come out of the woods if she had heard him.

"I'm sure he didn't." The detective folded Bruce's phony confession and tucked it into his pocket. "He finished the confession by saying he left the premises thinking Dustin had already killed you."

Chapter 25

Dazed from Pratt's long account, Star silently welcomed her visitors' departures. After removing his shoes, Hauk lay down on her bed and offered the comfort of his uninjured arm.

"How are you feeling?" He stroked her back through the gap of her pink hospital gown.

"I'm not sure." As her mind processed the events that crossed generations, she drew imaginary lines over his chest. "This is mind-boggling."

"Dragging you into that Model T investigation precipitated these events." He tucked her head against his chest. "I wish I could have spared you this ordeal, but I can't think of anything I could have done differently, short of not hiring you, which I almost did... didn't... do."

"Sooner or later, the truth would have resurfaced, Hauk. I'm very grateful I didn't face those monsters alone." The strong beating of his heart echoed against her ear, grounding her, like an anchor in the middle of a storm. "Should I ask why you jeopardized our happy future by almost not hiring me?”

“Because...” A silent sigh expanded his chest. “Because the last female diver I hired stole my artifacts and sold them to the highest bidders. Before you ask, I wasn’t romantically involved with her, but she still played me. Maybe if she’d been a man, I would have seen the red flags. Then again, the few women I dated behaved in similar ways, so I took her betrayal personally. After I lost Macey, I went to see Dylan. He recommended you, but I didn’t want a female diver, so I asked for his second-best diver. He called me pigheaded and sent me to the basement to meet you.” Hauk tightened his embrace. “You possessed the expertise I needed, but you were also everything I wasn’t expecting. Forthright, bold, strong, unpretentious, and that battle scar on your cheek, it commanded respect. Despite my unfair opinion of women, I offered you the job—and you turned me down.”

She had sensed Kyle’s animosity and distrust, but Hauk didn’t only give her a chance despite his prejudice, he gave her two chances. In his place, she would have fired the diver who almost severed her air supply, but Hauk saw something in her that she couldn’t see at the time. Worth.

“Did you really think I would accept your proposition just because you dangled a nice Model T in front of my eyes?” she teased, grateful that he looked deep beneath her surface. "Dylan said I could trust you, but if he'd told me I would fall in love with you, I would have questioned his judgment from Beaver Creek to St. John's. Still, it was all worth it, and I wouldn't hesitate to go through that ordeal again if it meant falling in love with you and finding the truth."

All those years ago, the murder of her family created a void inside her and locked a deadly secret within her mind that she had never been able to explain. The truth set her free to fill her life with the names and beautiful faces of the family who once loved her, and the family she wished one day to build with the man she loved.

Hauk kissed her hair. "Would you like to talk about Vanessa?"

"Vanessa lives inside my heart, but she died in that river. The night Ella rescued me, I became Star Fisher. This is my name and I will keep it. Does that make sense?" When he didn't answer right way, she tilted her head up. "Hauk?"

"I was hoping—" Gazing adoringly at her, he smiled. "I was hoping you'd consider adding Ludwig to your name."

"Adding?" He couldn't mean what she dreamed he meant, could he? "Are you proposing?"

"Yes. I am." His smile broadened. "I love you, Star Fisher, and whether you choose to add Ludwig to your name or not, I would very much love to become your husband.

Would you make me the happiest man alive and marry me?”

Without a shred of a doubt, she knew he was the man she wanted to spend the rest of her life with. “Yes, I would. Yes, I will.”

“I’m yours for the rest of my life, and whenever you need to talk about your past, I’m here to listen.”

Feeling loved and safe in his embrace, she let her mind travel back to Bruce Robert’s misleading confession. “When my fath— when Adrian Humphrey—”

“Adrian Humphrey was your first father, havfrue. You should call him as such. I’m sure wherever he is, he’s extremely pleased that one of his daughters survived.”

All her life Star imagined her father being someone who walked in and out of her mother’s life without giving a damn. It never occurred to her that he might have cared, that he might have loved her as much as Jimmy loved her. “My father Adrian’s car accident wasn’t an accident. Do you think he died believing his entire family perished because he discovered those allegations?”

“He didn’t mention the connection to the police when they interrogated him.” Hauk whispered in her ear. “I’m guessing probably not.”

Deep in thought, she caressed his bristly chin. “Do you think Eleanor’s lawyer son, Paul Robert, knew about the murders when he offered you all that money to stop the salvage operation?”

"He acted on behalf of his mother, supposedly to spare her some grief. How much Eleanor told him, we may never know, but nothing suggests that he was involved."

"You're probably right." There was no evidence to link Paul Robert to the murders or the attempts on her life. "I don't remember opening the door to Bruce Robert or seeing Dustin Carver in the bathroom, but Vanessa did and she tried showing them to me in my nightmares. I doubt they would have recognized me after twenty years, but they never forgot Vanessa's scar. Carver, he... he killed Jimmy's sister because she saved me."

"Witnessing Carver's atrocities sealed her tragic fate. That she didn't betray you brought immense comfort to Jimmy."

While Star didn't understand why Stella Fisher didn't go to the police right after she escaped the attack, Jimmy still found closure in her sacrifice. "What kind of monster slaughters children?"

Hauk stroked her back. "No punishment will ever erase the horrible crimes that Carver committed, but he's dead. He will never hurt you or another human being again."

While Carver met his fate, Bruce Robert's guilt remained to be proven in court.

"Detective Pratt will never be able to implicate Eleanor Watson in the murders, will he?" While Star didn't want anything to do with Eleanor's estates and the blood money responsible for the death of her family, she still wanted justice for the small child she once was.

Hauk kissed her forehead. "Once charged and convicted of your attempted murder and Carver's murder, Bruce Robert may change his story and decide to take his former stepmother with him."

"You really think a jury will believe the prostitute who claims Carver was with her across town when the truck hit me?"

"While it pains me that you will both have to testify, neither one of you has any reason to lie. She heard part of their incriminating conversation around the same time you saw Robert at the hospital and were hit by his truck. And let's not forget his fingerprints on the dog's collar. A jury will have a hard time believing Robert had yours or Carver's best interest at heart when he showed up at the shack."

"Robert left me to die in the woods, but you saved me. You never stopped looking for me." With Hauk by her side, she would never face life's hardships alone again. "Thank you."

"Not finding you was never an option, and I'm so proud of you for escaping."

"Almost escaping." Ironically, the dog scared her more than Carver. "Hauk, you don't want a dog, do you?"

"Not really. Why?"

She rubbed her scar with her fingers. "I hate dogs."

Hauk coughed up a chuckle. "When the kids beg for a pet, I promise we'll buy them goldfish, not a dog."

"A kid with a goldfish?" Amused by the images popping into her mind, she shook her head. "Sure."

* * *

The shift in the conversation and Star's enigmatic response threw Hauk for a loop.

Children had never entered any of their conversations. Lots of things were never discussed between them. Actions always seemed to speak louder than words, and they were—he was careless. In the middle of passion, they created a tiny life together. Star agreed to become his wife, but was she ready to embrace motherhood? Was he wrong to assume she would be as thrilled with the news? "Okay... what's so funny about goldfish?"

She wrinkled her nose. "Well, I don't think I've ever seen little blond kids pulling wriggling goldfish on leashes."

A weight lifted from his shoulders at the way she alluded to their future children. "Would you like us to have children?"

"Yes, and I'm hoping you do to."

Oh, yes. Many of them. He sneaked his injured hand out of the sling to tenderly caress her stomach. "Our little blond miracle is already growing inside you, havfrue."

"You mean..." Her hands joined his over her stomach. "I'm pregnant?"

Any lingering uncertainties he might have held vanished as he watched her fall in love with their unborn child. "Yes, and baby is fine."

Her dark brown eyes narrowed in suspicion. "Did you ask me to marry you because I'm pregnant?"

"No, I didn't, and you can check with Jimmy." Hauk twined her fingers with his. "I asked his permission before he told me you were pregnant. He's embracing grandfatherhood with delight and I'm embracing fatherhood with extreme blissfulness." *And great fear.*

A radiant glow enveloped her entire person. "Who else knows about baby?"

At the motel, Hauk had resisted the temptation to tell Kyle and Scott, thinking she might enjoy their reactions. "Well, I did stop to see Arnie at the hospital. I had to tell someone."

She rolled her eyes, visibly amused. "And what did Arnie say?"

"That I was a lucky guy." *The luckiest guy.* "And that he would fight with Jimmy for the title of grandpa."

The soft laughter bubbling in her throat filled his heart. "Can you take me home? Wherever home is."

"I have a studio above Aunt Hilda's garage, but I wouldn't call it a home." It was more like a luxury storage unit that he occasionally visited. "I'd rather we accept Jimmy's offer to live at the cabin until we build our own home. In the meantime, the doctor wants to keep you under observation for a few days."

Her hand stilled on her tummy. "Is something wrong with baby?"

"Baby is fine, havfrue, but you are dehydrated and you're fighting an infection. You need the IV for a while longer."

Without uttering a single word, Star snuggled up against him.

He looked at her suspiciously. "That's it? No argument? No complaint? Nothing?"

An impish smile adorned her face. "From time to time, I have to give you the illusion you're winning."

"Is that so?" he teased, grateful for the future she gave him. "I love you. Now close your eyes. You and baby need to rest. I'll be right here when you wake up."

Vanessa's spirited nature lived on, and with any luck, all their children would possess that same spirit.

The End

The story behind *Deep Beneath the Surface*:

Years ago, my daughter was exploring underwater wrecks on the Atlantic Coast. The descriptions she gave of the shipwrecks were eerie and fascinating, and they ignited my imagination. As far as I know, she has never seen a Ford Model T underwater, but she was the inspiration behind Star. To thank her, I wrote her a cameo in the story.

I hope you enjoyed reading *Deep Beneath the Surface* as much as I did writing it.

J. S. Marlo grew up in Shawinigan, a small French-Canadian town in Québec. She married a young military officer, raised three spirited children, and enjoyed many wonderful postings in different parts of Canada. She isn't sure where time flew, but decades later, she ended up in Alberta with her husband, spoiling four amazing grandchildren and writing Canadian mysteries under the Northern Lights.